LANDS END

*Looking northeast toward downtown San Francisco from the window of
SFPD Officer Phil McManus' condominium in the winter of 1976*

BILL FOX

LANDS END

KEZAR
BOOKS

San Francisco, California

Acknowledgements
"At Last"
Songwriters: Gordon, Mack / Warren, Harry
At Last lyrics © Sony/ATV Music Publishing LLC
Copyright: EMI Feist Catalog Inc.

"Power of Love"
Writer(s): John Victor Colla, Huey Lewis, Christopher John Hayes
Copyright: Huey Lewis Music, Cause And Effect Music, Kinda Blue Music,
WB Music Corp.

First printing, Kezar Books, San Francisco, May 2015
Copyright © Bill Fox, 2015 all rights reserved

LIBRARY OF CONGRESS CATALOGING-IN-PUBLICATION DATA

Library of Congress Control Number: 2015943111

Fox, Bill
Lands End / by Bill Fox
p. cm.

ISBN: 978-0-9963322-0-0

Printed in the United States of America
Set in Adobe Garamond Pro and ITC Blair Medium
Cover and interior design by Tom Joyce/Creativewerks

The most beautiful people we have known are those who have known defeat, known suffering, known struggle, known loss, and have found their way out of the depths… Beautiful people do not just happen.

———————————

Elisabeth Kubler-Ross
Swiss-American Psychiatrist
1926-2004

WHEN I DIDN'T WAKE SCREAMING
The pounding had subsided now
And I lay still afraid.
Like gun blasts beating home again,
Oh! "Only if I'd stayed."

———————

SHARI WEISS
1971

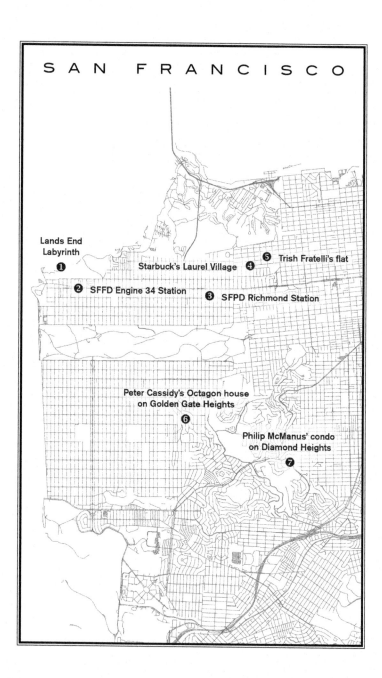

SAN FRANCISCO

Lands End
Labyrinth
❶
❷ SFFD Engine 34 Station
Starbuck's Laurel Village ❹
❺ Trish Fratelli's flat
❸ SFPD Richmond Station

Peter Cassidy's Octagon house
on Golden Gate Heights
❻

Philip McManus' condo
on Diamond Heights
❼

1

SUPER BOWL SUNDAY
JANUARY 31, 2010 · 2330 HRS

I'm done now, and I know it.

San Francisco Police Officer Phillip Matthew McManus slumped hard in his seat in the fifth-floor Hall of Justice conference room. He stared across the large rectangular table at Homicide Inspector Arthur Lahey and four members of the department's Command Staff led by Deputy Chief Michael Turner.

No one cracked a smile when the Deputy Chief—in a tone so grave it sounded like he was kidding—said, "Officer McManus, in accordance with department procedures and pending a further hearing, you will be placed on sixty days of unpaid administrative leave. I'm directing Dr. Rector, the department's psychologist sitting there at the end of the table, to conduct an evaluation when we're finished here."

Turner's eyes bored into McManus. "Any questions, Officer?"

McManus shook his head.

"I need to get your star." Turner reached his hand toward McManus, who sat up and unfastened star #1125 from his uniform shirt, and then placed it on the table.

The department will tighten ranks and move on. They always do. McManus watched Turner pick up his star and, without further comment, leave the room.

As throats cleared, McManus' career flashed before his eyes. *The excitement of being part of San Francisco history: Zodiac, the Zebra killers and the SLA, Golden Dragon Massacre, White Night Riot, Loma Prieta…am I history now?*

The 59-year old McManus glanced across the table at his immediate supervisor Sergeant Jack Grogan, 30 years his junior. The brown-nosing 29-year-old Grogan flashed a Cheshire-cat smirk at McManus, and then followed the Deputy Chief out the door.

You little cocksucker, you haven't seen the last of me. I guarantee you that. McManus slumped back in his chair and blew out a deep breath as the last three officers departed, leaving him alone with Dr. Howard Rector.

Shit, to save my career now I gotta go one-on-one with the shrink. Do I even want to save it? Maybe if I'm lucky, I'll have a heart attack. McManus stared at the doctor like a child seeking love from a dispassionate parent. When he saw Rector looking back at him like he was a piece of shit, McManus placed his palms on the table to steady his equilibrium…*I had my chance to avoid all this out at the Labyrinth Cliff.*

"Phil?" Rector took off his glasses.

McManus watched with curiosity as Rector's expression transformed into a look of professional empathy. *Maybe I could just reason and plead with him. I got the best argument a desperate cop could have. The job is all I got.*

"You were a good police officer, Phil," Rector began. "Nobody can ever take that away from you."

McManus looked down at the mahogany table, fighting to maintain his composure before he lifted his chin to meet Rector's gaze. "But, I wanted to go out with more dignity than this." He wiped a tear from his eyes. *Man he's studying me like a map.*

"It's a tough thing you've been going through, Phil." Rector cracked open a bottle of water and handed it to McManus.

No shit, Doc. He took a mouthful to moisten his mouth, and then chugged the rest.

"Part of being a cop is being resilient and thick-skinned," Rector said. "But everything we deal with out on those streets can stack up without us recognizing it."

The roaring in McManus' ears returned, just like he had experienced at Lands End. "What am I supposed to do tomorrow morning when I wake up?" *Rector's mouth is tightened. I guess he didn't like the question.*

"Phil, I'm your friend. We're all trying to help you, so you need to talk about this."

McManus chuckled and shook his head. *You're not my friend. None of you guys are my friends. Right now, it's your job not to let the department keep a liability around.*

He took another sip of water and blew out his breath. "Everybody's got their shit. You deal with it and move on. That's what you do when you're a cop...not a pussy. You don't bring anything up unless you really want to have a problem." He wiped his mouth with his shirtsleeve.

Rector shifted in his seat and looked down at his notes.

"I can handle this shit, Doc," McManus continued. "I don't have a problem. I'll be fine after a good night's sleep."

Rector jotted something onto his notepaper, and then he looked up. "You happy, Phil?"

McManus smirked. "I've never given that much thought, Doc. No, wait. Oh, yeah, I'm real happy. I can see how much I'm valued around here after 37 years in the business."

"What are the things you want to live for?"

"Well, I don't want to lose my job, for one."

Rector made another note. "Then I'm confused by your behavior lately, Phil."

McManus looked away and avoided eye contact until Rector asked, "Phil, I see from your personnel jacket you have no next of kin. Never married, no kids, no siblings, parents deceased..."

McManus interrupted Rector. "Just tell me what I have to do to keep my fuckin' job."

Rector cleared his throat and spoke in a more official tone of voice. "You made the SFPD your only family, Phil, so be advised..."

"So be advised." Fuckin' guy sounds like he's talking on a department radio frequency. And he says he's my Friend... yeah, right.

"You're not just leaving a job; you're leaving your family —your support network and all the things that make a family: love, conflicts, and shared experiences."

McManus shifted in his seat and looked down at his hands.

"Phil, if you haven't noticed, this place is changing. It's getting to be like the NFL. At 32, you're past your prime around here, and it all starts passing you by. America values youth. It's not 1966 anymore. The Baby Boom Generation isn't on the cover of *Time* magazine. The problem is that a lot of guys our age see holding onto this job as holding onto their youth."

McManus felt his stomach drop and his anger rise. *Fuck you, you self-righteous asshole.*

"Here's what's going down, Phil." Rector said, smiling now. "You can look at this as if your life is just starting. You've earned a 90-percent pension."

I don't have to listen to any more of this bullshit.

2

McManus sat in department vehicle 024 preparing to die. In a few seconds, he'd know if a brilliant white flash of light and St. Peter waited for him at the gates of Heaven—or if that, too, was all B.S.

He kissed his St. Michael medal and let it slip from his fingertips onto his chest. "Peace be with you," he whispered and crossed himself.

On his drive to the Lincoln Park golf course, he'd seen the dark wet fog billow in thick from the Pacific Ocean. *How prophetic.*

McManus fingered the seven blue-and-gold hash marks sewn onto the left sleeve of his uniform shirt—one for every five years of service. He touched his Silver Medal of Valor ribbon, hoping to invoke the courage it was supposed to represent.

Taking a deep breath, he leaned his head back against the seat and stared out the windshield into the abyss. McManus closed his eyes for a moment, and then shut off the radio car's mobile video terminal. The electronic glow disappeared, and darkness enveloped the interior of the car. He reached toward his right hip and unsnapped his service weapon.

Just do it!

He pulled the black SIG P226 from its leather holster and laid it on his lap. A metallic click echoed through the car's interior as he lifted and cocked the weapon, and then placed the anodized steel barrel into his mouth. His lips puckered from the chemical taste of the gun-cleaning solvent, Hoppe's No. 9.

Steady even pressure on the trigger—just the way the department trained you.

The weapon shook and rattled against his teeth. He waited for the sudden snap of the trigger, but heard only the cynics at the SFPD laughing about his demise. McManus flinched and gagged. *Fuck them!*

He jerked the weapon out of his mouth, pushed open the door, and stumbled out of the radio car. The door rebounded and struck him on the knee. He gasped, sucking in the foggy night air. McManus bent forward at the waist and vomited. Once, twice, three times. He groaned and puked a fourth time.

A dog howled somewhere out in the fog.

What's that? He stood up still holding his weapon. Wiping the corners of his mouth with the back of his hand, he spit, and then looked around.

Shit, did anybody see me? He re-holstered his weapon and reached inside the radio car to call headquarters.

"Richmond Six," McManus called.

"Richmond Six, go." The response was immediate, perhaps because the dispatcher sensed the adrenaline edge in McManus' voice.

"Richmond Six, I'll be out of the car investigating a 415 barking dog, possibly injured, in the vicinity of the Labyrinth Cliff at Lands End, copy."

"Ten-four." The dispatcher hesitated, and then asked, "Are you requesting back-up?"

Yeah, right. "Negative at this time, Headquarters."

McManus locked the radio car doors. The wind was picking up. He centered his hat on his head, and then swept the area with a luminous beam from his heavy antediluvian five-cell Kel-Lite, a relic from the '70s.

I can't see anything. Sounded like a dog howling along the golf cart path that parallels the fourth hole. This wind's as loud as a siren. Jeez, I'm just about to kill myself, and I'm looking for a damn dog…gotta keep moving.

Walking in the familiar direction, he felt cold drops splattering onto him from an overhead canopy of eucalyptus and Monterey cypress trees. *Would everyone have known it was a suicide from the hole blown through the roof? Well, daaah! What a great legacy I'm leaving…remembered as a "pussy" by the cops and condemned to hell by the Catholics for a mortal sin. Walking in this fog tonight feels like I'm inside a cotton ball. It's disorienting. Come on fog, lighten up. You're supposed to be my soulmate, not my tormentor.*

When he reached the Lands End Coastal Trail, darkness limited his visibility to a few feet. He swept his Kel-Lite back and forth. *This area used to be the favorite dumping ground for the bodies of pimps and drug dealers until the Park Service chained these trails closed at dusk.*

McManus descended a wooden staircase of 124 steps leading down to a promontory called the Labyrinth Cliff, where a circuitous path created from gathered stones lay inches from the precipice overlooking the Strait of the Golden Gate.

Do I really want to do this? Do I have a choice? The Lands End Labyrinth was his sanctuary, the place that provided refuge when his doubts, fears and the mean streets of the city challenged his resolve. But when he reached the Labyrinth, he tossed the Kel-Lite into the dark, cold, and fog. *This is the end. Let's just finish it.*

Two hundred feet above the jagged rocks and violent surf, the ground was wet and covered with loose gravel. After a few steps, McManus lost his footing, slipped, and fell. His chin scrapped against a rock and split open.

Can you believe this shit tonight! He pushed himself up on his hands and knees as warm blood ran down his neck and under his collar. Then he stood up.

Like a sneak thief, the gusting winds snatched his hat from his head and it tumbled into the ocean, tempting McManus to follow. He stood still, feeling the wind flutter his trouser legs like flags. *If I change my mind, do I have to go back to the same place? I feel trapped. Which way do I go?*

He spread his arms wide and screamed into the emptiness, "Help me."

McManus stamped the ground in frustration, and the earth gave way, pitching him forward. He fell hard on his hip, bounced once, and slid through the loose gravel toward the water two hundred feet below. Rocks slashed his uniform trousers, grating the skin on his knees and palms as he clawed at the earth, trying to stop his slide.

This is it!

Pain exploded through his groin as he slid over a rock, but the rock didn't crush his balls—instead, it performed a miracle and snagged the gold buckle on his Sam Browne belt, jerking him to a stop. Hanging by his gun belt over the water, he screamed again, looking down, not daring to move.

I'm still alive! What did I do? What will I do?

If he died now, it wouldn't be a suicide, but no one would ever know for sure. Nevertheless, the department would consider his death a "Killed in the line of duty," just to avoid any stigma of a cop suicide. He would be a hero—honored with a dignified police funeral.

Bigger in death than I ever was in life. But I don't want to die!

His right foot, which had twice betrayed him, found a toehold. McManus crawled his way back up the precipice to level ground. When he reached the top, the wind stopped blowing. He walked slowly back up the hill to his radio car.

Wow! All those years of picking up the pieces after a suicide, including my own mother's. And now I realize all it takes is just a moment of weakness…

Back at the Lands End Coastal Trail, McManus stopped. He turned off the Kel-Lite and took a deep breath. He could feel the stinging in his hands and knees and the gash on his chin. *I'm sure I don't look too good…*

A rustling sound in the brush nearby caught his attention. He turned the Kel-Lite on and played the beam toward the noise. He saw the glint of a dog's eyes. Then the animal turned and disappeared into the brush.

McManus followed the moving sound. When he came to the junction of the trail and the cart path, he saw a German Shepherd. Shining his light around, he caught the dog's eyes behind a eucalyptus tree. The dog barked, and when it jumped forward, he drew his weapon. The dog skidded to a stop. Its sad eyes looked at McManus, who was holding his weapon and Kel-Lite in a combat stance. Feeling foolish, McManus re-holstered his weapon for the second time in an hour.

I'm all set to blow away a vicious animal…and I get you. "What are you doing out here?" asked McManus with a sigh of relief and a smile.

The dog turned back and pawed the ground near the base of a nearby tree. McManus shined the light toward a pile of fallen leaves and branches.

"Oh, shit," McManus said, feeling the shiver go up his spine when he saw the body.

It lay atop the eucalyptus pile. The scene was surreal. *What the fuck is going on here? I'm about to kill myself, and I find a dead body...*

He stepped forward to take a closer look. The victim's sweat pants were pulled down to his ankles exposing his bloody genitals. The dog whimpered while he circled the body. McManus held the light on the corpse's face: his lips were blue, frozen in a ghastly scowl. McManus' heart pounded as hard as it had on the promontory. The deceased appeared to be his age. He wore a navy fleece jacket with "SFFD" embroidered on the left breast.

McManus leaned in closer and saw the primary colors of the Irish man: green eyes, white hair, and a red nose. A strong, dignified face, aged by life and alcohol—clean-shaven, mouth ajar. His teeth appeared to be intact and even whitened. On the corpse's right hand was a gold St. Ignatius High School class ring. *This guy looks familiar.*

McManus held the light to the man's chin. A dimpled scar about an inch in length appeared just left of center. He recognized the scar tissue on the man's nose, a common football injury. *I got one of those. Sacred Heart game—junior year.*

Then he shined the light on the victim's angry eyes. *That's what I'd looked like if...*

McManus' mouth tasted like pennies, and he felt nauseous. His face flushed. It wasn't seeing a dead body that upset his stomach. The dead had become the detritus of his job, another mess that someone else would clean up and discard in tomorrow's trash. He wasn't even supposed to care about who died.

What sickened him was that he had locked eyes with the death stare of a corpse he knew. *FUCK! His head is almost cut off. Face is a bloody mess, I haven't seen him in years...but I know who this is.*

For the second time tonight, he turned and vomited.

McManus returned to the radio car parked next to the fourth-hole tee box. He radioed Headquarters about the 802 coroner's case and requested Homicide and the necessary units to respond. His body ached.

How fucked up is all this? He thrust his hands deep into the pockets of his police parka and settled in.

I'm out here to kill myself and I find him...of all people. I've seen other cops crack from the emotions of the job. It's ugly and sometimes been fatal. Never thought I'd be one of them. I've been protected by my sarcastic nature—first developed in the white-hot crucible of St. Ignatius High School. When I got to the SFPD, I saw how being just another emotionally disconnected cop was a great shield that allowed me to handle anything...for a while.

McManus also never thought about "pulling-the-pin," even though retirement was the pot of gold at the end of the rainbow—the goal every cop anticipated from the day he or she entered the department. Like most street cops, he just wanted to move on to the next thing. But what would that be? He shook his head as his mind replayed the dog pile of 37 years' worth of every dead body, every beaten child, every DV, every "He said, She said," and every "Do I or don't I shoot?"

Most cops lived by the power of the uncluttered mind. They cared, but knew it was in their best interest to detach. Never, ever, internalize even the most heinous act. If they could hack it, being a San Francisco cop was just the greatest job in the world. A regular paycheck with plenty of overtime, futures assured by a 90% pension and the chance to carry a gun. At the end of their watch, they left everything hanging in their lockers—until they returned the next day.

But McManus couldn't detach. It was just who he was. Chatter always filled his mind. He never forgot anything. Situations needed to have the proper closure before he could let them go and move on. He felt responsible.

Someone has to uphold the Social Contract: "We don't trespass unto others." But things keep stacking up and are never resolved. Every tomorrow, I go out again, and it's the same thing. There's gonna be a dead kid on the ground, murdered by his own. And another one the next week, this time around the corner, killed because of mistaken identity. Then the week after that another one dead because he was in the wrong place at the wrong time. The week after that, another caught in the crossfire. And all I can do is dwell on it and hope it's not me that's laying there in the street some night. The images never go away...and there's nothing I can do to stop it.

McManus rolled down the window and spat.

Cherry blossoms, Indian summers, NFL playoffs, the Indy 500...The miracle of love has always been fool's gold. I can't feel anything anymore. I've got no retirement plans. The universe of golf courses and rest homes makes me shudder. I would no sooner sign a contract to live in one of those assisted living centers than spend another day answering to a 29-year-old boss. Only thing I enjoy on this job anymore is the ball park security at AT&T Park. Not a bad gig, getting paid to watch the Giants play...Way better than responding to 2798 Turk Street, Apartment 4B, to listen to Lydia taunt Roscoe again about his manhood, telling him, "If you's was any kinda man..." I was there last week. I'll be there this week...Maybe next week Lydia will finally have achieved her goal of "suicide by Roscoe"—followed by his arrest for her murder. Baseball season's still four months away. Sure hope they manage to win a World Series before I die.

In the adrenaline rush of being a San Francisco cop, McManus had found a demanding test for his courage and ability. Along with moments of heroic exhilaration, he got the feelings of power, superiority and recognition, thinking they kept him young. He loved the uniform, a strange kind of fame and celebrity like being Dirty Harry or Bullitt. A lot of guys dreamed of being cops, but never made it. He had. He was Somebody.

So how can I give this up? Especially when I have no plans, no purpose, and nothing to look forward to after leaving the department. Can I walk away from all this without destroying myself? Maybe Mom was right. She'd always warned me: "Phillip, don't ever get your hopes up. Just when things go good, they go bad."

When he saw headlights of the responding units, McManus checked his watch—0157. To help them locate the crime scene, he activated the radio car's overhead warning lights, which painted the fog into a garish red-and-blue tableau. He got out of the car and met Homicide Inspectors Arthur Lahey and Frank Anderson.

"Supposed to be fuckin' Christmas Eve," Lahey said, stepping out from his dark blue unmarked car. "Got a big fire going over in the Haight."

"Whatever, Beluga," McManus responded.

Lahey gave him a gentle punch in the shoulder, a throwback to the days when he was a giant-sized left tackle, while McManus played outside linebacker on the 1966 St. Ignatius city championship football team.

Of all the people I don't want to see tonight. Of course, Lahey catches this case. Some people always seem to show up in your life.

Lahey had shadowed McManus since first grade at St. Anne School and all the way through the 122nd Recruit Class of the San Francisco Police Academy in 1972. In elementary school, the over-sized Lahey was nicknamed "Baby Huey," after the 1950's cartoon character. All the kids had mocked him except McManus, who actually respected Lahey's physical strength. Like the cartoon character, Lahey remained blissfully unaware of the ridicule about his size and clumsiness. When he finally realized he'd been the school yard joke, Lahey senselessly blamed McManus and never forgave him.

They were both big men. Lahey was just bigger, and he still competed in powerlifting events at the Police Olympics. But seventeen years of murder investigations had reddened his nose and creased his face. When his brown wavy hair turned white, his nickname changed from "Baby Huey" to "Beluga," and he liked it.

McManus led Lahey and the other investigators down the cart path and through the fog to the body. The LED light from a video camera illuminated and recorded the scene as the CSI techs began their perfunctory investigations.

Lahey pulled on a pair of blue rubber gloves. "Holy fuck, somebody's got anger management issues. The guy's head's almost cut off."

Now, in the light of the camera, McManus could study the attack. It appeared to have come from behind and was swift and sudden—a stab wound to the base of the skull. The victim had collapsed on the spot from a severed spinal cord. Two slash wounds across the left side of the victim's neck were prominent, one alongside the jaw, the other at the base of the neck. The jugular vein and carotid artery, both severed, had bled out. The wounds were long and deep—three or four inches—with the stubs from the small bones of the neck sticking through black globs of coagulated blood. Three slash wounds had shredded the victim's groin. A bloody testicle, still attached to his body, lay on the eucalyptus leaves beneath the victim.

Merry Christmas. Shit, someone this violent was wandering around out here. How did I miss 'em? That's another problem with being a cop in this city. Can't tell who the bad guys are. They don't wear florescent jumpsuits that say, "County Jail" out on the streets. Then, even if I'm super polite and respectful, I'll jack somebody up in San Francisco who looks edgy or out of

place, and inevitably he'll turn out to be Mr. Model Citizen,
whose crime is that he's different.

But sure as hell he'll know the phone number to Internal
Affairs and ABC7 to complain how the cops profiled and
harassed him. After a while, why bother. People are more
afraid of the cops than the crazies. And maybe they should be.
We're all on edge. We just see too much shit and violence, and
we know what can happen.

"We'd better get the haz-mat suits on for this fucker,"
Lahey said as he walked back to his car.

While Lahey suited up, his partner Frank Anderson
left the main crime scene and swept the beam from his
Kel-Lite across the brush, highlighting nothing but shadows. McManus knew that when daylight came, a wider
and more thorough search would commence.

When Lahey returned, he knelt down next to the victim.
"The guy's got golf shoes on. Where's his bag and clubs?"

Lahey went through the turned-inside-out pockets of
the victim's dark fleece jacket while McManus stood nearby
and watched him work. Despite the cold and fog, sweat
dripped down McManus' face.

Lahey finished with the body and stood up. "For
Chrissakes…you don't kill somebody like this for his
fuckin' golf bag. What's wrong with people?"

"What do you think it's like to die like that?" McManus
asked.

Lahey puffed his cheeks out like a blowfish. He looked hard
at McManus as if he had just passed gas in a closed radio car.
"What?…You missing the Y-chromosome or something, now."

Then he motioned to the Crime Scene tech with the camera. "Make sure you get some close-ups of the pockets. Looks like this guy's been plucked. Got a robbery homicide here."

Lahey got out of the way of the camera and walked over to McManus. "By the way, what the fuck happened to you? Looks like your mother tied a steak around your neck and let the dogs loose."

"Tripped in the dark."

"Better get that looked at."

McManus shrugged. "I'm fine, but we know this guy, Beluga."

Lahey looked back at McManus. "Pockets plucked. No ID on him."

"I think we can make him. Got on an S.I. class ring. Haven't seen him since the last team reunion in '06," McManus said.

Lahey leaned closer to the victim's bloody face with his light. Anderson returned from his search of the immediate area.

"You barf, McManus?" Anderson was a small man—nicknamed "Friendly Frank." His outgoing manner helped when he and Lahey interrogated a suspect with the old good cop/bad cop routine. "We got a puddle of puke over there and a lot more up by your radio car."

McManus turned his palms up, "Yeah, I'll claim 'em. Had a bad pizza for lunch off a food truck."

"Sumbitch, that's him," Lahey said after he inspected the body. "I haven't made any of those team reunions for a while."

Anderson leaned forward to have a good look.

I've seen enough. Never liked the bastard. Thought he had all the answers back in high school. And he treated me like shit. Arrogant asshole. Probably deserved what's happened to him. McManus looked away and listened to the moans of the foghorns from the nearby Golden Gate Bridge.

"You okay, McManus?" Anderson asked.

"That's Pete Cassidy—our old team captain," McManus said. "Beluga and I played football with him at S. I. He was the quarterback when we won the championship. Then he played at Cal and for the Raiders. He was Deputy Chief in the fire department."

Anderson recoiled. "Oh, this is just great."

Recognizing Cassidy's name, Anderson threw up his arms in disgust. "We got the most famous guy in the fire department. Former NFL player. And he's found murdered —with his balls chopped off—out here at Lands End. Fuck me, the Jakeys are going to be all over us to cover up the details of this fiasco. This is like one of those '70s satanic gay murders we used to catch out here all the time."

"Nah," Lahey said as he chewed hard on a piece of gum. "We got a whole new generation of gay guys in this town now—gay sex is mainstream." Lahey blew a gum bubble until it popped. "They don't have to come out here and troll anymore. That's old school."

"We talking an 800 crazy then?" McManus asked, trying to join the conversation.

"Homicide between gays definitely raises havoc," Anderson said. "And this is definitely overkill. They're worse than domestics."

"I remember one on Masonic Avenue around Haight, where the guy had a broom handle shoved all the way up his ass," Lahey said. "When we got there, the guy who did it was doing his housework—pretending nothing happened."

McManus flinched. *That's how I feel right now... "pretending" to be on duty when a couple minutes ago I was headed to wherever Cassidy is now.*

The banter swirled about him like some bad LSD trip.

"What's the deal with the knife in the neck?" Anderson asked.

"It has to be some sort of specialty knife to do that kind of damage," Lahey said. "There are no signs of a struggle."

"He probably lost consciousness in a couple seconds and died quick," Anderson said.

"Then when he's down...I mean, somebody's really pissed off here; look at his balls hanging by a thread," Lahey said.

"If you're pissed and trying to chop somebody's balls off, don't you finish the job?" McManus asked.

Lahey shot a dismissive glance at McManus. "I wouldn't know. Can't recall ever being in that frame of mind myself."

"Was somebody lying in wait for him then?" McManus asked.

"There's a lot of rage here. Stabbed him from behind, then came around and got him in the throat," Lahey said. "You see his golf bag or clubs lying around?"

A pair of headlights caught their attention.

"Oh, fuck," Anderson said, recognizing a television news van.

"McManus, chase those guys outta here. Establish the media perimeter at your radio car."

Relieved to be leaving the gruesome scene of the crime, McManus walked back up the hill to his radio car. When he got there, a bearded obese videographer with a media ID card dangling around his neck, struggled to get out of the van.

"Gotta stay back here, guy," McManus called out to the driver of the van.

"Can I just get an establishing shot of you and the radio car with the crime scene in the background, officer?" he asked.

"Yeah, sure," McManus said. *I believe in the power of a photograph. I wonder if, on this night, a photograph would reveal the paradox within me. The department's personality tests described me as "quiet and reserved, with an unusually rich inner life." The test also had recommended a career in counseling or the clergy.*

Lahey and Anderson released McManus from the crime scene at 0245. He drove out of Lincoln Park back to Richmond Station. The fog had thinned, and in the distance, he could see the lights of downtown San Francisco twinkling on Christmas morning like an eerie mirage.

The car was warm and his torn hands hurt from holding the steering wheel. *Sure didn't expect to be alive.*

He pulled into the bus stop at 20th Avenue and Geary, rolled down the window and took ten deep breaths—a relaxation technique taught him by a therapist. Then he looked across the intersection.

Shit, I'm at 20th and Geary. I gotta get out of here. Always avoid this place like the flu. It's where all the crap in my head started, over there. Christmas '78. Reggie and Sarah Howard. They never had a chance when that big honker pick-up nailed them in the crosswalk. Then the rear wheels rolled over her face. I'm still pissed the insane driver only got a year in the County Jail. Let's get the FUCK OUTTA HERE!

Cold air blew in through his open window and helped clear his head. He restarted the car and drove back to the station.

The officers on duty were both busy when McManus entered and signed off. *Whew! Don't have to tell anyone the details of what went down out there.*

He walked back to the locker room and hung his gun belt in his locker.

Startling him, the whiney voice of his immediate supervisor, 29-year-old patrol sergeant Jack Grogan, called out his name.

I hate that dipshit's voice. I want to cover my ears when he uses that command and control tone they taught in the Academy. Aaaaaaaaaaaaagh! That felt good—even if Pee Wee Herman over there didn't hear it.

With his dainty effeminate mannerisms, quirky facial expressions, and slicked back hair, all Grogan needed was a red bowtie to complete the picture of the comic fictional character from the '80s.

McManus muttered, "Here," without lifting his head as he rested his foot on a bench and tied his shoes.

Grogan walked up to his locker. "McManus, why were you not wearing your hat at the crime scene?"

McManus hesitated before answering. *Guys like Grogan are becoming the majority of SFPD supervisors. They test well on promotionals and move up the ranks, but they're lost out on the street because they have zero interpersonal skills.*

Grogan's USF law degree and sycophantic nature had earned him the nickname "The Boy Sergeant Who Would Be Chief."

"I was just showing respect for the deceased, Sergeant Grogan." A smile crept across McManus' face.

"Don't be truculent with me, officer. What happened to your chin?"

McManus' smile disappeared as he reached up and felt the dried blood. The new breed of SFPD supervisor picked up on the little things they knew how to handle.

They chastise you for not wearing your hat but are incapable of asking if you were okay. "I tripped in the dark," McManus said.

"And why were you not coming up on your radio when we called you?"

"When?"

"Just before you managed to come up with that coroner's case of yours."

"It's in the report I gave Homicide."

Grogan stiffened. "Okay, smart guy. We'll deal with this tomorrow night."

McManus stood up and towered over the Gen Y sergeant, who barked, "And I'd advise you not to call in sick on Christmas night, McManus."

McManus closed his locker.

"Did you file your papers yesterday?" Grogan asked.

"No, I was busy."

Grogan blew out his breath in frustration. "You're going to be 60 years old, McManus. The city's going to take care of you with a nice 90% pension. If you want to keep working, be a mall cop. It's a new day around here. I just don't want you around these kids on the watch. You're contaminating them."

Fuck you. McManus stifled his laugh and left the station through the back door. He went out to the parking lot, opened the door of his black Camry, and collapsed into the seat. He could feel the chill from his tee shirt, soaked with perspiration. It was 0315. He sighed and inserted Sade into the CD player. The pounding rhythm of "Paradise" lifted his spirits. McManus turned the volume up full blast.

It's Christmas morning. Who the fuck is asleep on Christmas morning?

The fog was rolling in again. McManus decided to race it across San Francisco to his place atop Diamond Heights. He cheated by breezing through the red light at the deserted intersection of Fulton and Stanyan, and then made a steep climb up 17th Street into the hills above the city where his top-floor loft awaited him. The condominium complex boasted gardens and trickling waterfalls, as well as hawks, owls, and, from time to time, wild parrots. This was his refuge. *This is all I have to show for my life.*

The condo was the tradeoff he'd made for the horrors of the job he endured nightly. A place to lick the wounds inflicted by the job. He'd moved in at age 22 after graduating from the Police Academy, using money from the sale of his late mother's house to purchase the place. Wood beams and floor-to-ceiling mirrors made the condo seem larger than its snug 500 square feet. The basic beige-and-tan décor proclaimed "I'm not gay." Whenever he walked to the garbage chute, he always left the front door open to let his curious homosexual neighbors know his status.

A framed two-by-three-foot movie poster of Steve McQueen as Bullitt hung on one wall. Magazine cover portraits of JFK, Vince Lombardi, and Hugh Hefner were grouped together on another wall. A picture of "The Catch" from the 49ers' first Super Bowl season hung over the fireplace—a reminder that magic and miracles could happen. On the coffee table, a neat stack of recent *American Police Beat* and *Sports Illustrated* magazines epitomized McManus' two interests—cops and sports. On a close-by bookshelf was a faded black-and-white team photo of the 1973 SFPD championship softball team with McManus standing in the back row. Two players to the left of McManus was Dan White, who was an ex-cop and firefighter elected to the city Board of Supervisors. He later resigned, and in a fit of rage, assassinated San Francisco Mayor George Moscone and gay-activist Supervisor Harvey Milk in 1978.

The most spectacular feature of the room was a 12-foot bay window opening onto a sweeping panorama of the Bay Area. McManus could stand at his window and see half of San Francisco and five neighboring counties: Alameda, Contra Costa, Solano, Sonoma and Marin. On clear days, he could also see Napa County through the tripod mounted telescope. Like a huge wall-mounted aquarium, the city's ever-changing moods and delicate beauty were on constant display.

In the mornings, McManus would sip his coffee and watch the conveyor belt of headlights on the Bay Bridge flowing into the city—grateful he wasn't among them. Sunsets in November were remarkable, appearing to set the Financial District skyscrapers ablaze in dazzling shades of gold and orange.

At night during baseball season, he liked to stand in the open window and watch the glistening lights at the downtown ballpark. When the winds came out of the east, he could even hear the distant roar of the crowd. Without leaving home, he could watch the Blue Angels' airshows and fireworks displays over the Bay.

The view was McManus' sanctuary—shielding him from the traffic, noise and trauma below. When he'd been a rookie cop, this view made him feel like a centurion, looking out at the kingdom he was empowered to protect.

Lately, though, the view left him feeling pensive and lost. When he'd gone to work hours earlier, he'd said goodbye to the place, never expecting to return. That afternoon he'd cleaned, dusted and vacuumed in anticipation of Homicide's arrival and their "turning the place" during the investigation into his death. He hadn't wanted his fellow officers to think he was a slob.

McManus downed two quick shots of Blanton's Single-Barrel Bourbon Whiskey and went to the bathroom to pee.

Hung above the toilet, at eye level, was his framed Honorable Discharge from the United States Army. It served as a constant reminder of his capricious good fortune compared to 59,000 of his Baby Boomer Vietnam-generation contemporaries who never came home. McManus had spent his military career in the Reserves at the Presidio Army Base in San Francisco, assigned as his Commanding Officer's driver. The CO was a cop-buff and loved to "cop talk" with a real-life San Francisco police officer.

Washing his hands in front of the mirror, he cursed the tired old face looking back at him. The bags under his eyes had ballooned; the hair around his temples now the color of cigarette ash. He cleaned and shaved the area around the gash on his chin and closed it with a butterfly bandage. Then he bandaged the scrapes on his hands and knees.

When he was done, he walked back into the living room and slid open two windows. The curtains billowed. *That breeze feels good. Exactly what I need right now—or is it?*

McManus spun the dial on his iPod until he found the haunting Miles Davis trumpet solo "Generique." He lit the gas-fueled fireplace and wrapped himself in his mother's old hand-knit red-and-yellow 49er blanket. Then, with drink in hand, he stood at the window and felt the warm familiarity of the bourbon as he watched the shifting tides of the fog over the city's skyline. *How many people sleeping in those new downtown high-rises know they're build on Bay landfill that will turn to Jell-O in the next big earthquake?*

Growing up in San Francisco had taught McManus to be fatalistic. So had his job. *Everything's destiny and fate...*

McManus poured another Blanton's, this time on the rocks because he loved to suck the ice cubes. From the bookshelf next to the fireplace, he pulled his white cloth-covered high school yearbook, *Ignatian '67*. He wanted to remember Cassidy and the details of the Thanksgiving Day city championship game. McManus and Cassidy had attended the all-male St. Ignatius High School run by the iron discipline of the Society of Jesus and governed by the spirit of AMDG (*Ad Majorem Dei Gloriam:* "For the greater glory of God and the Salvation of Man.")

AMDG was a call to overcome life's struggles and pursue excellence in order to give that glory to God. This religious concept resonated with McManus in contrast to the dysfunction of his childhood. As a Catholic school boy in San Francisco, he dreamed of becoming a football player and a "Gentleman of S. I." When he made the team, he found the outlet for overcoming the inadequacies in his life. *Best moment of my life was playing on Turkey Day for the city championship before that huge crowd! Back in those days I had some purpose and direction. Where did it all go?*

McManus settled into his beanbag chair and spread the yearbook across his knees. He thumbed through until he found the eight pages devoted to Varsity Football, AAA Champs and saw the faded green clipping from the *San Francisco Chronicle* sports section dated Friday, November 25, 1966. He unfolded and read the headline that described his life's one shining moment.

Late TD Gives S. I. 21-14 Win
To Take SF City Championship

McManus set the clipping aside and studied the black-and-white photo of the play. That picture was good—outstanding even, considering that the student yearbook photographer had shot it 40 years before auto-focus, ten-frames-per-second motor drives, and digital manipulation. Probably taken from the sideline, maybe ten yards from the play, it showed McManus' back to the camera. He'd worn a white mud-covered uniform, jersey number 86 and appeared to have just collided with Perper, the Lowell defensive back facing the camera. McManus was reaching up for the ball suspended above Perper's shoulder. Behind them was Colin O'Connell, number 82.

McManus had rerun the play in his mind thousands of times over the years, not wanting to forget how it had felt. *Never again have I felt such determination and inner peace— as in that game. Things just all broke right that day.*

McManus closed the book and got up. He finished the last trace of Blanton's and turned off the lights, leaving the condo illuminated only by the fireplace flames. His cuts and bruises hurt. He opened the grate, stepped back, and threw the empty shot glass as hard as he could into the fireplace. Shards of glass exploded like a bomb onto the carpet.

Merry Christmas, stupid shit. At least you're alive.

3

While children tore open gifts and the world watched what St. Nicholas had brought, McManus slept two hours. He awoke to the wail of Brian Jones's harmonica and Charlie Watts pounding out "2120 South Michigan Avenue" on the snare drums—his punishment for forgetting to reset his alarm clock.

Fuck me. McManus stared at the ceiling and heard water rush through the pipes in the next door condo. The sound flooded him with scenes from last night's chaos. Touching his chin, he realized it was no nightmare. He winced and tightened his core muscles, and then swung his legs over the side of the bed. *I'm getting older, and I can feel it.*

McManus winced again, this time from the chronic tightness in his lower back. Whenever he experienced this sensation, he needed to align his spine before making his way to the kitchen. Then he would shuffle stiff-legged to the refrigerator. This morning he looked inside and found a half-bottle of two-percent milk, a package of hot dogs, and a decorative glass bottle of Coca-Cola he'd received as a Christmas promotion from the Diamond Heights Safeway.

He poured a glass of milk and grabbed some Oreo cookies to settle the remaining acidity from last night's six ounces of Blanton's. He rinsed the glass, yawned, and then walked to the bay window. On the way, he stopped to feed the blue veiltail Betta fish he'd named "Floater" because it never seemed to move.

He pulled back the curtains to see that Christmas Day in San Francisco was going to be foggy and gray. Dots of light sprinkled through the mist from cars headed into the city on the Bay Bridge. *Where are they all going on this Holy Day? Where will I be going…now that I need to start making decisions again? I guess I'll be going to this afternoon's retirement brunch, after all.*

McManus shook his head, closed the curtains, and went back to bed.

FRIDAY
CHRISTMAS DAY 2009 · 1200 HRS.

The last thing McManus wanted to do on Christmas Day was celebrate his imminent retirement with a bunch of retired cops. But he was their guest-of-honor, and it was a free lunch at "America's Oldest Italian Restaurant" in North Beach.

"Enjoy, sir," the maître d' said to McManus as he led him to the Godfather Room. McManus respected the place's Old World dignity and the wait staff dressed in tuxedos. He was glad he'd made a last-minute change from his usual brown A-2 bomber jacket to a navy cashmere blazer. The maître d' pulled the room's maroon curtain back to reveal the ten retired members from McManus' 1972 Police Academy class, who met monthly to check on each other's well-being.

"Where the fuck you been, asshole? You're late," said his former partner Guido Donatelli amidst the hoots ringing out from the other nine.

McManus' face flushed as the maître d' turned around and left.

"Just because you were on the news this morning, Kid, doesn't mean you can show up any old time," continued Donatelli, who had given McManus the nickname "Kid" when he started losing his hair at age 32.

The retired members of the 122nd Recruit Class crowded around McManus to greet him with handshakes, hugs and laughter. All the ex-cops were either single, divorced, widowed, bald or gray. From the day they had entered the department as 22-year-olds on Monday, September 11, 1972, to police the streets of San Francisco, they had begun to lose their innocence. Domestic relationships had pretty much been destroyed, so it wasn't a surprise that this Christmas Day party had no wives, girlfriends or children.

McManus' history of the heart was no different. His last serious relationship ended with the woman declaring, "You're certainly friendly, but you definitely have 'No Trespassing' signs." She was right. McManus never allowed anyone to pass under the yellow crime-scene tape that surrounded his life. He had no energy to invest in true intimacy. The moment things turned serious, he bolted for the door.

It's Christmas. And I have no another place. No other family to see. This is pathetic. I'm not sure what's going on here, but I see several police-trained eyes darting around the room looking for someone or something suspicious. Could their well-honed instincts sense what happened last night?

"Okay, everybody fuckin' sit down, and let's get this thing started," the class president Rich Dryden commanded.

McManus took his seat at the head table next to Dryden, who had founded the "Group of Ten." Chairs scraped the floor. Soon a piece of bread was hurled at McManus' forehead. The eighth grade boy's mentality had set in. The warm glow of approval belonging to the SFPD, and this fraternity of brave and professional men, gratified him. For the moment he forgot about Grogan.

The waiters paraded in holding steaming trays of linguini and clams high above their heads. Dryden poured McManus a glass of wine, stood at the head table, and tapped on his water glass for attention. The room quiet, he turned to smile at McManus, "Phil, I got something I want to say."

Does he know? Sure he does, they all know what happened last night? I'm embarrassed to be here.

"Phil, you know the difference between your civilian friends and your cop friends?"

McManus shook his head. *Where the fuck is this going?*

"Civilian friends will take your drink away. Cop friends will pour you another and make sure you get home okay. We're all brothers in this room, Phil. We've seen and experienced stuff none of your civilian friends can imagine —much less want to hear about. We're your family here. Remember that."

More hoots and applause broke out.

Dryden continued in an official tone, but with a smile, "You need to know how happy we are about your retirement and for joining us today. We wish you the best for your future, Phil. And we hope you will join us here often."

The group stood and applauded while Dryden gestured to McManus. "I know you've never been a big talker, Phil, but would you like to say a few words?"

The applause grew louder.

McManus now stood up and smiled at the friendly faces. Dryden embraced him and patted his back. McManus took a deep breath. "I…I really appreciate this, guys…truly…"

his voice barely audible over the applause. "But, you know what they say these days: 59 is the new 49…"

A voice interrupted him. "So you braggin' you can get a hard-on without the blue pill?"

Laughter exploded through the room.

I have no idea what I'd do in retirement. McManus looked down and fidgeted before answering. "Not really, but I'm having a hard time pulling the pin right now, guys. I can still do the job."

A tense silence settled over the room as his academy classmates looked at one another in disbelief at his candor. He was refusing to perform the one final act of duty. "Pulling the pin" off his uniform was the last thing a cop did before he retired, and McManus was avoiding a rite of passage. He sat down. Then staring at the table to avoid eye contact, he sipped wine.

The silence continued, broken only by the sickly hack of somebody's cough and Dryden's angry voice. "You're out of your mind, McManus. You better get your ass down to that Retirement Board NOW before they have to wash your fuckin' brains out of a radio car some night."

He did know—didn't he?

Dryden pointed his finger at him. "Remember I said that."

———————

FRIDAY
CHRISTMAS DAY 2009 · 1645 HRS.

McManus sat in front of his locker at Richmond Station, and with a sinking feeling in his stomach, read the yellow Post-it note stuck to the door: **"SEE ME!!! Sgt. J. Grogan #3419."** *Killing myself was supposed to have solved all of these problems.*

He looked at the uniform and gun belt hanging in his locker. They both looked alien to him. *I don't belong here.*

McManus inserted the pin of his sterling silver police star through the eyeholes of his uniform shirt and dressed for work. It annoyed him that the department now issued only silver-plated stars to new officers. The star was important. Just like the gun. He was a "uniform cop." People didn't see Phillip Matthew McManus. They just saw his gun and star. He was ambivalent about that and had long ago decided to make the uniform work for him, not against him. If people only saw the star and gun, he'd hide behind the uniform and let it make the decisions.

This became his defense, and it represented his being in charge. But many times he felt like an actor wearing a costume—one that came with power and expectation. Because he was in a police official's uniform, people expected him to solve their problems. When he couldn't, he felt their wrath and scorn. Then he used the rules, having learned it was far easier to be "a cop in uniform" following department procedure, than trying to reason with people who didn't want to be reasonable.

McManus finished dressing and strapped on his service weapon. He closed his locker and walked into the assembly room for the lineup. Someone had attempted to brighten the room with a poinsettia and a wreath. Near the booking desk sat a pitcher of eggnog and a large plate of cookies, most likely baked by the wife of a young officer who had to work on Christmas. McManus had traded watches with 24-year old Benson Tran, so the young man could be home both Christmas Eve and Day with his wife and new baby.

The lieutenant called the watch to order, and McManus stood at attention in the lineup. He answered "Here" and received his usual radio-car assignment—Richmond Six, with the 7 PM prisoner transfer to county jail. Christmas shifts were either very quiet or very busy. McManus hoped tonight would be the latter—good for a hot prowler or car chase. He wanted the hours to pass quickly.

He glanced down the lineup of men and women standing next to him as the lieutenant read the list of the night's assignments. *The torch has been passed to a new generation. Where's Murphy, "Irish" Horan and McIntosh these days? Do they know they've been replaced by Chan, Ali and Hernandez? The new guys wear the same blue uniform as the old ones, but I don't feel comfortable with these new people. They all have fresh faces and strong youthful bodies. Shit, the women are in better shape than most of the guys. The new recruits were all born after I entered the department. Many adopted San Francisco after growing up elsewhere. Some are foreign born. And they all glow from having spent Christmas morning opening gifts with their young families. I don't*

want to think about it. When was the last time I opened
presents on Christmas?

Grogan wasn't in the station when the lineup conclud-
ed. McManus picked up a clipboard in the assembly room,
munched on a Christmas cookie, and then waited for him.
Meanwhile, he read the investigative report on the coroner's case at Lands End. As he suspected, the victim was
Pete Cassidy.

Grogan's yelling his name startled McManus, who
looked up from the report and then followed the sergeant
into his small cubicle. Grogan sat down, opened a black
three-ring binder entitled SFPD Patrol Officers' Manual,
and flipped through the pages.

McManus took a seat on the other side of the desk and
crossed his arms. *No wonder this guy always has a scowl.*
I'm old enough to be his father. Too bad. If I was his father,
I would have kicked his ass.

Grogan carefully spun the Patrol Officers' Manual
toward McManus, summoning him with a curled index
finger to his desk to read the "Uniform Dress Code" section.

McManus sighed as he got up.

"Officer, you may think you got all the answers around
here. But from what I can see, you're either stupid, don't care, or
you're senile, and I'm not going to stand for that on my watch!"

McManus' face stiffened and his ears rang.

Grogan continued, "The men and women on this watch
need to know they can count on you to do your job correctly
and not be a danger to them. At this time and place, I don't
think they can count on you, officer."

McManus had two choices. Shoot Grogan or walk out of his office. He walked out, but knew not to slam the door. He got into his radio car, started the engine, and jerked it into gear. The car jack-rabbited forward. He drove a block, and then pulled into a bus zone, his head hitting the steering wheel. A dozen people waited there for the 38-Geary bus, and one woman from the group peered in through his car's passenger window. She knocked on the glass.

I hope she doesn't think I'm having a damn heart attack. McManus nodded he was okay and pulled away.

He drove eastbound on Geary Boulevard to Mz. Brown's Feedbag in Laurel Village for coffee. *I'm pathetic. I shouldn't be seen in public, but I need coffee. I gotta headache that just won't quit.*

The coffee shop was deserted when McManus arrived. He took a seat at the counter and saw his favorite waitress, Flo, whose hair was tied into a gray-streaked bun. Sometimes she wore it long, and he liked it better. She came up to him, smiled, and took his order for coffee.

Maybe Grogan's right. Am I losing my edge as a street cop? When his knees started to give out two years ago, McManus transferred from the Crime Prevention Unit downtown to the residential Richmond Station out in the fog belt, bordered by the ocean and Golden Gate Park.

Richmond's supposed to be the rest stop before we collect our pensions. This would be the perfect place if it weren't for that little dipshit, Grogan. Why the hell did they put him out here to stir up crap? McManus had grown to like Richmond, where he got to work a solo radio car. That freed him from dealing with a partner's predilections and interpretations of the law.

Flo placed a dark tan mug in front of McManus and filled it with steaming coffee. She reached under the counter for a smiling Santa Claus doll and set it next to the mug. After she flipped the switch in Santa's ass, the doll lit up, and "Jingle Bell Rock" played from inside its plastic belly.

"Merry Christmas, Big Guy," Flo said. She leaned over the counter and planted a friendly kiss on McManus' cheek. "You know how many Christmases I've worked in this place, McManus?"

I'm just not in the mood. He shook his head.

"Twenty," she smiled.

McManus looked up at her with a weak smile. "Merry Christmas, Flo."

"You have a good Christmas?"

"Had better."

She studied him in the flickering light of a broken fluorescent tube and tapped her bottom lip with her pencil. She whispered, "Maybe you just need someone to fill your stocking."

"Maybe," McManus said. "But my stocking has too many holes."

For the time being, flirtation was as far as McManus went with Flo, but today he simply wanted to drink his coffee with someone nice. He watched the dancing Santa Claus and finished his drink.

I like her legs and her confidence, but her eagerness around me is like puppies in the pound all jumping for attention. I like the quiet ones back in the corner. He left her a twenty dollar Christmas tip and walked out the door without looking back.

FRIDAY
CHRISTMAS DAY 2009 · 1830 HRS.

Two other radio cars responded with McManus to the prowler call on 30th Avenue.

"You guys secure the back and the Anza Street side. I'll talk to the Reportee and make the search," McManus said, as he walked up the stairs of the white stucco apartment building with a red tiled roof. The woman, who had called, waited at the top of the steps.

"I'm so embarrassed," she said. "It was probably just a cat or something."

"What did you hear and how long ago?"

"Sounded like somebody jumping into the apartment's backyard about ten minutes ago. I made sure my back door was locked and called you."

"Ma'am, please go outside and wait by the police cars while we search. You got any dogs or animals back there?"

"No," she said.

McManus smiled as he notified the units he was going to go into the dwelling and down the back stairs to search. He drew his weapon and took a deep breath. Once inside, he shut off the lights in the kitchen to allow his eyes to adjust to the darkness. After pausing and listening, McManus unlocked and opened the rear door. He pulled the SIG P226 tight against his ribs to prevent a suspect from grabbing it out of his extended arm. *This is standard stuff. No one's going to be back here. The squeal of tires and the squawk of police radios would have scared even the stupidest of the stupid to flee the scene.*

McManus stepped out onto a wooden porch. The aromatic mix from dozens of meals cooking in restaurants on Geary Boulevard accosted him. *Hey, don't let yourself get distracted here. It's routine unless you don't pay attention.*

He pulled out his Kel-Lite and checked the condition of the stairs; then, one step at a time, he descended. A plank creaked. *What the fuck is that? Are these stairs going to hold up? A thousand nighttime searches, why am I shaking now? Just follow procedure and trust your instincts, McManus. This is stupid. I can see risking my life to save someone in a burning building. But risking my life searching someone's backyard for a prowler? Jeez. Shouldn't be here, anyway. I should be dead. But I gotta do this. I'm gonna look like a fuckin' coward if anyone sees me shaking.*

He pulled the gun tighter against his ribs to keep his hand from trembling. The backyard was a ten by thirty-foot patch of grass with only a short juniper tree in the southeast corner. *No place to hide back here.*

When he reached the ground, McManus increased the pressure on the SIG's trigger and swept the yard with the narrow beam of the Kel-Lite. *See, nobody's back here.*

McManus took a deep breath. "Richmond Six. Code Four, backyard's clear."

FRIDAY

CHRISTMAS DAY 2009 · 1930 HRS.

McManus arrived late at County Jail #9 with the 7 PM prisoner transfer. He instructed the detainee, who wore a suit and no tie, to take a seat on the bench near the booking counter, and then he unclicked the handcuffs.

This place always make me nervous. I can't stand the noise and that putrid stench of body odor. That's worse than the blood and guts at a shooting. McManus looked around at the bars and bulletproof glass, and then at the sheriff deputy's pallor. He shut his eyes and wondered who might be waiting at home for his gray-suited prisoner, whose silver Mercedes S550 filled with wrapped Christmas presents and a baked turkey had sideswiped a parked car on Geary Blvd.

McManus secured his weapon in the gun locker. Jail procedure required officers to enter the county jail unarmed. He then handed a bag containing the prisoner's belongings to the desk sergeant. McManus was surprised to see Inspectors Lahey and Anderson standing near the booking counter. Both looked tired and in need of a shave.

"When you get done there, Phil, let's grab a cup of coffee in the back, okay?" Lahey said.

"Sure thing, Beluga," he said.

McManus booked the prisoner and then followed Lahey and Anderson along a well-scrubbed concrete floor to the guards' lounge, their footsteps echoing in the hallway. Lahey carried a brown shopping bag.

What's up? Lahey never invites me for a coffee. This has nothing to do with sharing the holiday spirit.

In the lounge, McManus found the coffee pot and poured a cup, ripping open two sugars since there was no cream. He sat down at a steel-gray table bolted to the floor across from the two inspectors.

"Rich Dryden told me you're not retiring now—how come?" Lahey asked.

News travels too fast through the SFPD. "I just don't want to retire right now."

"Fair enough," Lahey answered, chewing on the end of a pen. He didn't lift his eyes off McManus, who turned the cup of coffee in his hands and remained silent.

Sometimes that guy seems like a psychic. He's the best homicide inspector in the department and always catches the high-profile murderer.

"That mean your tour guide career is on hold?" Lahey asked.

McManus' shoulders sagged. *What the fuck does it look like?*

The previous Christmas, McManus had moonlighted as a city tour guide for a bus company owned by two retired SFPD captains. He'd left hints that it had been more fun than patrolling the streets and might be his next career.

Lahey cleared his throat and looked at Anderson, who nodded once.

"We're up against the wall with this Cassidy murder, Phil."

McManus lifted his eyes. He'd never heard Lahey stumped, and he'd never been asked to help in his investigations. Anderson leaned forward while Lahey continued,

"We got no leads, no suspects, and lots of media. We just wanted to pick your brain in case we missed something last night. You were first on-scene."

"We pulled all the radio transmissions you made last night," Anderson said and slid a time-log of McManus' activities across the table to him.

"Check that out and see if the times and runs look right."

McManus put on his reading glasses, feeling his heart pound.

"You went out of service at 0102 on an investigation," Anderson said. "Then you weren't heard from again until 0128."

Caught in both of their stares, McManus didn't move or breathe.

Lahey paused with his eyes on McManus. Then he said, "Communications called you several times for a 10-13 update, but you didn't answer. In fact, at 0127, they started a car rolling to check on your well-being. Thirty-five seconds later, at 0128, you came up on the air saying you'd found a body. What was going down, Phil?"

Lahey stopped talking. He pressed his fingers together in a quasi-prayer.

McManus licked his lips and drew in a short breath. "I didn't hear them calling me. Honestly. This is the first time I've heard they were trying. You guys know you don't get good radio reception in that area. I didn't hear anything."

Lahey dropped his hands on the table and slid his fingers back onto his lap, leaving streaks on the steel. He turned to Anderson.

"What were you looking for out there?" Anderson asked.

"A barking dog. It sounded like it was hurt," McManus said, avoiding Lahey's penetrating stare. "I got out of the car because I couldn't drive any further, and then went looking to see if it was caught in a bush or something. It was the dog that led me to the body."

"Why didn't you call for backup?"

"What, for a barking dog?"

"When was the last time you talked to Cassidy?" Lahey asked.

"Like I told you last night, I haven't seen him since the class reunion a couple years ago."

"I remember you two didn't get along too well back at St. Anne or S.I.," Lahey said.

"That was grammar school." McManus stared at Lahey.

"Is there anything you didn't put in the report that you can remember? What about Cassidy's car? Did you see it?"

What the fuck are they thinking? Pinning me to Cassidy's murder because of what went down when we were in school? Everyone knew we were rivals. But murder? This is bullshit! "There were some cars parked up by the Legion of Honor," McManus said. "I just secured the crime scene and waited for you guys—figured you'd check out the cars."

"You ever see Cassidy out there before?"

"Never," McManus said.

"You think he was on the Down-low?"

McManus shrugged. "I got the same questions about him you got."

"How about the dog?"

"I guess he just wandered away when everybody showed up. I didn't think anything about it, to tell you the truth."

Anderson got up and turned on the TV, which hung from the ceiling. He popped in a DVD.

This is not good. McManus grew more uneasy as he watched the video load.

"Okay, Phil," Anderson said. "We want you to watch something."

The close-up image of McManus shot by the television crew at the crime scene appeared on the screen. For a moment, the silence of the room startled him. He would have preferred the cacophony of inmates than to hear his heart beat like this. He rarely sweated under pressure, but now he could feel the beads forming above his brows. *I make a shitty liar. But I'd rather be pegged as a murder suspect than as trying to off myself.*

"Now it's a little hard to see on this screen, Phil, but last night you looked a little rough around the edges. How'd you get those scrapes on your face?"

I'm fucked. McManus shifted in his seat. "Again, it's like I told you last night, I was walking down that cart path near where I found the body and slipped on some of those eucalyptus seedpods. They're all over the place."

Lahey drew his hands together again, steeple-like, fingertips barely touching. "How's your food poisoning today?"

"Where was this food truck you ate at, so we can advise the Health Department?" Anderson added.

"I can't remember," he said. "Do you remember where you ate yesterday?"

"Sodini's on Green Street," Lahey said. "Linguini with clams in a white sauce."

"What kinda B.S. is this? You guys think I'm a suspect? Thirty-seven years in the business together and you bring me up here to the prison to separate me from my weapon …you got that little respect for me?"

Lahey looked stunned, as if McManus coldcocked him.

"You really think I'd kill a guy on-duty, pull his pants down to blow him…then hang around for you guys to investigate? On Christmas?"

"Calm down, Phil. We've all been in this business long enough to know anything is possible. We're just checking out the what-ifs."

"Screw your 'what-ifs.' Mirandize me," McManus said. "It's that little cocksucker Grogan, isn't it? He put you up to this, didn't he? He's been screwing with me, trying to get me to retire since he got out to Richmond, to show the kids on the watch how tough he is."

Anderson leaned forward in his seat. "We got a 26-minute window of time we can't account for," he said. "And you got cuts and scratches all over your hands and face. Those are some big red flags, Phil."

Lahey pulled a small digital camera from his briefcase. "We need to get some pictures." He photographed McManus' injuries, studied the images, and then turned the camera around to show McManus.

Shit, I look like something a rat in the sewer would chew on…

"Okay, you can go now," Lahey said.

McManus rose from the bench, feeling his face flush.

They walked to the door. Anderson stopped and looked at him, "One other thing we wanted to ask you. You lose anything out there?"

"Where?"

"Lands End."

"No," he said. *Should I have said that?*

Lahey and Anderson smirked at each other.

I don't think they bought it.

"Okay, Phil," Lahey said. "We'll be in touch."

FRIDAY
CHRISTMAS DAY 2009 · 2030 HRS.

No one in the SFPD could see this demonstration coming. The crowd was small at first, maybe 25 dissidents, marching up Market Street, heading to City Hall. Many wore black watch caps and bandanas to hide their identities. Some beat on bongo drums; others carried black flags. But in the age of social media, a disgruntled crowd could gather quickly to protest a police shooting allegedly of a transient African-American man or even over the right to lie on sidewalks drinking wine in brown paper bags. "#Police War: No Justice—No Peace," read the Twitter posts.

The perfect storm of civil disorder could go down on Christmas night when police staffing was at a bare minimum. This evening's call for help went out right after McManus left the Hall of Justice. Responding with red lights and siren, he reached City Hall within minutes.

"What's this?" he asked another cop as they parked their radio cars on the McAllister Street side of the building. The growing crowd in front of City Hall chanted, "No Justice—No Peace...They got away with murder." They waved banners proclaiming, "SFPD Has Blood On Their Hands."

Hats and bats time. Let's get it on. McManus grabbed riot gear from the trunk of his radio car. Whistles echoed throughout the Civic Center Plaza as McManus joined a line of twenty helmeted cops in the City Hall rotunda waiting for orders. Meantime, police radios crackled with ominous reports from Union Square of window-smash burglaries, citizen assaults and holiday decoration destruction.

To the former St. Ignatius and Sacred Heart football players who'd joined the SFPD, this now felt like the adult version of the Bruce/Mahoney Trophy Game. City Hall was under attack and needed to be defended.

As long as I'm here...NO FUCKIN' WAY these creeps are getting in here to destroy the joint. McManus pulled down the protective face shield on his helmet, ready for battle.

Intent on taking over City Hall, protestors tore the gilded handles from the building's front glass doors. They used them as battering rams to break out the windows, attempting to gain entrance through the locked doors.

"What's the hold-up?" one cop yelled.

"I'm waiting for orders," the lieutenant-in-charge responded.

The yelling and screaming grew louder. McManus watched the front doors of City Hall give way under the rioters' weight. Three people tumbled onto the marble floor. He heard the crowd roar its approval, sounding as if the 49ers had just scored a touchdown. The line of twenty cops braced for an imminent attack. McManus tightened the grip on his baton. But no demonstrators ventured further into the building.

What the fuck is going on?... They're backing off without a fight? McManus lifted the protective face shield. Wiping his brow, he smelled the acrid odor of burning rubber wafting through the rotunda.

"They torched the radio cars," an officer yelled.

The lieutenant-in-charge could no longer control the frustrations of his officers. He released the floodgates and stepped aside. Like a broken hornet's nest, eight cops broke ranks and stormed out of City Hall onto McAllister Street.

McManus joined the remaining officers in a wedge formation for their mutual protection. Together they lock-stepped forward with thrusting batons to disperse the mob.

He caught sight of their radio cars fully engulfed in flames and the lone-wolf officers trapped by gangs of protestors. *This crowd seems different. They're standing their ground and spitting at us. They think we're abusive? What about Lahey and Anderson abusing me? Do I even want to be in this fight?... HELL, YES...You wanna fight? Let's get it on you guys.*

For over an hour, McManus waged hand-to-hand combat with rioters while the crowd roared, fires raged, whistles blew, and sirens blared.

Reinforcements finally arrived from the district stations, and the cops managed to form a protective blue wall around

City Hall. Standing shoulder-to-shoulder, they held batons ready to challenge rioters.

Soon a thin, light-skinned African American woman with a hoodie sweatshirt stood a foot from McManus pointing toward his hip and screaming in his face, "You're a coward! You're a coward! You have a military weapon." Others moved forward, crowding in next to her. A second woman shouted in his face, "You have no right to do this!"

I swear to God. If I look these women in the eyes, I'm going to fuckin' lose it. Stay cool, McManus, Stay cool. He gritted his teeth and swallowed hard.

Standing four feet behind the women was a white man in his early 20s holding a video camera.

OK, cameras are rolling... Best Behavior now—Stay Cool.

Speaking with a foreign accent, a third woman jabbed her finger at McManus and shrieked in his face, "This is a democracy! You are violating my Constitution Rights as an American citizen to protest."

McManus focused his eyes beyond the women and noticed three young white men with full black beards and black watch caps pulled tight, standing silently together.

Those guys are trouble. They're going to pull something here in a minute. I can just feel it. They're too quiet. They're using the women to distract us. Gotta watch 'em...Fuck!... Get out of my face, will ya lady.

"Shame on you! No More Police Shootings, Shame on you! No More Police Shootings," chanted the line of protesters.

Another woman gave McManus the finger and shook it in his face. "Slave...you are the new form of slave." She uncurled her finger and pointed to the gold numbers on the side of his riot helmet. "You're just a slave. Slave Number One, One, Two, Five." You're a fuckin' slave of the fuckin' rich people."

Stay Cool! Stay Cool! McManus watched the women move down the line of officers calling out their stars numbers. Anger was building in the cops' eyes.

McManus had turned his attention back to observe the three men in watch caps when through the smoky night sky, a rock found its target just above his already torn-up right knee. A searing pain shot through his leg.

"Fuck!" he screamed as he fell to the ground, pushing his palm against his leg to stop the bleeding.

McManus looked up and caught sight of a young dissident laughing at him. Wearing a black hoodie sweatshirt, he was inside the screaming throng of people taunting the cops.

McManus staggered back up to his feet. *You're mine, dude.* He lumbered decidedly toward the young man whose laughter stopped, and fear now showed in his eyes.

"Here come the Pig, Here come the Pig," the crowd taunted.

Suddenly the area turned into a psychedelic light show as flashes from dozens of camera phones captured McManus thrusting his baton into the hooded man's mid-section. McManus' hands burned as if a swarm of bees had stung him. Mustering all his strength, he whacked the doubled-over protestor in the ass with his baton.

Collapsed on the ground, the man screamed, "You got what you wanted man."

Two officers stepped forward and dragged him away, arresting him for failure to disperse and assaulting a policeman.

Helped by two other officers, McManus limped toward a waiting ambulance. He stopped, turned, and looked back at the man as he was pushed into the paddy wagon.

"Who's laughing now, asshole!" McManus yelled.

4

McManus awoke a few hours later in his condo from a dream about his mother walking in bloody peanut butter on a blue tile floor. He jerked up in bed. *Shit! Why am I STILL thinking about that day, now?*

He checked the bandages covering the contusion and three stitches on his right thigh. Then he hobbled to the wet bar and pulled the horse-and-jockey stopper from a new bottle of Blanton's. He took a swig and looked up through the bay window. *Whoa! Rain sounds like pebbles hitting the glass. And that wind... Guess this the start of another El Niño weekend?*

McManus shook his head to clear his sinuses and pressed his hands against his eyes. Pain shot from the torn flesh on his palms. The phone rang. He checked the Caller ID. It was his former police partner, Guido Donatelli. McManus picked up.

"You hear about Tony Mannella?" Donatelli asked without saying, "Hello."

"No," McManus said.

"Brace yourself…bad death."

"Oh God, No!" *He just retired!*

After 34 years in the SFPD, Mannella had planned a dream vacation to Italy to celebrate the start of his new life.

"He was with his family on that long flight," Donatelli said. "Heard he developed a blood clot. When he got to the hotel, he collapsed and died."

"Jesus." *The guy was a devout Catholic and he dies on Christmas Eve in Rome. Wow!* McManus slumped down in the green bean bag chair in front of the window and took another slug of Blanton's.

"Can you fuckin' believe that?" He picked up the jockey stopper and threw it against the wall, leaving a hole.

McManus wiped his eyes. "One of the good guys and now he's gone."

"Might as well have pulled the pin from a hand grenade," Donatelli said.

McManus listened to the sound of the rain hitting the window. "What is it about pulling the pin? Most cops seem to fall apart as soon as they retire."

"You know what it is. We're all wound up on adrenaline. We don't know how to relax."

Ain't that the truth, Thank God for Blanton's.

After an awkward silence, Donatelli spoke again. "Ole Tony-boy would have gotten a laugh out of that picture of you on the front page of the *Chronicle* this morning."

"What are you talking about?"

"You haven't seen the paper?"

McManus hung up the phone and reached for the Blanton's. He took another swig. This time he swished it around like mouthwash before he swallowed. He walked to the front door and retrieved the paper. Filling the top half of the front page was the color photo of a cop with "1125" on his riot helmet. The cop's eyes bulged like a catfish, his police baton poised above his head ready to strike.

Swell overnight I'm now the poster child for police brutality. FUCK THOSE PEOPLE! They're anarchists. If they were serious about changing the world, they'd be storming City Hall demanding an application to join the SFPD.

McManus called in sick for a legitimate reason, to lay low for the weekend. Blanton's and Advil helped dull the physical pain, but nothing seemed to stop the film loop running 24/7 in his mind. He flinched at the double feature of him hanging by his gun belt off the edge of a cliff, followed by his inability to dodge a rock hurtling out of the smoky darkness.

The phone rang again.

Fucking phone. Go away! That constant ringing is as tormenting as Mom's warnings that something's always going to go wrong. What the fuck do they want? The notification of pending charges and my suspension for brutality? The call from

Homicide with more questions about Cassidy's murder? Or is this is the end—disguised by the department's Post-Traumatic Stress Crisis Intervention team checking on my well-being. Take your pick.

Rain poured all weekend, and McManus didn't go outside. Instead, he watched the 49ers end a depressing season on a winning note, beating the hapless Detroit Lions 20-3. After the game, he lay in the beanbag chair and looked out the bay window to watch the clouds form and re-form.

At least I don't have Cassidy's problems. Who'd he piss off? Hell, who didn't he piss off? If this investigation goes any further, I'm going to need to call the POA for a lawyer.

MONDAY

DECEMBER 28, 2009 · 0430 HRS.

What's that mysterious rumbling in the closet? What's in that strange burlap sack? Something's thrashing around in there. I need to call a snake charmer.

"*You gotta Spitting Cobra snake there mistah,*" *he said through his thick Indian accent.*

"*Well, just get it out of here,*" *McManus screamed.*

"*Nothing to be afraid of,*" *the charmer said, picking up the sack and untying the knot. The sack shook, and then slipped through the charmer's hands to the floor. The cobra slithered loose and flared its hood...McManus saw his mother's face on the cobra's body.*

He awoke from the nightmare, drenched in sweat. His heart was racing like a NASCAR engine.

I gotta get going. I gotta clean this house. Is it her again, more of her, "Just when things go good," bullshit? She was always saying that dusting calmed her mind and vacuuming was the only exercise she needed. He went to the hall closet and pulled out the vacuum cleaner. He unwound the cord, plugged it in, and then ran it over the green shag rug.

They got me on an assault charge. That guy is gonna sue the shit out of me and the city. Even though I was the one hit by a rock—just like the NFL—second guy into the fight always gets caught. Maybe I could claim Diminished Capacity or something. Can they take my pension? No. Ha, Ha, I'm under their old plan.

McManus' typical middle-of-the-night vacuuming pissed off his neighbors, who sometimes would pound on the door—but not this morning. He shut off the vacuum cleaner, rubbed his eyes, and stared up at the wood-beamed ceiling. After an eye-opener of Blanton's, he walked to the bay window where the fog was coming back in. *At least my soulmate hasn't abandoned me.*

He stood at the open window and watched the mist linger atop Twin Peaks—as if to catch its breath after the four-mile push inland from the Pacific. Then little fingers of fog, like wax melting from a candle, cascaded down the south side of Twin Peaks. When it reached the intersection of Burnett and Portola Drive, it fanned out in all directions. Within moments, the view from McManus' condo disappeared.

Feels like I'm in an airplane dipping into a cloud.

"Very pretty out there. Haven't seen you do that in a while, Foggy," he said.

McManus was a San Francisco kid who loved the fog's quirky character. Especially on mornings like this when it appeared as a ghostlike supernatural force. Over the years, McManus and the fog developed a system to communicate. McManus would pose a question or make a statement. If the fog agreed, McManus would feel the wind ruffle his thinning hair. If the fog didn't agree, the air was still.

Who needs Google when I got Foggy and Blanton's?

"Foggy, guess what? I think the years are taking their toll."

A puff of wind came through the open window.

5

Something was up when McManus entered the station locker room on Wednesday night. Benson Tran, the young cop with whom McManus traded watches on Christmas, and who normally chatted about his new son, changed into his uniform without acknowledging him.

He also noticed that Greene, the civilian station duty officer, was avoiding him. When McManus asked him about getting a new battery for his PIC radio, Greene picked up a telephone. McManus could hear the dial tone.

Roddick, the station keeper, stood in the business office watching the scene play out. Finally, Roddick glanced right and left, sidled up to McManus, and whispered, "Grogan passed the word—we're not supposed to talk to you."

Locking eyes for a moment with Roddick, McManus stiffened his upper lip and then curled it into a smile. *At least Roddick's got some balls.*

"Okay, thanks," McManus said.

Roddick shook his head and walked away.

6

The next night, a rare New Year's Eve blue moon heightened McManus' trepidation as he drove to work. When he arrived, he found the neighborhood around Richmond Station transformed into a media encampment. Three television satellite trucks, their transmission masts extended, blocked a lane of traffic double-parking in front of the station. *I can't believe no one hasn't ticketed those TV trucks yet.* Inside, he watched Grogan in the middle of the assembly room, bathed in camera lights and surrounded by reporters.

"What's up?" McManus enquired in the locker room as he changed into his uniform.

"Grogan made a grab on two guys in the Cassidy murder."

"No shit."

McManus shook his head and went back out to the assembly room. He stood on the outer edge of the reporters listening to Grogan describe how, an hour before, patrolling along El Camino Del Mar Drive, the glare from the setting sun caused him to reduce the speed of his radio car to a crawl.

"At this time, I heard the sound of breaking glass and observed two suspects wearing baseball caps entering a parked, silver Honda CRV." Grogan then began to read from his notes, stumbling over the pronunciation of Russian names.

"These suspects have been identified as Aleksey Vladimirovich Khamuttshikh and Sergey Abramov. Both are 24-year old Russian college students. They are in this country on tourist visas. Their hometown is St. Petersburg."

Grogan looked up from his notes and said, "That's the St. Petersburg in Russia, near the Baltic Sea, not the Atlantic Ocean, for those of you who don't know."

This story's off the charts. A criminal's stupidity and a cop's good fortune are responsible for most arrests. But, this is 100% pure-grade shit house luck.

"I then exited my patrol car and confronted the suspects at gunpoint inside the vehicle," Grogan continued. "At this time, one of the suspects, Mr. Khamuttshikh, flashed a gold San Francisco firefighter's badge in the hopes, perhaps, I wouldn't shoot him."

"Apparently, unlike in Russia, the San Francisco police department has a policy not to shoot suspects caught in the commission of an auto burglary."

McManus' stomach churned upon hearing Grogan's glibness. *So this is the hip new world of the SFPD. Never heard of a patrol cop calling a press conference to talk up an arrest he'd made.*

"We have now been able to determine that the gold San Francisco Fire Department badge belonged to the deceased, Deputy Chief Peter Cassidy."

THURSDAY
DECEMBER 31, 2009 · 1730 HRS.

A light rain fell on New Year's Eve traffic as McManus patrolled the district.

"Richmond Six," called the radio dispatcher. "Arguello and Geary, the Doggie Diner. Says here, check on the well-being of the cook." The dispatcher paused, and then added, "Maybe he ate one of his hamburgers. See if he's keeled over in the back. Interview the manager."

A hamburger didn't make the cook keel over—it was old John Barleycorn.

The odor of cooked onions breezed throughout the intersection of Geary and Arguello as McManus arrived at the "Dog" and parked in front in the bus stop. Standing outside in a cloud of greasy gray smoke, the manager Juan glared at him.

This guy's really pissed. What did Colin do now?

"He's your friend, McManus. Get his ass outta here.

He showed up drunk Christmas Eve and now tonight. One more time…HE'S DONE!"

Time for a little sucking up. McManus nodded. "No problem, Juan, I appreciate your courtesy. I'll take care of him. Christmas Eve, you said?"

"Yeah, he was so fucked up, I sent him right home."

Inside, Colin O'Connell was leaning against a counter lighting a cigarette with unsteady hands. He wore a grease-soiled white tee shirt sporting the Doggie Diner logo—a wiener dog wearing a bow tie and chef's hat.

McManus and O'Connell had known each other since their Midget League baseball days at St. Anne School. Their friendship had flickered on and off over the years as O'Connell was spiraling downhill, spending most of his time in bars or fencing stolen property.

McManus had tried to help by getting him the cook's job when he was released from county jail two months before.

"Come on, Colin, let's go." McManus pulled the cigarette from O'Connell's lips and threw it to the ground. Then he grabbed his arm and pushed him outside and into the backseat of the radio car.

"That guy is a fuckin' idiot," O'Connell said.

And you're not. "He is the boss, stupid shit."

"Yeah…well, I got a 139 IQ, McManus, what was yours?"

McManus slammed the back door shut and got behind the wheel.

"What the fuck," O'Connell complained as he pounded his fist against the Plexiglas partition that separated the front seat from the back.

"Shut up or you're spending the night in jail."

"You're taking me to jail on New Year's Eve, asshole?"

"SHUT UP!"

McManus glared at O'Connell through the rearview mirror and saw him slump back into the seat. His clothes still reeked.

Jeez, now the fuckin' car's gonna stink of grease and onions all night. "You used to be great in everything—now you're just great at making a mess."

O'Connell sulked in silence as McManus wheeled the radio car into traffic on Geary. They headed toward 16th Avenue where O'Connell lived—in the same house they'd played in as kids. The memories flooded in.

The cookies his mother Deirdre used to bake. Both our fathers dying. O'Connell nearly losing his own life drag racing on the Great Highway. O'Connell losing the football scholarship to Cal. Grad Night when he showed up high on LSD and circulated around our capped and gowned classmates, telling them not to worry about the military draft because he was "God" and he'd just ended the Vietnam War. The guy's a TOTAL FUCK. What the hell am I doing here?

McManus cut through the park and stopped for the light at Ninth and Lincoln Way. He noticed a large New Year's Eve crowd waiting to get into the Little Shamrock bar.

"You can drop me here," O'Connell said.

McManus looked at him in the rearview mirror. "You hear who got murdered last week?"

"Who doesn't wind up murdered in this fuckin' town?"

Does he or doesn't he know? "Pete Cassidy." McManus checked the mirror again. O'Connell sat up. *He's really shocked.*

"Oh, man, how?"

"Stabbed at Lands End…I found the body," McManus said.

"Serves him right. He was a total dick."

"Look who's talking. And you were the paragon of virtue?"

O'Connell raised his voice and made no attempt to hide his contempt for McManus. "You were jealous 'cause Cassidy got more ink in the papers than you did. You ever get your name in the paper?"

When the light turned green, McManus kicked the accelerator, throwing O'Connell back into his seat.

"You're going to the funeral, right?" McManus yelled above the roar of the engine.

O'Connell struggled to sit up. "No fuckin' way."

Jerk.

McManus braked hard sending O'Connell hurtling forward this time against the Plexiglas partition. *That thing separates us in more ways than one.*

He turned around and stared back at O'Connell. "You know what, Colin? Get over it. That was over forty years ago."

O'Connell spat at the Plexiglas.

That's classy. "You could have achieved all the stuff he did, but you drank it away. You had some kind of death wish after the accident."

O'Connell leaned forward. "I was drinking for the exact opposite reason you were, Phil. You were always trying to find yourself. I was trying to forget."

THURSDAY
DECEMBER 31, 2009 · 2345 HRS.

Fifteen minutes left in this fuckin' year and the rain's falling harder. That's a bad sign…What the hell do I have to look forward to in 2010? Returning to patrol, he wheeled the radio car onto a narrow pedestrian pathway just inside Golden Gate Park. Ahead on the rain-slickened path, the car's headlights reflected the bare feet of a meandering teenaged girl, who turned around and squinted into the bright lights.

Blondie looks fucked up. She have any idea where she's at? Oh brother, she needs more protection than that drenched wool shawl over her head. What the hell is she doing? What has she been doing? He activated the red and blue emergency lights and aimed the high-intensity spotlight at her head. She extended her middle figure.

Are you kidding me little girl? He slammed the car into park and called for backup.

"Richmond One, responding. What do you need?"

Another fucked up hippie chick… But I can't say that over the air. Can I? "Juvenile X, wandering in the rain barefoot on the path in the Panhandle at about Oak and Cole. May be under the influence, copy, Richmond One?"

"10-4, two blocks away, be right there."

The girl glared at McManus as she stood shivering under a thick grove of eucalyptus trees.

Don't look at me like that you little slut or I'll leave you out here for the wolves. "What's your name, Miss?"

"I love to smoke pot and wiggle my toes." She laughed and stuck out her tongue.

"Is that your first or last name?"

"You're funny, Blue Meanie."

"You gotta a name, don't you? Did you take anything tonight?" *You look pretty spacy to me, sweetie.*

She rocked back and forth for a minute. "Oh, I've had several LSD trips, but not tonight. Acid does nothing for me. I like to smoke pot. It…"

"Okay I got it."

The headlights of another radio car appeared.

It's going to kill the rest of the night dealing with this kid. We're going to have to take her into protective custody and try to find her parents. Typical bullshit. Why am I wasting my time?

"There's a weird New Year's party goin' on in that place," she blurted out, pointing across the street.

McManus looked over to the five-story Queen Anne apartment house and saw flickering lights on the top floor. "What are they doing?" *All of a sudden she's not such a snot…*

"I think they're going to make a human sacrifice. There's a baby girl—she's only a couple days old…"

I know this building, a turn-of-the-century dump, waiting to be converted into posh condos next to the park when the economy turns. For now, it's just transients, druggies, and police calls.

Help arrived in the person of Joe Garibaldi, another loner cop without a family to be with tonight. "Whatcha got?" he asked.

"Don't know exactly, but she says there's some kind of weird stuff in that apartment across the street."

"There's always shit going down in that dump," Garibaldi said.

The girl was still rocking, her eyes glassy like she was going into a trance. "They're going to throw a baby into the fireplace. You better hurry up. They're laughing about it. Said they'd do it at midnight to celebrate New Year's."

What the fuck. Who throws a baby into a fireplace? "Who's the 'They'?'?"

"Those people are freaky. Into Voodoo or something. I got outta there. One of them just had that baby. It cries too much."

"Did someone say they were going to throw the baby in the fireplace at midnight?" Garibaldi asked.

"I think, maybe…the Black Eel said it."

"Who the fuck is the Black Eel?" McManus asked.

The girl shook her head. "He lives there. He gets all his bitches high, and then fucks 'em."

This some old creep? "How old is this guy?" McManus asked.

"Maybe thirty," she said.

"Which apartment?" Garibaldi asked, staring at the building across the street.

"The top one. Looks like they could have a fireplace going," McManus answered.

"It's nearing midnight." Garibaldi glanced down at his watch.

"I don't mind telling you that Voodoo shit freaks me

out," McManus said. "I was in New Orleans one time for the Super Bowl and learned all about it. Too many cops there think Voodoo has the power to make them drop to their knees and bark like dogs."

"Really?" Garibaldi said. "Then, we'd better call the 30-car."

"Good luck gettin' him. Ya think Grogan has any balls? He's not going to risk taking any blowback from having to make a decision that might be controversial. You watch. Call him and he'll make a traffic stop or have to go back to the station to take a piss before he gets here."

McManus did a visual check of her for weapons, then opened the back door of his radio car. She got in and lay down on the seat. He locked the door and called for more backup. Then the two officers crossed Oak Street and entered the apartment. They climbed the stairs, playing their Kel-Lites on each step. The building smelled of piss and burning marijuana. Scattered about in the hallways were filthy straw mats, and the walls were covered with crayoned drawings. The pair stopped on the stairway and listened to what sounded like several women chanting.

"Maybe the chick's not BS-ing us," Garibaldi said.

"I think you're right." Should we wait? *Come on Grogan, where the fuck are ya?*

When they reached the top floor, they saw a faint glow coming from under the door of an apartment at the end of the hallway.

That grass smell's getting stronger. It's too quiet here. Maybe we tipped them off.

The two drew their weapons. Garibaldi pressed his back against the wall and followed McManus down the hallway.

Then the chanting started up again. A baby screeched.

Shit. McManus holstered his weapon. "Cover me." He stood in front of the apartment door and raised his right leg to drive the heel of his boot into the wood just above the knob.

The jamb splintered apart as the door swung open, revealing a smoky haze backlit by a fireplace. Inside, three nude women, heads bowed, their hands pressed together, sat cross-legged on the floor around a large white table-cloth. Another woman held a large glass bong. She looked up and coughed. McManus ran into the room and saw a small bundle lying on the table cloth.

"San Francisco police. Nobody moves," he said.

He dove in between them and scooped up the bundle from the floor like he was recovering a fumble on the foot-ball field. One of the women leapt to her feet and from behind grabbed his hair.

"Fuck," he screamed as the bundle fell from his hands, spilling clothing onto to the floor. *I can't believe that chick just tore the hair outta my head! Where's the baby?*

A scream came from another room.

Garibaldi entered the apartment and pushed the naked woman off McManus. She held up the tuft of McManus' hair in her hand and screamed at him, "You're a machine who will never know love."

She looks like a crazed animal caught in a trap. This is not good.

The woman turned and threw his hair into the fireplace.

FRIDAY
JANUARY 1, 2010 • 0400 HRS.

McManus spent the rest of the watch writing reports and finding protective custody for the baby and the barefoot young girl. The women were a different story. They all possessed medical marijuana cards, so they could only be booked for child endangerment and battery on a police officer.

McManus refused medical treatment to his scalp. *It's a new year—but so far, the insanity hasn't changed. The shit's gonna hit the fan on this one. Am I Voodoo-cursed now? What's up with this "I'll never know love" crap? What if I'd waited for Grogan? No, Dipshit was off making a fuckin' traffic stop.*

On his way home, he stopped by O'Connell's place.

"Happy fuckin' New Year, McManus," O'Connell said opening his front door.

"Dude, it's four in the morning. You still drinkin'?" McManus pushed his way inside.

O'Connell stood at the open door trying to steady himself. "Hey, you can't arrest me in my own house."

He's always been a happy drunk. But now Old John Barleycorn has squeezed the joy out of him. His skin looks like tissue paper, and his arm bruises are as big as oranges. O'Connell has run off everyone who's ever cared about him except me. I've got that fucking Catholic guilt, and I'm all he has left.

That loyalty's still costing me $116 a month. Should never have co-signed his student loan 20 years ago. The dick had enrolled *at St. Mary's College, and then he never finished classes. He totally ignores the monthly payments. WHAT A FUCKIN' ASSHOLE! Well, I'm the stupid asshole because I'm still writing checks.*

Once well-kept, O'Connell's two-story Doelger box was now a neighborhood eyesore, a far cry from the house he'd grown up in and inherited from his mother. The front of the house was equal parts exposed stucco and peeling beige paint.

How could he have let this place go to shit? Another example of his total lack of responsibility. That's his real problem… and why he's in a death spiral.

Chris Berman, the ESPN announcer, was delivering Montreal Canadians highlights in French from the TV set. Still wearing the onion-and-grease-stained T-shirt, O'Connell had slumped onto a couch in front of the TV.

"You may be my oldest friend, Colin, but I can't keep saving your ass," McManus said.

"Yeah, right," O'Connell laughed.

McManus shook his head. He looked around and noticed flies crawling along a pile of plates in the kitchen sink. "Your Mom wouldn't be happy if she saw this place. You ever wash the dishes?"

"No, but have at it, McManus."

McManus couldn't help himself. He turned on the hot water, scattering the flies. "Still eating Lucky Charms, I see." He reached into the cereal box next to the sink, shook it, gave it sniff, and then grabbed a handful.

"Hey, man, don't be eating my food," O'Connell hollered from the living room.

"You owe me, asshole."

Friend, you were once a natural in everything. 4.0 at St. Ignatius High School and All-City in both football and baseball to boot. Even had the best car in school, thanks to your mom on your sixteenth birthday—a canary yellow 1966 Jaguar XKE 2+2 coupe.

But you didn't have any of it long. That Friday night out at the Great Highway, drag-racing Cassidy, you skidded up the ice plant center divider and launched into that terrifying series of end-over-end flips. Then you managed to walk away with only a cut nose and hand…but minus one sweet car and that full-ride scholarship from Cal. Too bad they rescinded the offer, giving it instead to Cassidy after hearing about the accident.

"What time you got to be at work tonight?"

"Nine."

"Think you can make it?"

"I always make it."

Oh yeah sure. Think I'm going to help you? It's the dishes and I'm outta here. He turned and headed for the door. "I expect to see you at Cassidy's funeral."

"When is it?"

"You get to work by nine. You can find out for yourself."

FRIDAY
JANUARY 1, 2010 · 0445 HRS.

McManus turned on the windshield wipers. They squeezed across the glass. *I want to be nice to Colin, but he's always been an asshole. Couldn't even come to my defense that time in the school yard. That lunch-time basketball game back at St. Anne when I blocked out Cassidy for a rebound.*

My elbow grazed Cassidy's ear as I came down with the ball. Then he punched me from behind in the kidney and I crumpled to the ground, crying. The game stopped and every-one watched him taunt me. Then O'Connell appeared behind him. I thought Colin was my friend and would kick his ass. So what's he do? He boasted: "Yeah, if you can't run with the big dogs, McManus, stay on the porch."

Asshole.

FRIDAY
JANUARY 1, 2010 • 0545 HRS.

McManus climbed to the top of the staircase and looked into the bathroom. His mother, naked and bloodstained stood in a black puddle. She caught sight of him staring at her.

"NO!" she screamed and began chasing him. He turned and ran back down the stairs, glancing over his shoulder at her. Both her hands were missing. Blood sprayed from the stubs of her arms onto the walls and ceiling as if it were water coming from a fire hose.

McManus woke, saw the time, rolled over and went back to sleep.

Flo smiled as she placed the plate of bacon and eggs in front of McManus. "Speak," she said.

McManus, in uniform, dutifully got off his stool onto his hands and knees on the floor. Flo then reached under the counter for the smiling Santa Claus doll. After she flipped the switch in Santa's ass, the doll lit up and "Jingle Bell Rock" played from inside its plastic belly.

"Dance," she said. McManus rocked back and forth to the music.

"Good Boy," she said. "Now bark."

McManus barked.

"McManus, you're a good doggie." Flo then tossed him a piece of bacon.

McManus woke, saw the time, rolled over and went back to sleep—again.

The weight pulling on the buckle of McManus' Sam Browne belt finally burst apart sending him falling backwards from the rock into the night and the frigid air and the black water

and the crashing waves onto the rocks. He screamed.
McManus woke, saw the time, and got up.
Happy Fuckin' New Year.

7

An Honor Guard carried the casket containing the body of San Francisco Fire Department Deputy Chief Peter Cassidy down the front steps of St. Anne Church. In uniform, McManus stood with hundreds of firefighters, issuing a final hand salute. The casket passed under a huge American flag hung from the extended aerial ladders of two SFFD truck companies as a solo bagpiper played "Amazing Grace."

Look at this. Everyone is stunned by the murder. But something's up. I don't have a clue...and I was there.

Across Judah Street, McManus saw Lahey and Anderson standing with a group of civilian mourners. Nearby, mixed in with the media contingent, the video guy from CSI photographed the crowd.

Who looks guilty around here? Who's nervous and fidgety? Who's really outta place? It's not unusual for a killer to attend his victim's funeral.

As the hearse pulled away from the church, McManus noticed the familiar face of Rich Falkenburg, a member of McManus' 1972 SFPD Academy Class. He had transferred from the police department to the fire department in 1977 and joined Cassidy's SFFD fire college class.

"Hey, nice picture in the *Chronicle*," Falkenburg said.

"Yeah, thanks," McManus laughed and hugged him. "Where you at now?"

"I'm out-the-line as the driver at 34 Engine, getting ready to retire," Falkenburg said.

"That's like stealing," McManus shook his head.

"So, when are you going to pull-the-pin?"

McManus didn't respond.

"There's not going to be a burial," Falkenburg said. "Cassidy's will requested cremation, and his ashes are to be scattered at his favorite spots throughout the city. Kezar Stadium is one of them. Why don't you come to Fahey's where a bunch of us are getting together? The bar's going to be closed to the public, so we can drink in uniform. You ready to drink, McManus?" he winked.

MONDAY
JANUARY 4, 2010 · 1330 HRS.

The shining red COCKTAILS sign above the brown barn doors was a familiar sight to first responders throughout the city. By the time McManus arrived, the sun had burned off the morning marine layer.

McManus didn't recognize the firefighter in his dress blue uniform posted at the entrance. The Jakey gave him the once-over and saw the name "McManus" embossed on his uniform's name tag. The fireman smiled and said, "You're okay—you're Irish." He swung open the door. McManus nodded and entered.

On the bar, a table shrine displayed Cassidy's personal memorabilia, including a dozen family photographs.

Yes, minus the coffin, this looks like the typical Irish wake. But the mood is different, not the raucous affairs I'm used to. Gotta be a courtesy to the family. "I'll have two fingers of Blanton's...thanks."

"Don't carry Blanton's," the bartender said. "How about three fingers of Jack instead?"

"Sure, why not," McManus said, and then turned back toward an argument at the front door.

"He's my friend, motherfucker," screamed Colin O'Connell, dressed in jeans and a gray sweatshirt, with his hands on his hips glaring at the uniformed bouncer. The firefighter drew himself up to his full 6-foot 4- inch height and pulled the door closed.

I'm not getting involved in that one. Everybody's dressed in uniform, and he shows up looking like a shit bum... Way to go, Colin. McManus sipped his Jack and watched a red-faced old firefighter kneel to pray in front of the shrine, and then struggle to rise from his knees. Once upright, the tear-faced old man leaned forward to kiss the top of Cassidy's battle-scarred fire helmet. Its gold shield read "SFFD Deputy Chief" with his initials "MPC."

The widow, Gina Cassidy, stood with a solid steady gaze in a receiving line. She'd removed the black lace floral veil she'd worn during the funeral service. McManus studied her greeting the old firefighter. She reached out, brushed away his tears, and gave him a hug with a reassuring smile.

After a moment, the old firefighter smiled, too.

That's nice. Gina could be sweet... when she wanted to be. Still a gorgeous Italian woman, trim and stylish, even in her late 50s. Almost as pretty as the picture in their wedding announcement 35 years ago. How about that? Cassidy got the Homecoming Queen.

McManus finished his drink and walked over to the table shrine, which contained three helmets—each from a different era of Cassidy's life. McManus recognized Cassidy's white St. Ignatius football helmet with blue "S. I." stickers on the sides. It sat next to Cassidy's silver-and-black Oakland Raiders helmet and his soot-covered white fire helmet. Next to the helmets was an official National Football League game ball. Painted silver and black, the ball honored Cassidy's five solo tackles on kick coverage during a 1974 game against the San Diego Chargers.

A smoky-smelling SFFD turnout coat with "Cassidy 1125" painted on the collar hung from a chair beside the table. His black #17 Raiders home game jersey, with "Cassidy" in silver letters across the shoulders, hung from another chair.

McManus stood in front of Cassidy's shrine and saluted. Releasing the salute, McManus realized Gina, her two kids and a woman firefighter had been waiting for him. Embarrassed, he walked forward to greet her. When she saw the SFPD uniform and his name tag, her eyes lit up. "Phil McManus. Thank you for coming," she said.

My junior year at S.I. I was head-over-heels in love with her. She was the Homecoming Queen and Cassidy's girlfriend. Rank has its privilege. He was the quarterback of the football team—I was only an outside linebacker. She was a senior at Presentation High—I was a junior. No chance with her, I'd thought, but one night Gina Fratelli and I fucked.

It was unbelievable! Recognized her one day at Candlestick when I was working security, and she had her purse snatched with her car keys inside. She had no way of getting home. Made the report and said if she could wait until I got off-duty, I'd drive her home to get the spare set of keys. Told her I'd played with Cassidy at S.I. She said she remembered me from the catch that won the Turkey Day championship game. We talked about Cassidy playing for the Raiders. She said they broke up right after high school when he went to Berkeley and she went to nursing school at USF. She was working in the Franciscan Treatment Room at St. Francis Hospital.

So I drove her to her place in Twin Peaks. Used the old credit card trick to slip the lock, and opened her front door. She was impressed and invited me in to stay for a drink. I couldn't believe it. Maybe it was the uniform and the gun, but we were in her bed in ten minutes. Never fit so perfectly into a woman. Felt like I was touching the Face of God. She wrapped her legs around my hips and trapped me inside her. Then she just sort of went limp, and that's all it took.

Best fuck I ever had. God, I was in love with her. Drove her back to Candlestick that night to get her car. She gave me her number. Really thought she was a woman I could marry. I could see myself being in love with her and our two kids living in Novato or Pacifica and being really, really happy... Didn't turn out that way. "Mrs. Cassidy, I'm sorry for your loss."

Gina Cassidy smiled, put her hand on his arm, and thanked him with a nod. *Her sincerity surprises me. I wonder if she even remembers.*

She turned and introduced her son, Emmett, dressed in a black suit and tie. *Emmett's got a firm handshake.*

Gina next introduced Katie, their daughter. *So this is "Kickin" Katie Cassidy? She's the spitting image of her mother when she was in high school. I've read about her career as the goalkeeper for the USF women's soccer team. She can kick a ball 70 yards in the air.*

McManus shook Katie's hand, then looked back at Gina. *Is she checking me out?*

His eyes drifted to the floor. *What should I say to her now?* "Gina, I was the one who found Pete's body at Lincoln Park."

Her face went pale.

I'm an idiot. That was really insensitive. McManus tilted his head to the side in a gesture that said, "I'm sorry," then reached into his pocket, pulled out one of his SFPD business cards, and handed it to her. "If there's anything I can help you with, please call me, Gina. I'm so sorry for your loss."

Gina took the card and pulled him into her embrace. She rested her cheek on the Silver Star pinned to his chest. When she released him, she kissed his cheek. With a slight tremor in her lips she said, "Thank you."

Wow. What was THAT all about? Wish she could have felt that way back in the day. She never returned any of my phone calls. Finally, one day I just went to her house. She opened the door with a pissed-off look and said, "I thought you would have gotten the hint." Wham, bam! I felt sick and stupid. What a fucking bitch!

Standing next to Gina was a sturdy, athletic-looking woman, dressed in the "Class A" navy blue uniform of a San Francisco firefighter. The woman, also in her 50s, had rolled her hair into a bun. She had brown eyes and 1/4-carat diamond studs in her ears. *She looks like an emergency responder, confident, emotions in check, perhaps ready to say something sarcastic to mask her pain.*

"Phil McManus," Gina said, "This is my sister, Trish Fratelli."

He shook her hand. *Those callouses on her hand feel like I'm shaking hands with a car mechanic. She's really tall. Must be at least, five-foot-ten. Can almost looked me in the eye.*

"Trish, Phil found Pete's body."

Trish Fratelli's eyes locked onto him.

McManus returned to the bar and ordered three more fingers of Jack. Falkenburg joined him. "You know what's weird?" he asked.

McManus wrinkled his face. *Where's this going?*

"If Cassidy hadn't sprained his ankle, he never would have become a fireman."

McManus arched his eyebrows and shook his head.

"The week before the '71 entrance test, he's playing for Cal at Arkansas. He sprained his ankle and couldn't play for six weeks. Bad news/good news deal. It screwed up his season and would force him to make the NFL via the free agent route. But the next Saturday, instead of playing in a game, he was able to limp over to San Francisco and pass the SFFD written."

"Sometimes it's better to be lucky than good," McManus said. "That guy had everything going for him. A great house in Golden Gate Heights. Marries Gina Fratelli, the Homecoming Queen. And with something like that at home ..."

Jeez, I'm starting to get a heat-on. Well, time to ask Falkenburg the million dollar question. "Why do you think Cassidy was out at Lincoln Park, trolling for some guy to suck his dick?"

Falkenburg stared at McManus like he was an asshole.

Is it the question or my tone that caught him the wrong way?

"I know what you're thinking," Falkenburg said. "Cassidy's no saint. But he had enough cachet around here not to have people speculating and trashing his rep, if you know what I mean." Falkenburg swirled the ice cubes in his

Jack Daniels and took a sip. He continued to give McManus the stink eye. "It would be in your best interest, McManus, not to stir up that kind of shit around here tonight."

"Fair enough," McManus said. *Something's not right here.* Falkenburg stood up and headed for the restroom.

Phew…better stay clear of that question the rest of the night. Look at her over there. Across the bar, McManus caught a glimpse of Trish Fratelli surrounded by a group of female firefighters, all of whom she towered over. He watched Fratelli tilt her head back, cast a sideways glance at him, and smile.

Oh that's interesting. There's something about her eyes and posture. I betcha she's pretty good firefighter. Better shut it down, though. This isn't the time or place to hit on her. Then he gazed in her direction again and saw her coming toward him. She carried a glass of white wine.

"Okay, I remember who you are, now," Fratelli said. "The Turkey Day game. You and Colin O'Connell. Right?"

McManus chuckled.

"It's always better to be lucky than good, McManus," she said.

McManus smiled. *That burn scar on the side of her neck? Wonder how she got it?*

"What's Colin O'Connell doing these days?" she asked.

"You didn't see him?"

"No, I know he's not in the fire department. S. I. Irishman. Is he a cop?"

McManus shook his head.

"Then he's either a priest or a drunk," she said.

McManus smiled to himself. *That's pretty perceptive sweetie.*
Fratelli swirled the wine in her glass.

"I made out with him one night up on Turtle Hill at one of the football team drink-ups," she laughed. "My sister was appalled. She was the Homecoming Queen there with Pete—and her little sophomore sister stole the show by kissing a senior as everyone cheered."

"That was you?"

"Yep."

Those Friday nights up on Turtle Hill were the best. The football team would gather there afterwards to discuss the game. Then all the Presentation girls would show up together. It was so pretty at night on top of that hill looking out at the sweeping vista of the city.

"You go to Prez?" he asked.

Fratelli raised her glass in a salute and smiled. "Started at Presentation, but finished at Lincoln. My parents were mortified. One daughter was the perfect four-point-oh and Homecoming Queen. The other got kicked out of the school."

"Better to be lucky than good, I guess," McManus said.

Fratelli feigned indignation by placing her hand on her hip. She took a sip from her wine. "Touché, McManus," she grinned, while not losing eye contact.

Her voice turned sincere. "I appreciate you coming to honor Pete. He was a great brother-in-law."

She looked down and appeared lost in thought. Then she looked back at him and said, "Well, McManus, maybe we'll cross paths some night out on the front lines."

"Where do you work?

"Thirty-four engine. Out there on Pt. Lobos at 41st Avenue."

"Maybe we will," he said. "I work midnights at Richmond Station."

McManus nodded and watched her walk away to rejoin the group of women firefighters. *I think there was more she wanted to say...No ring. Great ass. Wonder what her story is?*

Falkenburg returned.

"What's with you and the Fratelli sisters tonight?" he asked.

"What's her story?"

"Don't light the pilot light just yet. She's on my crew at 34, and maybe you'll get lucky, but she's a fuckin' dyke. She owns a lesbo bar down the street by the beach."

You're shitting me. Is everybody in this town gay now?

"See the dingy-looking blonde next to her?"

McManus looked at the woman wearing a black pantsuit, who appeared to be much younger than Fratelli.

"That's her new roommate, or playfellow, or whatever dykes call their significant other. She's a social worker at the General. They started going together a couple months ago," Falkenburg said, swirling a fresh Jack in his hand.

Well, so much for that idea.

"Got a great story about her," Falkenburg said. "Fratelli used to be straight 'til a couple years ago. Then she started hanging out with this smokin' hot Cuban bitch with Bette Davis eyes. The Cuban used to drive Fratelli to work every morning in her white 735i BMW and park in the firehouse driveway to drop her off. This is down at Station 16 in the

Marina. During the change of watch, there'd be a dozen guys standing around waitin' to get relieved. Fratelli would show up, get out of the car, and then stick her ass out as she'd lean in the car window to say goodbye. The Cuban's eyes told you all you needed to know about what was going down."

Oh My God! I can see it, now. McManus smiled at the story.

"Fratelli's taxi service didn't last long," Falkenberg continued. "One of the guys on the crew told a cop friend, who pulled the Cuban over one morning and wrote her a '500d' tag for parking in the driveway of a firehouse."

"What an asshole," McManus said.

"Yeah, Fratelli thought so, too. She's actually a pretty good fireman, but sometimes she doesn't want to be part of the group. After she met the Cuban, she became standoffish to the rest of the crew...I guess it was understandable." Falkenberg took a drink.

"A lot of the Jakeys then absolutely loathed having women in the department when she first got hired. To them, having a dyke in the department was the ultimate insult—a stain on the uniform. Most of those guys have retired now, and the years have passed. Things seemed to have mellowed out. But we all wonder why Fratelli's not more open. She's a mystery. Take your pick. Never know what's going on inside her head. She whipsaws back and forth between being a dyke and being a bitch," he said, shaking his head. "Good luck if you're gonna make a run at her."

I'm getting drunk...Better shut it down. McManus grunted a yawn. He looked across the bar at Fratelli and sighed.

Okay. I'm in love. Been awhile. Nothing's in the pipeline. Why am I always attracted to women who aren't available? Shit, I'd better eat a corned beef sandwich and take a walk before I try to drive home.

8

O'Connell fiddled with the thermostat in his living room be-
fore the heater roared to life. It spewed a dirty cloud of dust
and mildew causing him to break into a coughing jag.

"Good thing I don't smoke," he said between coughs so vio-
lent they sounded like his lungs were tearing loose. Suddenly, he
stumbled backwards. A choked gurgle came from deep within
his weary throat as his hands clutched at his chest. Blood poured
from his mouth and ran down his chin. His eyes turned vacant.
O'Connell collapsed against the wall and slid to the floor. He
was dead before he hit the ground.

His soul, wearing a white #82 St. Ignatius football jersey
appeared above his body at the exact instant a guy who looked

like James Dean entered the room wearing black Ray-Bans,
under which his bloody eyeballs dangled.

"Come back a year from tomorrow," O'Connell's soul said
to McManus. "That is if I don't go with him, first," he laughed
pointing toward James Dean.

What the fuck is this?

The phone ringing next to his bed jarred McManus
awake. He opened his eyes and felt like he'd been drugged.

The morning sun peeking through the crack in the curtains blinded him. He pressed his palms to his forehead,
careful not to trigger a back spasm, and then rolled over
onto his side to answer.

"Officer McManus … are you up?" asked a vaguely familiar female voice. "This is Gina Cassidy…I-I spoke with
the priest at St. Anne and decided to call you."

Catholic priest? What the fuck do I have in common with
a Catholic priest? Why me? McManus slumped back onto
his pillow.

"I need to talk to you about the investigation," she said
in a plaintive voice.

Swell. "Mrs. Cassidy, I'd like to help, but I'm not the
investigating officer. That's Inspector Lahey and his partner,
downtown at the Hall of Justice." He sat up in bed and
shifted the phone to his other ear, and then rubbed his eyes
with his forearm until he could focus.

"I know that," she said. A long silence followed before
she spoke again. "I think they're covering something up. I
need to see you."

Oh, great!

After dressing, McManus found two berry-flavored antacids in the medicine cabinet and popped them into his mouth.

Maybe it's time to cut back on the drinkin'...or just stick with Blanton's... Shit, I'll worry about that later.

He went out to his Camry, which was parked on the street. Before driving off, he wiped the morning dew from the windshield.

Going to finally see the inside of that showpiece. It was Cassidy's football money that got him one of the most unique houses in all of San Francisco. Watched it being built from my bedroom window when I was a kid. When did they start calling it "The Octagon"? The three-story wood-framed house perched on steel piling on Pacheco Street looks just like a fire watchtower. How appropriate.

McManus found a parking space and walked toward Cassidy's house. With the sun at his back, a cold northwest breeze greeted him. He gazed straight ahead from high atop Golden Gate Heights toward the Marin Headlands and Mount Tamalpais. Resembling the figure of a sleeping lady, the mountain's eastern slope lay strikingly pristine in the morning light. Suddenly, he saw a burly Latino man wearing a brown wrinkled suit leave Cassidy's house. The guy spotted McManus and shot him a hard-ass look.

There's that scumbag Rodriguez. What the fuck is he doing?

Rodriguez was a disbarred attorney who served both sides of San Francisco's legal and cultural divide. At night, speaking Spanish to mostly Mexican clients, Rodriguez worked as a bail bondsman. During the day, he transformed himself into an intimidating process server in affluent white neighborhoods.

At the Cassidy home, Gina was holding a brown envelope and papers when she opened the door for McManus.

Rodriguez probably dropped off that stuff. She doesn't look happy. "Did you get subpoenaed or served?"

"How do you know that?"

"I've seen that guy around."

"I got served," she said looking frustrated at the pages of legal-sized documents.

Gina led him into the house and out onto a veranda that circled the top floor of the octagonal house. She blinked her swollen eyes to adjust to the sunlight.

A sleepless night, I bet. Trying to dull the pain with Cabernet?...or something stronger? "A house befitting of the S.I. Homecoming Queen, Gina," he said, trying not to sound too patronizing.

She turned toward him and smirked. "Pete's dream house—not mine. This homecoming queen would have been happy living down there in the Avenues in a Doelger box. Pete was the one who needed the 'look-at-me' showcase. I just needed my family...You want coffee?"

Who are you kidding, Gina. This place is all you. I don't believe that story for a minute. He watched her ass sway out of the room and turned to take in the panorama across Golden Gate Park toward the conspicuous twin spires of St. Ignatius Church. The glass and metallic surfaces on the church's façade were ablaze with sunlight.

After a few moments, she returned with two coffee mugs and nodded toward the church. "When I woke this morning, I wondered if the fires of Purgatory had cleansed the sins from my husband's soul, and if he finally might be experiencing perfect joy and inner peace in Heaven."

Whoa? How's that? I'm sure Pete's not worrying about any Catholic bullshit. Obviously, Gina's a different story. Apparently her faith in the virtues of the Catholic Church, marriage and family have never wavered. Pretty old school, I'd say…but really hard to buy. Let's just get on with whatever.

He took a mug from Gina and followed her through an open sliding glass door back into the house.

"We call this the Observation Floor." She waved her right hand around the room displaying 270-degrees of unobstructed floor-to-ceiling windows. The white carpet and drapes contrasted with the high-gloss black-lacquered furniture. The only color in the room came from an abstract painting featuring the eras of Cassidy's life with his black Oakland Raiders uniform and his white SFFD chief's helmet.

They sat facing each other in twin wingback chairs with a coffee table between them.

Look at that fuckin' bling! Gina's the quintessential trophy wife. How much did that four-carat solitaire diamond and the gold Rolex set Cassidy back? Holy Shit! She'd never have gotten that outta me. God, she's still SO stunningly beautiful…even with what looks like a royal hangover.

"I remember when you were the May Queen, Gina." He smiled recalling the memory of her leading the procession of classmates through St. Anne Church to lay roses at the statue of the Blessed Virgin Mary.

Gina shot him an anxious look. Setting down her mug, she sat straight up and clasped her hands in her lap. "Curious you should mention that. It's exactly what I was thinking yesterday during the service. Where did all the time go? You ever marry, Phil?"

We might have. He shook his head and said, "No."

"Let me tell you something about marriage, then."

Okay, this should be interesting. He watched her lips tighten in anger.

"It was a disappointment. My marriage had high artistic potential, but it went unrealized. The pieces to create a masterpiece were in place, but my husband always remained aloof."

Gina shifted in her seat, her voice cold and distant. No mistaking the hard edge to her words.

"When I think of the essence of being Irish, Italian and Catholic—the ideals of marriage and family are all inseparable," she said. "Sadly, Pete didn't see it that way. He never accompanied our family to Sunday Mass. Trying to be cute, he'd tell me he was a CEO. You know what that means?"

Knowing Cassidy, this is gonna be good. He shook his head again.

"Christmas and Easter only," she said in defeat.

That's classic! What a dick thing to say to your wife.

"When I asked him, 'Why,' he'd stiffen and assume the role of the pontificating philosopher. He used words like hypocritical, outdated, and boring because he knew those words cut right to my heart. Then he'd just dismiss me by explaining he'd fulfilled his spiritual obligations by watching TV—the Sunday services of the First Church of the National Football League." She tossed her papers on the coffee table and sat back, looking worn and disgusted.

McManus lowered his eyes to the stack of legal looking documents on the table.

"Now, I've got a lawsuit to contend with from someone I thought was an old friend. Him and his son, the sociopaths. They have a complete lack of empathy. We just buried Pete and they're suing. Claimed we misrepresented a problem with a water leak when we sold them an apartment house. A tenant let her toilet overflow for a couple days, figuring if she claimed a storm caused the damage, she wouldn't have to pay her rent."

McManus folded his hands and listened.

"$200,000 worth of damage! It happened AFTER we closed on the place." Gina shook her head and sighed. "It's curious. Now that Pete's gone, I'm dealing with messes I had no idea he was involved in. Who was Pete Cassidy, really?"

Whoa. "Excuse me?"

"I tried to stay in the background regarding Pete's business transactions. He dealt with the outside world and let me run things around here. I found my satisfaction making a comfortable home for him and my children."

"Well, your windows are spotless, Gina," he said with a smile. *Darned if she's turned into a Stepford Wife. Maybe I could get her to come over and do mine...and me.*

"Thank you. I enjoy housekeeping. It gives me a sense of accomplishment. I wanted to be the good wife for Pete, and I admit I liked the solitude. In fact, it was sort of my meditation."

The house phone rang. Gina didn't make a move to answer it. It rang again. "Probably some solicitor." She let the phone ring until it stopped.

Let's see if she remembers we were lovers. "You still a nurse?" he asked, shifting in his chair.

Gina sipped her coffee and frowned.

She remembers, but what the fuck good is that going to do me. And what the hell am I really doing here?

"No. I got my nursing degree from USF, and then worked at St. Francis Hospital for a couple years. I enjoyed that. It's where I met Pete, again. He was finished with football and had just joined the Fire Department. He proposed, and when we got married, he didn't want me to work."

"Why's that?" *Might as well let her finish the story. I do want to find out where she's at right now. Then we'll get down to business.*

"Pete saw himself as an old-school breadwinner and sole provider. Said he wanted a large traditional Irish/Catholic family. Fortunately, we stopped at two. I hadn't resisted the idea of being a wife and mother because that's how I'd envisioned myself when I was growing up."

McManus sighed. "I lost my father, and my mother *had* to work," he said.

Gina nodded without comment.

The notes from Paul Hardcastle's mellow instrumental "Rainforest" played from the state-of-the-art sound system. McManus looked around and stared for a moment at the expensive-looking painting.

That abstract doesn't look like something Cassidy would cough up big bucks for. McManus took a sip from his mug and let it linger in his mouth, trying to taste any difference in the expensive blend she'd probably used. *Just tastes like coffee.*

"Nice service yesterday," he said struggling to find anything to say. "At the wake, I got a chance to talk to your sister, Trish. Didn't realize she was in the Fire Department, too. Haven't seen her since high school. We talked about those Friday nights up on Turtle Hill. Remember them?"

The mention of her sister caused Gina's face to tighten in anger again.

Sibling rivalry I suspect. Gina looks pissed.

"My sister and I don't see each other often, pretty much because I don't want to get caught up in her dramas. But now she's got this roommate who's a real loose cannon. Quite frankly, it's disgusting how they're living. Imagine how I felt to see her little playmate at my birthday party. She really didn't have to bring her to the funeral yesterday."

A house sparrow chirping outside brought Gina out of her seat. She walked to close the sliding glass door.

Great posture, great ass. Probably from years of yoga and Pilates. Wonder what she's like in bed now?

"Here's why I wanted you to come over, Phil. The detectives have asked a lot of questions about why Pete was at Lands End. You know why? What have you heard? It sounds to me like they're trying to cover up something."

McManus shook his head. "I'm just a patrolman, Gina. They don't tell me anything. I just found the body."

Gina seemed to flinch when he said the word *body*. "I wasn't home when he left," she said defensively. "I think he was just out there taking a walk. Or maybe he was golfing. He loved practicing on that fourth hole. Told me he dreamed of getting an Eagle on it. Sometimes after the course closed, he'd just play that hole over and over again."

McManus smiled. *Cassidy was always pushing it.*

"So why are they asking ME all these questions? I feel like a suspect."

Okay, I get it. We're here about the investigation. "Gina, Homicide's work is very thorough, and it's never cordial. Most murders are committed by relatives, and either they're solved within the first forty-eight hours or they never are."

Gina looked stunned. "You mean they think I did it? Murdered my own husband? For the love of God, how can they possibly think that?"

Well, duuh! You mean the thought never occurred to you. The spouse is always the first suspect.

She sat back in her seat as McManus watched her complexion redden.

"Well, then, I'm glad I didn't tell them that Pete wanted a divorce. I don't trust those guys."

Whoa! Wait a minute! Cassidy wanted a divorce? "Say that again!"

"It hadn't happened yet. So maybe it wouldn't have happened, and I saw no good reason those detectives should know."

Hold on lady. You're in total denial, here. Jeez, how stupid am I for coming over here now? Is this a set-up? She had Rodriguez standing at her front door to ID me. Fuck! How would she know Lahey's squeezing me as a suspect? Maybe she's working some sort of deal with him to get me. What the fuck is going on here?

"You gotta tell Homicide about that, Gina," he said as he stretched out his arms toward her and turned up his palms. "That opens up a whole new can of worms. Divorces can end up with all kinds of issues. People can get so mad they want to kill someone. Did Pete give you a reason?"

"I don't know if you'll understand this, Phil," she said with sadness in her voice. "But I was afraid. Pete could get extremely angry. My husband was like my father. They were both vicious men."

Gina looked away before continuing. "Pete's aggressiveness was always lurking just underneath the surface, especially when he was drinking. He was abusive ... and I didn't want him to turn on me. I'd seen my father blow up over nothing, time and time again." She paused to fight back tears.

"What made everything worse is that I couldn't get along with my sister Trish because she was so jealous of me. In her eyes, I was the idolized daughter. But I did feel sorry for her when my father went for her after beating up my mother."

Well, shit, Cassidy had a place to fill with Gina. He was a bad ass Oakland Raider and had an image to live up to. He shook his head. "I'm sorry to hear all of that, Gina."

"What am I supposed to do, Phil?" Her pleading eyes did make him want to help her in some way.

"Well, the first thing you gotta do is contact Lahey and his partner downtown at the Hall. Best to tell them the story exactly like you just told me," he said. "But don't mention I came here or this conversation."

They looked at each other for a moment without speaking Gina nodded sadly.

Okay, I gotta get out of here before we wind up doing something that really complicates this thing. "I think we're done here now," he said and took a step toward the door.

"Phil," Gina said grabbing his right elbow. He stopped and looked back.

"I've always thought my heart was either my biggest strength or my biggest weakness." Her eyes were red and watery. "I've never been able to decide which."

He studied her for a moment. *I have no way to respond to that one.*

9

The radio crackled to life as soon as McManus got behind the wheel of department vehicle 024: "Richmond Six. Respond to near the seventeenth hole of the Lincoln Park golf course. 909 Mr. Williams, regarding found property."

"Richmond Six, responding." *Another bullshit run about nothing. Wonder what this guy's got?*

McManus wished he could enjoy the twilight time as he drove through the outer Richmond district, but his sour mood wouldn't allow that. On the seat next to him lay the pink copy of the District Attorney's Rebooking Information File. The DA "dismissed in the interest of justice" all charges against the Voodoo women, including the assault on a police officer. The DA warned McManus that he was also vulnerable to a false arrest suit. *Typical. San Francisco's more afraid of the cops than the crazies.*

He rolled down the car window, took a deep breath, and noticed how quickly people seemed to be walking around on this Friday night. *Everyone's got great plans for the weekend now that their workweek's done. Not me. Mine is just starting. Something's wrong with this picture.*

From the car, he noticed a brown, barren Christmas tree lying in a gutter at Twenty-Eighth Avenue and California Street. *That's sad. Two weeks ago that tree was the centerpiece in some family's home. I can see the parents taking pictures of their kids tearing open presents under that tree. Well, I guess the tree did its duty and then just gets tossed out in the street and forgotten… No wonder the world's fucked up. Nobody's got sentiment anymore.*

Charles Williams, a 6-foot 8-inch black man, stood in front of his 9.6 million dollar home on El Camino Del Mar and waved down McManus' radio car. Parked in front of the house was a cream-colored Drophead Coupe Rolls. Inside the three–car garage sat a red Ferrari F50 and a black Hummer H2. The Hummer appeared to have bulletproof glass and armor.

Driven past this place a million times and always wondered why Daddy Warbucks left his ghetto cruiser outside in the fog. With the garage door open, I see why now. Holy Shit! McManus parked and approached.

Williams held a German shepherd on its leash. The dog was built like an Abrams tank. It sniffed at McManus' shoes when he got close. *That's a bad-ass looking guard dog. Looks like he could take me with one bite... Wait a minute...I've seen that dog before.*

The man pulled the dog away. "This is Uzi. I'm Charles Williams, the man who called."

McManus nodded and studied the dog more closely. *That's it! Uzi's the dog I almost shot just before I found Cassidy's body. Williams must own him. What's the deal here?*

"I got something you might be interested in." Williams led McManus inside his Spanish-style mansion. Wagging his tail, Uzi followed them. They walked across the mottled white Italian marble floor through the vestibule, and then through two sets of French doors into a sitting room with a floor-to-ceiling stone fireplace.

Been in almost every home in Sea Cliff and never saw anything close to this. Makes Cassidy's classy place look like a tenement. "You play in the NFL or the NBA?" McManus asked.

Williams looked at McManus and smirked. "I'm a businessman. KYA Management. Stands for Kiss Yo' Ass. I handle athletes' money; then I make them more money."

McManus nodded and looked out the window at the view of the Golden Gate Bridge. Distracted, he didn't notice Williams bring out a fluorescent-colored scuba diver's knife.

"Look like a murder weapon to you? Could be connected to the murder of your fire chief, you think?" Williams held the knife by the blade and handed it to McManus.

Oh Shit. Any usable evidence on that knife is contaminated now. McManus reached into his coat pocket and pulled out a clear plastic evidence bag. "Just drop it in there."

Williams placed the knife into the bag. "The dog found it in the bushes when we were walking."

McManus sealed the bag. "The dog have it by the handle or the blade?"

"Handle, with lots of slobber dripping on it. Figured there weren't going to be any fingerprints left."

Smiling at the image of Uzi with the knife in his mouth, McManus called Homicide. "Is Uzi a family pet or a working dog...looks like he could be pretty aggressive if he had to be."

"Yeah, I picked him out special. He's a professionally-trained guard dog."

"Does he stay in the house or outside?"

Williams eyed McManus cautiously. "I let him wander the grounds...can't be too careful around here. We're backed up against the open space. A lot of freaks out here."

McManus nodded and stared again through William's large living room window at the Golden Gate Bridge. "You ever get tired of that view?"

"Would you?"

FRIDAY
JANUARY 8, 2010 • 1800 HRS.

Inspector Lahey accompanied Williams and McManus along the pathway next to the seventeenth fairway. Using Kel-Lites, the trio followed muddy trails soft from the recent rains. After about five minutes, Williams stopped and directed his beam into the bushes.

"Here," he said.

"How do you know this is it?" Lahey asked.

"X marks the spot." Williams pointed to a clumsy "X" he'd drawn in the mud with the toe of his shoe.

McManus looked at the heavy underbrush. *The knife's location is about three quarters of a mile from Cassidy's murder site—that's well outside the perimeter of the evidence search.*

Lahey made notes in his report book and took pictures.

"Thank you, Mr. Williams," Lahey said. "We appreciate your help. You and Uzi can go now."

"Just glad to help the police." The dog barked as Williams turned and went home.

Lahey looked hard at McManus. "Cute trick, McManus, contaminating the evidence."

Fuck you. "Me? Screw you, Beluga. You aren't gonna get any prints or DNA off that thing. The weather out here probably washed it like a dishwasher. Besides, you know this is some sorta gay beef gone bad. You got a 59-year-old family man and fire chief wandering around Lands End on Christmas Eve, and he winds up with his balls chopped off."

"We're just following procedure here."

McManus scoffed. "You know the dog I saw out here near Cassidy's body was a German shepherd."

"We'll check it out."

Colin O'Connell sat on the curb with his head in his hands as traffic flashed by the Doggie Diner on Geary Boulevard. His manager, Juan, stood behind him. As McManus parked in the bus zone, Juan ran up and pointed back at O'Connell. "He's your friend, Officer. He's done. I've told you if he shows up drunk one more time…"

McManus nodded and held up his hands. He walked over to O'Connell, who had rolled over on the sidewalk and was resting his head on his arm. McManus tapped O'Connell on his foot with a nightstick. "Let's go, Colin."

"Is he gone?" O'Connell looked up cross-eyed.

"Yeah, and so are you," McManus said shoving O'Connell into the back seat of the radio car.

As soon as he pulled the car away, he turned to the back. "I try to take care of you, Colin, and you do this shit. We're done. Roll over and die, pal."

"Screw you, McManus. Remember us at halftime of the Turkey Day game? You didn't quit then, and you won't quit now. We were the 'Miracle Team.'"

McManus pulled the radio car over and parked. He turned around and looked at O'Connell, who lay across the back seat curled in the fetal position in pain.

This is now the defining moment in both our lives.

43 YEARS BEFORE
THANKSGIVING DAY
NOVEMBER 24, 1966 • 1215 HRS.

"Time to take your diapers off and be men." St. Ignatius football coach Lou Paganini shrieked, as he chased his team through the tunnel leading back to the Kezar Stadium locker room. He'd just watched their asses get kicked by Lowell during the first half of the San Francisco city championship game.

"If you quit now, you're contemptible and have no honor." His caustic voice echoed in the dusty tunnel.

The sound of metal-tipped cleats echoed on the concrete floor as McManus and O'Connell bowed their heads on entering the locker room. They found side-by-side stools in the back. McManus picked up a towel off the floor to wipe dirt from a bloody scrape on his forearm before taking a seat.

The team doctor stuck his head in the locker room door and asked, "Anybody hurt?"

Not the right question to ask in front of Paganini.

"They ain't hittin' hard enough to get hurt," the coach growled back at the doctor.

With Paganini, the angry man ruled the room. His black horn-rimmed glasses fogged over as he stared out, waiting for everyone to quiet. Then he assumed his gorilla stance that had earned him the nickname, "The Goon."

"What you have in your mind controls what you do with your body," Paganini croaked.

McManus and O'Connell stared at the floor along with the rest of their teammates.

"Here's the deal, fellas. Don't ever expect much in this life—you suffer now for your salvation in heaven. You gotta suffer before you can celebrate. Look up here, will ya?"

Everyone looked up as Paganini reached into an equipment bag. He pulled out a thick white candle and placed it on the floor. "Anyone can have a Roman's appetite for victory," Paganini screamed with disdain. "Very few have a Spartan's will to suffer for it."

He next pulled out his battered Marine Corps lighter, and with two flicks on the wick, he lit the candle. Then he ripped off his fogged glasses, and with rage-filled eyes, stared into the face of every team member, one by one. The coach's eyes felt like two burning torches to McManus.

"How badly do you want to be champions?" Paganini demanded as he lowered his palm into the flame. "Is your will to win stronger than your pain?"

An hour later, when a last-second pass bounced off McManus and into O'Connell's hands, they had their answer.

FRIDAY
JANUARY 8, 2010 • 2145 HRS.

"McManus, I don't feel well," O'Connell cried from the back seat.

"What's wrong?"

O'Connell answered by puking.

"Shit." McManus jumped from the car and pulled O'Connell out of the back seat, just in time to watch him throw up again onto the sidewalk.

He's fucked. That's gross. The vomit looked like bloody coffee grounds.

FRIDAY

JANUARY 8, 2010 • 2245 HRS.

An hour later, McManus stood in the hallway outside Treatment Room Five at St. Mary's Hospital.

"Your friend has a GI bleed. Looks like his liver is going out on him," the female doctor said.

"Fuck," McManus said, and then apologized to her.

"We're going to give him some blood and see how he does. We should have him stabilized in a couple days." The doctor patted McManus on the back and left.

He nodded his thanks and returned to the treatment room. O'Connell was alone, lying on a gurney awaiting admittance upstairs to an ICU room.

"Just like halftime of the Turkey Day game, Colin? 'The will to win is stronger than your pain.'"

"I don't think so, Phil. I'm so tired." O'Connell's words were muddled because of the tube delivering oxygen through his nostrils.

FRIDAY

JANUARY 8, 2010 · 2250 HRS.

Hopefully, some police work will take my mind off O'Connell. At least being back in service I can do some good...theoretically, anyway.

In the next hour, he handled a blocked driveway complaint on 22nd Avenue and a bill dispute involving a tourist from Des Moines at a restaurant on Clement. The Iowa woman couldn't believe San Francisco prices and shouted at McManus, "You're a big help!"

The streets quieted. McManus welcomed the lull. *Tough couple of hours. Need to eat. Hope my favorite restaurant is still open.*

He drove out Geary Boulevard toward the Cliff House. Brake lights lit up the roadway as he descended the hill at 48th Avenue and Point Lobos. There he saw a tall skinny vagrant standing on the sidewalk waving both arms for cars to stop. Barely visible in the darkness, a small black-and-brown dog was running back and forth across the lanes of traffic. McManus turned on the red warning lights and pulled his car to a stop in the left lane. He got out and saw the terrified animal sitting in the middle of the roadway. *Hope a drunk driver doesn't come roaring over the top of the hill.*

He took off his police parka, hoping to trap the animal with it, but the frightened dog bolted off—directly into a pair of approaching headlights. McManus dove forward, throwing the parka around the animal. *Ouch. There goes the scabs on my knees.*

A white pickup truck roared two feet from his head and threw dirt in his face as he held his arms tightly around the dog.

McManus stood up and got off the road. Meanwhile, the animal was struggling to get free, but McManus managed to jumped into his radio car and throw it onto the passenger seat. The dog wiggled free of the parka, just as he slammed the door shut.

Last week, I'm trying to shoot myself. This week my best friend is dying of alcohol abuse. And now I almost get splattered all over the road trying to save a dog. What the Fuck! This some sort of cosmic bullshit? But jeez! I feel like Superman… Helluva a lot more invigorating than being dead in the water off a cliff.

He drove down the street to the Cliff House, parked in front of the fire hydrant, and shut off the engine. McManus' heart pounded like the hooves of a galloping horse as he glanced at the dog looking up at him.

"You almost got me killed, little doggie, so don't cause me any problems now, okay?"

The dog turned and barked at a man knocking on the passenger window. McManus recognized the vagrant as the man who had been warning drivers at the top of the hill. McManus opened his window and motioned for the man to come around. *What's this guy want?*

The man rounded the car and leaned in the driver side window, two inches from McManus' face. *Cheap wine breath, Phew!*

"Officer, my name is Tyrone, and I'm pissed."

"Back up a little bit, please. You're pissed?"

The man wore a tattered pea coat with a black watch cap pulled tight over his ears. "Meaning no disrespect to you, Officer, but this mo'fuckin' white bitch threw that dog away."

"Excuse me?" *What the fuck is this 'meaning no disrespect,' shit?*

McManus warily got out of the radio car and patted the vagrant down for weapons. Finding none, he got back in the warmth of the radio car.

"So what were you saying, Tyrone?'

"Likes I was sayin'…the bitch wuz carryin' the dog in her big ole mo'fuckin' purse and screams. Then she grabs the dog by its colla' and throws it on the mo'fuckin' sidewalk."

"What'd she do that for?"

"Cuz, the dog shit her purse."

"How'd you know that, Tyrone?" McManus stifled a laugh and looked down at the dog licking its lips.

"Fa' God's sake. That's what she was screaming."

"So what happened next?"

Tyrone cupped his hands around his mouth to amplify his voice.

"She screams as loud she can, 'Fuck you, Carly. Be homeless if you want.' Then she gots in her car and just drives away. Almost caused an accident, too, backing out into the traffic real fast."

"What kind of car?"

"White, fancy."

"You get the license plate?"

"No, sir."

"What happened next?"

"After she gone, the dog jist runs out in the street after her."

"So the woman called the dog Carly?"

"Yes, sir."

McManus checked the Yorkie for a dog license. She didn't have one.

Shit there goes dinner, now. The Cliff House's closing soon. Maybe they'll give me a break and still serve me. McManus opened his incident report book and began to write out Tyrone's narrative for his police report.

Off in the distance he heard the furious high-pitched whine of a powerful motorcycle winding out and gathering speed.

"Whatta ya use for an address, Tyrone?"

Suddenly, the high-pitched whine went silent, and an instant later, the violent sound of exploding tires and metal grinding on the pavement echoed over the area. A solid thud, the sound of glass exploding, and then silence.

McManus looked up from his notebook and saw an orange glow lighting up the darkness over the hill. *What the hell?*

McManus fired up the radio car, turned on the red warning lights, and sounded the siren. Tyrone jumped back from the window, a look of horror on his face as he looked up the hill. McManus threw the car into reverse and backed out onto Point Lobos Avenue. *Hope nobody's coming.*

Then he slammed the car into drive and headed up the hill where a crowd of people were waving frantically at him.

Arriving on the scene, he turned on his high beams and parked in front of a half-naked man lying twisted at a grotesque angle in the middle of the street. Nearby, flames were spewing forth from an overturned Miata sports car, which lay atop a demolished glass bus shelter.

"Richmond Six, Code 33—urgent," McManus radioed.

"Richmond Six with a Code 33—go," the dispatcher responded.

"Richmond Six to Headquarters," McManus repeated.

"Richmond Six."

"Richmond Six to Headquarters, Code 33," repeated McManus again.

"Can any unit copy and relay? Richmond Six has a Code 33."

"Richmond Six, Code 33."

"Richmond Six, Go."

"Richmond Six. I have an on-view major 519, a couple hundred feet down Point Lobos Avenue from 48th Avenue, opposite the Merrie Way parking lot. Copy?"

"Ten-four," responded the dispatcher. "Are you involved?"

"Negative, Headquarters. I am on scene. Request fire department, Code 3. We have an overturned burning vehicle and victims in the street. Also, request at least two 408s, Code 3, as we have an unknown number of victims at this time. Copy?"

"Ten-four."

"Richmond Six. Also, request additional Richmond units for traffic control, a supervisor and a traffic unit. Copy."

"Ten-four."

McManus sprang out of the radio car and felt his whole body trembling. *Holy Mary, Mother of God, pray for us sinners now and at the hour of our death...*

He closed the car door to prevent the dog from getting loose and knelt beside a man in his early 30s whose badly mangled head was covered in fresh blood. The man's pants were around his knees and blood trickled down from a large wound in his groin.

McManus ran across the street toward the flaming car. He stopped when he heard a loud snap and looked up. He jumped backwards no more than a foot and felt air pressure change as the top portion of the concrete streetlight whooshed down inches from him. It hit the street, exploding into a cloud of dust.

The onlookers gasped.

The bodies of an elderly man and woman lay on the ground next to the burning Miata. Apparently, they had been sitting in the glass bus shelter when the vehicle rolled over them. The body of another 30-year old male crumpled against the curb. *Holy shit, this guy's dead, too.*

Bystanders waved desperately to McManus and pointed up the street to 48th Avenue where halfway down the block a motorcycle lay on its side burning. Challenged by the weight of his gun belt and bullet-proof vest, McManus trudged up the steep hill. Flames illuminated a knot of people aiding a downed rider.

Sirens sounded in the distance.

A woman was holding the man's head in her hands, trying to prevent him from moving. "I'm a nurse," she said to McManus as he was rushing to aid the rider.

"Fire department and ambulances are en route," McManus told her

He saw the jagged bones of the rider's leg sticking out from the torn end of his jeans. The muscles surrounding the bones had contracted, and amazingly there was no blood. *Oh shit! Looks like a leg of lamb in a meat market.*

Using his PIC portable radio, McManus informed Headquarters of the location of a fifth victim. He requested an ambulance and engine company to respond to the scene. Sirens and flashing red lights now filled the intersection of 48th Avenue and Point Lobos. Engine 34 proceeded down Point Lobos to the burning Miata. Medic 14 appeared and headed down 48th Avenue toward McManus. When it arrived, two SFFD paramedics jumped out and quickly wrapped a tourniquet around the stub of the rider's amputated leg. By now, a huge crowd had gathered to gawk.

McManus backed away from the victim and felt someone tapping on his shoulder. He turned around.

"Officer, that man's foot is underneath the car over there," said a ghost-white woman pointing across the street.

"Thank you." McManus said and walked to the vehicle where he crouched down and shined his Kel-Lite beam underneath. There it was. The shoe was missing, but he saw a heavy wool gray sock and foot. Lying flat on the ground, careful not to scratch his star on the pavement, he pulled out the foot.

Gross! Surprising how heavy it is. Am I really doing this? He cradled the foot in both hands and walked back to the paramedics working on the rider. McManus stood out of the victim's line of sight holding the foot. *Hey dude, got your foot for ya.* To the paramedics, he said "You want me to wrap this up and leave it in the rig?"

One of the emergency workers looked up. "No, I'll take it."

Soon a TV helicopter was overhead, recording the grim scene. McManus left the motorcyclist and returned to his radio car to stand guard over the initial victim, now covered by a gray blanket. He awaited the arrival of the coroner. But Grogan got there first. McManus watched him get out of his car, center his hat, and stand with his hands on his hips, taking it all in.

What's Dipshit doing...pretending he's Patton?... Tell me he's not doing that... Holy shit, he is... He's actually imitating that scene where George C. Scott surveys the carnage. What a sick fuck!

Grogan looked toward McManus. He smiled and nodded at him. *Wow!... Maybe Dipshit is going to come over here and compliment me for taking charge of the scene.*

Grogan walked toward McManus standing over the mutilated corpse. He stopped, looked down, and chuckled. Then he walked away.

Asshole.

The coroner arrived to take possession of the body.

"Looks like the waste of a good dick to me, but he's really not my type," a female voice came from behind McManus. *What the fuck?*

McManus turned around. The voice came from a woman wearing soot-stained turnouts with "Thirty-Four" painted on the shield of her black New Yorker fire helmet. The helmet was pushed up on her head, revealing a cocky smile and her hair in pigtails. She looked familiar.

"Trish Fratelli, McManus, we met at Chief Cassidy's wake at Fahey's."

McManus nodded. "So what's your type, Fratelli?"

"Well, for starters, they can't have their heads caved in like that."

"Sounds like you've done this before."

Fratelli chuckled. "Oh yeah, I've done this before. One night out on the Bayshore Freeway, we were all stepping in this goop we thought was either motor oil or engine coolant. Turned out it was the victim we couldn't find. Commute traffic is a killer, McManus, if you let it get to you."

McManus smiled.

Fratelli dug into the pocket of her turnout coat. She pulled out two rolls of Life Savers. "Want one?"

Holding them in the palm of her hand, she offered McManus his choice of either Pep-O-Mint or Tropical Fruits.

McManus reached for the Pep-O-Mint.

Fratelli smiled.

When the coroner completed processing the victim, he asked McManus and Fratelli to help load the body into a bag.

"So, you averse to having coffee with a firefighter?" Fratelli asked as she grabbed for the victim's arms.

Wow. She's asking me out for coffee? "No."

"You live in town?"

The victim's head flopped back onto Fratelli's thigh making a popping sound, leaving a trail of blood and brain goop.

"Oops," she said.

McManus hesitated a moment. "Yep, up in Diamond Heights."

The coroner stepped forward to assist as they lowered the victim into a black body bag.

"Okay, how about Starbucks on California Street in Laurel Village?" she asked. "You be up by one o'clock?"

"Sounds great, Fratelli."

"Okay, Officer McManus. We'll celebrate being alive."

McManus nodded.

Fratelli turned and walked away as the coroner zipped the body bag closed. She stopped after a couple steps and turned back to McManus. "Oh, by the way, your Sergeant. He's an asshole."

McManus looked through his radio car's window after being released from the accident scene. For a moment, he was surprised to see the little Yorkie asleep on the passenger seat. The dog awoke, squeaked a bark, and sat up, wagging her tail when he knocked on the glass and opened the door.

I'm tired and still haven't eaten. I just want to go home, take a shower, and forget all this. But fuck, now I gotta write a report and take her to the shelter all the way downtown.

McManus drove to the all-night Safeway at 48th Avenue and Fulton. He went inside and bought two cans of dog food and a small bag of treats for Carly. *I'll just take her home with me and drop her off at the SPCA before I go to work tomorrow. Jeez, what's with Fratelli wanting to have coffee? There's something about that woman I really like. Too bad she's a dyke.*

10

His shower was hot and steamy as McManus sat inside it on a wooden bench scrubbing his hands and fingernails. *I'm no stranger to mayhem and death, but this one's hard to shake.*

Every time McManus felt his hands were clean, he remembered another scene from the accident, another vision of death, and he upped the intensity of his scrubbing. *Last night was ugly. The guy's head splattered like a dropped watermelon on Fratelli's thigh. That was almost worse than Cassidy's balls hanging by a thread.*

When the water cascading off his neck turned cold, he gave up. Carly barked at him as he stepped from the shower. She jumped up and scratched his shins as he wrapped a towel around his waist.

"Okay, okay. Get down." He bent over and pushed her away. The Yorkie sat at McManus' feet, cocked her head to the side and looked up at him.

McManus looked back, annoyed. "Sorry, sweetie, I don't think this thing is going to work out." *It's more than I want to deal with. I'll drop her off at the pound after I meet with Fratelli.*

McManus pulled on a pair of faded jeans and a black cashmere crewneck sweater.

"You hungry?" McManus opened a can of food, but before he could put it in the dish, Carly jumped up and ate it off the spoon.

"Relax!"

The dog sat in front of the bowl, looking up at him plaintively.

"Bon appetite," he said filling the bowl to the brim.

Carly eagerly gulped down every morsel of dog food and then began running in circles around the condo before she flopped on her back and squirmed side to side in ecstasy. *She's fun to watch. It feels good to laugh.*

Carly finished rolling on the floor, jumped up, and ran to the corner behind McManus' bed.

What's she doing back there?

"No!" McManus screamed as he watched her squat to poop.

Carly turned and looked embarrassed.

"Damn it… You don't poop there." Frustrated, McManus

watched her finish her business, and then got towels to clean the mess.

Carly hid under the bed.

"I'll deal with you later," he said. "I need to go meet someone. Be back in an hour. No barking."

SATURDAY

JANUARY 9, 2010 · 1255 HRS.

Fratelli waited at a small circular table along the side wall of the Laurel Village Starbucks. The sight of her jolted McManus wide-awake. She had combed out her pigtails and wore a black and brown stone bead necklace. A skirt with a hint of thigh had been traded for her bulky, blood-stained turnout pants. Rubber firefighter's boots swapped for a pair of sexy cordovan colored knee-high ones. The sooty black Nomex fire-retardant coat exchanged for a camel-colored, merino wool cardigan.

"You look great in real clothes," he said taking the seat next to her. *That sounded stupid.*

Fratelli grinned. "Yeah, those turnouts aren't much of a fashion statement. I guess I need to take mine in a bit at the hips."

McManus took a calming breath and sipped the coffee she'd bought for him.

"Black okay?" she asked.

McManus nodded. The mood inside Starbucks was as subdued as the foggy light coming through the front windows.

"You okay this morning?" he asked. "That was messy. Worst traffic accident I've ever dealt with. Get any sleep?"

"Yeah, like a baby," she said.

She kidding? "I keep seeing that guy's head flop back onto your leg," he said. "By the way, thanks for saving my uniform pants."

Fratelli shrugged, "We gotta look out for each other, McManus."

The conversation soon turned to old school friends and I-wonder-what-they're-doing-now? The more they talked, the more McManus relaxed.

Wonder if I can somehow ask The Big Question, "Are you still interested in guys?"

The bouncy beat and sultry tones of Sade singing "Paradise" played over the coffee shop speakers.

"Hold on a second." McManus got up from the table. "I've never been in this place early enough to get a cinnamon sticky bun."

A couple moments later, McManus returned with a pastry so large he had to carry it with both hands. Fratelli smiled. He offered it to her and she tore off a piece. He felt her fingers graze his.

"Here's to enjoying being alive," she said holding out her non-fat latte to McManus. He picked up his coffee, and they clinked cups.

"Rumor has it the passenger in the Miata was blowing the driver at the time of the accident," she said

McManus choked back a laugh on his coffee. *Did she really say that?* "At least, he died happy."

Two Jewish men attired in charcoal gray Brooks Brothers suits and yarmulkes walked in from Saturday worship at the nearby Temple Emanu-El. McManus watched them check out Fratelli. She didn't return their stares.

"So why did you join the Fire Department, Trish?"

"Money."

McManus nodded in agreement. "I remember hearing the stories about how hard it was when women first came in," he said wiping sugar from his fingertips. "So how did an EYE–talian gay woman handle all those old harps in the firehouse?"

Fratelli's face tightened. "I was once a New York City bike messenger, McManus... I learned not to complain. Living in the firehouse was cake compared to the place I used to work at. The restroom sign there read, 'Don't piss on the floor.' Pretty classy."

She paused and shook her head. "Let me tell ya. Pedaling a one-speed bike through midtown traffic and breathing diesel fumes for minimum wage. That was a helluva lot harder than pulling fire hose with an air pack on your back."

Fratelli reached up and pushed her hair back over her ear. "And, dangerous? Shit, a truck pulls out in front of you or a bus hits you, and all you're gonna be is a grease spot in the middle of West Fifty-Seventh Street."

The hair worked its way loose, again. "And I guarantee you. There'd be no flags flying at half-staff, no dignitary-filled funeral, and no official thirty-day mourning period."

Okay, I get it. Women can do anything men can.

"Things are changing, McManus. We won't be around

to see it, but 50 years from now women are going to be running the show. Government, corporations…"

McManus smirked. "Why do you think that?"

Fratelli smirked back. "The same reason blacks were allowed into professional sports. It's all about winning. Teams finally recognized winning was more important than maintaining segregation. Women can run things better than men because we don't have the baggage you guys do."

"What'd you mean?"

Fratelli pushed her hair back over her ear. "Guys worry about who gets the credit. Women just worry about getting the job done. When that day finally arrives, getting the job done will be all that matters…women are going to be running things."

McManus saw the two suits looking at him with dismissive sneers. *Fuck you guys. Why you lookin' at me? Don't think I'm good enough for her?*

"If women were to come together and unite," she said. "Things could really turn upside down in this country. It's about waking women up. We're still second-class citizens."

Oh boy, here we go. "Why do you think that?"

Fratelli pulled another piece from the sticky bun. She studied McManus as she chewed on it before answering. "What comes most often to mind in the psyche of women is… 'I'm not good enough; I really don't know what I'm doing. Unfortunately, that was the way I was raised—NOT to follow what really interests me and what I feel passionate about.'

"Instead, I'm groomed to be sure I'm attractive, so I can find someone to provide me with a sense of security. Every magazine cover I see in that Safeway checkout line is going to remind me: 'If I look a certain way; If I walk a certain way; If I dress a certain way; If I talk a certain way. I am guaranteed I'll be loved, and if I am loved, well then, I have security, and I'm going to be okay."

McManus dropped his eyes away from Fratelli's gaze and looked at the tabletop. *Okay, so do I sit here and just agree with her Women's Studies 101 lecture, or what?* He shrugged. "Those are all valid points, Fratelli. I'm not going to argue with you."

She looked at him with surprise in her eyes. Then reaching forward, she tore off another piece from the sticky bun. "So, McManus, are you like a Bullitt or a Dirty Harry cop?"

Thank you for getting off that subject, Fratelli. I was beginning to regret my meeting you. He blew out his breath. "Cute question, Fratelli. Probably neither. Most of the time, I feel like an occupation troop in the ghetto, protecting the rich whites from the poor blacks."

"Come on, McManus. Let's see a little creativity here... Bullitt or Dirty Harry?"

McManus hiked up his shoulders. "I always liked Dirty Harry's quote in *Magnum Force:* 'A man's got to know his limitations.' Great piece of wisdom because the prospect of death limits all people. To deny that is to deny the realization of the inevitability of failure."

How's that for an answer, sweetie? Oh, Fuck. Here comes Lahey. What's he want to do? Bust my chops some more?

"You sound pretty intellectual there, McManus. That the S. I. education?" she asked.

No, that's 59 years of living and paying attention. "Maybe I just see myself as what men really are…just trying to get by and survive," he said, before taking a sip of his coffee.

She stared thoughtfully at him for a moment and nodded.

She wanna hear more? Okay. "I guess to answer your question, I liked Bullitt because he was insubordinate to his superiors. And I liked his girlfriend, Jacqueline Bissett. When I was in the Academy, I bought the same style shoulder holster Bullitt wore. And off-duty, I always wore turtleneck sweaters."

Fratelli arched an eyebrow. "Ever marry, McManus?"

Interesting switch. I guess she's heard all she wants to know about Bullitt. She'll like my answer to this question, maybe. "No. Heard marriage is the screwing you get for the screw you got."

"Sounds like you were married," she chuckled.

"Never married."

"Nobody? You don't hit from the other side of the plate, do you?"

So how am I supposed to tell her, "Yeah I fucked your sister. Fell in love with her but then she destroyed my heart? "No. You know how it is. Warm hellos and sad goodbyes. The only woman I ever would have considered marrying…"

Be careful here! "There was a woman I met in '75 at a Giants game," he said checking for her reaction. Seeing none, he continued. "Didn't last long, but I think she ruined me for sex with any other women."

What'd I say that for? He blushed.

Fratelli laughed.

McManus sat back in his chair. *That was stupid. How could I say that? Oh fuck, here comes Lahey now with his hot chocolate. He's going to sit down with us!*

"How's your sister doing, Fratelli?" Lahey called out with a hint of sarcasm as he reached their table.

She seemed surprised by the question and nudged the troublesome strand of hair over her ear once again. "One thing you should understand about Gina and me, Inspector… It's not in a patriarchal culture's best interest to have women get along. We may be sisters, but there's a generation gap. We've lived different lives and have dissimilar life experiences."

"Whatever," Lahey sneered at her and then turned to McManus. "How are you doing today, big guy?" he asked rubbing McManus' shoulder.

Fuck you. You never let up, do you? "Everything's great, Beluga."

"Glad to hear that," Lahey smirked. "Say, why don't you guys just go get a room?" He called out as he turned to leave.

Fratelli watched his back. "That guy's such a fuckin' asshole," she said.

Well, at least she and I are on the same page about Beluga. "He and the other guy, Anderson, interrogated Gina and me and made us both feel like suspects."

"Part of the job." McManus shook his head.

Get a room? Lahey's never wrong. Always spot-on intuition. Does he know something about Fratelli? Does he know she's not lesbian? "So how is your sister doing?" McManus asked.

"With Pete gone?"

"Yeah."

Fratelli blew out a rueful sigh. "Good days and bad days. We all miss Pete…" Her sentence hung in the air. A glare appeared through the window as the fog started to burn off. McManus squinted and watched the 1-California electric bus unload passengers in front of Starbucks. Fratelli reached forward and, without asking, picked up the last piece of sticky bun and popped it into her mouth.

There's something really feminine about the way she does that.

As she chewed, she again studied McManus' face. "So, what's your deal, McManus?"

"My deal? What do you mean?"

"Come on. It's all over your face, and I don't mean the sugar. You've been doing this job, for what, thirty-plus years, and you still get the shakes about violence and death. And…you think a woman thirty years ago ruined you for sex. Wow. You still got a heart, McManus."

"What's your point?" He leaned back in his seat and turned up his palms to her.

"No point." Fratelli smiled and shook her head. "Gotta go teach my yoga class."

"You teach yoga?"

"You should come to class sometime. Would chill you out. Do you know the Veterans Administration is using yoga to help vets with PTSD?" Reaching into her purse, she grabbed a piece of paper and a pen. After writing her name, phone number and address, she pushed the paper toward him.

Getting up, she reached forward and shook his hand.

"Thanks for the sticky bun," she said.

McManus stood up and moved the table so she could walk past.

Fratelli stopped, turned back, and gave him a hug.

"Stay in touch."

Just when things go good. They go bad. I wasn't ready for her to leave. McManus watched her hips sway as she walked out the door and disappear into the crowd on California Street.

I WILL see that woman again.

SATURDAY
JANUARY 9, 2010 · 1345 HRS.

McManus browsed the candy rack in the gift shop at St. Mary's Hospital. O'Connell always got the chocolate munchies when he stopped drinking, so McManus bought his two favorite candy bars, a Twix and a Reese's. He headed to the ICU. But he arrived only to learn that O'Connell had left.

"Just missed him…checked out AMA," the nurse said.

Against Medical Advice, that's O'Connell. He's in no shape to leave the hospital. That crazy fuck. He's gonna die soon. He cursed and walked back out to his car.

When he got to O'Connell's house, he parked behind a Yellow cab in front of the house. He watched as his friend held open the front door for the cabbie, who labored up the steps under the weight of two cases of Gran Legacy vodka.

Are you kidding me! His Death Wish is likely to come true real soon! McManus got out of his car and followed the cabbie up the stairs. In the doorway, he watched and listened.

"Put it in the kitchen," O'Connell said. The cabbie placed the vodka on the kitchen table along with his business card. O'Connell reached into his pocket and pulled out two $100 bills. He placed one C-note under the business card and handed the cabbie the other.

"If I need something and I call you, you're going to get here like the fuckin' Fire Department, right, Raul?"

Raul nodded.

"What the hell is this?" McManus interrupted.

Surprised, O'Connell looked up. Then laughed.

"Get out of my house, McManus, before I call the cops."

McManus threw up his arms. "Fine, we're done."

McManus grabbed the front door, slammed it as hard as he could, and left.

SATURDAY
JANUARY 9, 2010 • 1400 HRS.

Carly's frantic scratching on the inside of the door greeted McManus when he returned home. *Shit, I completely forgot about her. Aaugh... Too late to drop her off at the SPCA, now. What's that smell? Damn it.*

Carly jumped up at his shins as soon as he opened the door, and then she started running around in circles. He followed the odor to the bedroom and found her poop near the bed where he scooped it up and took it out to the garbage chute. He always eliminated anything from his life that became an inconvenience and that would now include this dog. Carly sat by the bed when he returned. She looked at him with an apologetic expression.

McManus shook his head. *No, don't look at me like that.*

He opened the last can of dog food, fed her, and watched her eat. When she finished, McManus grabbed the unread *San Francisco Chronicle* off the kitchen table and laid it where she'd squatted. "Go on the paper, Carly."

The dog looked at him with a "You got to be kidding," expression.

McManus walked into the bathroom, shut the door, and took a piss. Carly scratched outside. When he opened the door, Carly again jumped up at his shins. He walked out into the living room, then nodded his head in appreciation at what he saw laying on the newspaper.

"Good job, Carly."

You know what? Fuck the SPCA. I'm keeping this dog.

SATURDAY
JANUARY 9, 2010 · 1530 HRS.

The front door was open when McManus returned to O'Connell's house. A pair of shit-stained jockey shorts lying just inside the door greeted him. From the dining room, he heard the familiar crash of ten falling wooden pins. He followed the sound and found O'Connell, hunched over the '60s-era "Skittle-bowl" game. He was about to swing a ball on the end of a chain to knock down the pins.

Man, I can't believe that's the same game we played with as kids on the same battered old table. "What the fuck did you do, Colin, check out of the hospital so you could come home, drink, shit your pants, and play Skittle-bowl?"

O'Connell looked up from the mess of score sheets and a half-empty bottle of Gran Legacy sitting on the table. He'd changed clothes out of his Doggie Diner clothes and now wore a pair of torn jeans and a yellow tee shirt with the image of Sponge Bob Square Pants smiling on the front.

"What are you doing back here?" O'Connell snarled.

McManus ignored him. He picked up the hospital paperwork lying on the table and read it. "Says right here, if you start drinking again, you're going to bleed to death."

"Fuck them. They gave me a couple bottles of Pepto."

McManus chuckled. "Sounds tasty. Vodka with a Pepto chaser." He tossed the paperwork back onto the table and toured the darkened house. The floors were littered with pages torn or cut from discarded magazines and newspapers. McManus walked into the master bedroom and studied the closet.

"You know, you still got Kathy's clothes hanging in here?" O'Connell's wife had died two years previously from breast cancer.

"So?" O'Connell yelled back from the living room.

"It's morbid."

Kathleen Driscoll, a nurse, had seen something in O'Connell that no one else could see—except McManus. She'd even dumped her first husband to marry him, McManus had been their best man. Now O'Connell was living off her life insurance.

McManus walked back into the living room and watched O'Connell set up the pins on the Skittle-bowl game for his next shot. "How about a game, for old times' sake?" O'Connell asked.

"Okay, let's play."

"I'm 'The Natural,' remember McManus? Four-point-oh, All-City football, All-City baseball. What was your grade point?"

McManus ignored him.

"I'll go first," O'Connell said.

Despite his intoxication, O'Connell's aim was steady. He knocked down all ten pins for a strike. "Don't fuck with me, McManus, I've always beat your ass at this and I still can," he hooted.

"Fuck you."

By the final frame, O'Connell held a slight lead as he took the ball and lined up his shot. "Watch this." With a smooth stroke, he sent the ball on the end of the chain arcing around the pole and into the standing pins. The ball exploded like a hand grenade scattering them all for a strike. O'Connell won the game by twenty pins.

"Swell," McManus said.

O'Connell smirked. "See, McManus, you don't always have to be great—just be great when you need to. Want to go again?"

Enough of this shit. McManus shook his head. "I told you, Colin. I can't keep bailing you out. You'd better check back into the hospital."

"Oh, he completely changes the subject after I kick his ass. You can leave now."

McManus glared at O'Connell and noticed his eyes looked cold and emotionless, the eyes of a shark. *The bond we shared throughout our lives existed only in my mind.*

He shook his head. "This ain't going to work anymore, Colin." He turned up his palms and walked toward the hallway. "The real world wants you to perform and you can't do it."

McManus closed the front door behind him without looking back.

11

Fratelli draped her thigh over McManus' hip and pulled him closer to her. He responded by sucking on her nipple. She squealed.

He woke up and took a deep breath, feeling the rush of hormones and blood sweep through his penis. *Sending a lesbian into my life. You screwin' with my head again, Mom? You gonna tell me, now, 'Don't get your hopes up, son…etc., etc., etc.*

McManus rolled over onto his stomach and pushed his groin into the bed. *Shit, what's goin' on? I'd like to think of myself as a believer. I used to talk to God all the time and thought he had my back. But now I'm not so sure.*

Miracles do happen—not killing myself out at Lands End was one. Who's in charge here? Am I really falling in love with an inaccessible woman? How does all this stuff happen? Who knows if I will ever see her again?

MONDAY
JANUARY 18, 2010 · 1335 HRS.

A No.10 white envelope caught McManus' attention when he dropped his mail on the kitchen table. His name and address were printed in large block letters in pencil. *Looks like a kid wrote it. Probably a flyer soliciting for some school fundraiser.*

When he tore open the envelope, McManus' blood ran cold. A note with letters and words cut and pasted from a magazine read:

U will die

Who the hell have I pissed off? Is this fallout from my front page picture nailing that guy? Maybe someone in his family? No wait. This has to be fucking Grogan. No one wants me gone as much as he does. But why? What's Grogan's deal? Why is he so intent on getting rid of me?

12

TUESDAY
JANUARY 19, 2010 · 1635 HRS.

A Coke can rattled through the vending machine in the locker room at Richmond Station. It dropped hard into the pick-up tray, and McManus reached in to retrieve it. He had "hot pipes"—a souvenir from ten straight nights of hard drinking after work. McManus opened the can and chugged it. He belched, long and loud, a sign of contempt for how he felt.

He entered the Assembly Room and took a seat. From a clipboard, he thumbed through all the incident reports during the past twenty-four hours. Nearby, the station keeper, Sgt. Louie Cardinale, sat behind a desk inside the business office reading the *San Francisco Chronicle.* He was ignoring the ringing phones because that was the civilian clerk's job.

The station's front door swung open, and sunlight poured in. Cardinale looked up and cursed. An elderly man struggled through the heavy door. The man stopped and held the door open for his equally slow-moving wife. Cardinale looked at Hoffmire, the civilian bent over a phone taking notes.

"Hoffmire, you got somebody at the window," Cardinale called to him.

McManus looked up from the reports and watched Hoffmire raise his hand and continue to talk on the phone. Cardinale fumed. The old man and his wife waited in the office foyer, looking at Cardinale through the bulletproof glass. Cardinale ignored them. The old man picked up the intercom phone in front of him. The phone inside the office rang.

"Hoffmire, you got somebody at the window," Cardinale called to him again.

Turning to look at Cardinale, Hoffmire cocked his head to the side and raised his eyebrows.

Cardinale remained seated and yelled to the old man through the glass. He pointed at Hoffmire, "He'll be with you in a minute—hang up the phone." The intercom phone continued to ring while the old man, confused about what to do, held the phone in his hand.

"Fuck," Cardinale screamed and threw a pencil at Hoffmire's back.

Suddenly Grogan's voice boomed from his cubicle loud enough to be heard in the business office. "You got the Russians' DNA. What the fuck else do you need to do?"

McManus saw Grogan on the phone and immediately knew that the "miracle arrest" of the Russians for Cassidy's murder was falling apart. He looked back at Cardinale, who had finally gotten up to deal with the old couple at the window.

"Maybe if you tried harder," McManus now heard Grogan shout. "Have you done a PCR process?"

McManus guessed that the crime lab guy on the other end was trying to explain to Grogan that the knife found at Lands End contained no fingerprints or DNA to link the Russians to the weapon. The wet, foggy, windy conditions at Lands End had most likely washed the knife clean. McManus chuckled and shook his head.

"MOTHERFUCKER," Grogan yelled.

McManus returned to thumbing through the incident reports and found a Coroner's Case Report filed at 11:35 that morning. His heart dropped.

16th Avenue. OH! FUCK.

```
Reporting Officers Barron, Star 1097,
and Mitchell, Star 4454, responded via
radio call to the above listed address
and met the Reportee McGloin, who
identified himself as the regular mail
carrier for the above listed address.
Reportee McGloin stated that three days'
worth of mail delivery was in the mail-
box and that he smelled an unusual odor
emanating from the residence.

ROs investigated, and recognized the odor
as that of a decomposing human body. ROs
```

```
then requested a supervisor, ambulance,
and SFFD to respond at the scene. Sgt.
Kvanvig, Star 6620, and paramedics
Drisdell and Dubois, along with members
of SFFD Truck 12 (Lt. Lopez), responded.
Lt. Lopez made forcible entry through
the front door of the residence under
the direction of Sgt. Kvanvig.

Upon investigation once inside the
residence, ROs observed the deceased
lying on the couch in the living room.
Paramedic Drisdell then determined that
the deceased had died of apparent nat-
ural causes and appeared to have been
dead for a period of longer than 48
hours. Coroner's unit was then summoned.
```

McManus dropped his chin to his chest to hide his tears. *O'Connell knew he could either drink and die, or he could stop and survive. But he didn't want to stop.*

He scanned the rest of the Coroner's Case Report and read how Barron and Mitchell had observed "several empty plastic half-gallons of Gran Legacy vodka scattered about the residence."

I can see Colin sitting on the couch, studying the label, wondering about the omission of the 'd'. McManus took a deep breath and wiped his eyes.

Death has a thousand or more doors. One night in high school, Colin had flipped an XKE end-over-end on the Great Highway racing Cassidy, and he lived…but then he spends the next 40 years in a personal hell and dies drinking from cheap plastic bottles of vodka while sitting on his couch.

Why was that? What purpose did it serve? McManus looked up as Grogan approached, carrying a brown legal-sized envelope.

"Here's your lawsuit from the Voodoo women—they didn't waste any time." Grogan's smirk was unmistakable.

McManus put down the clipboard and opened the envelope. He read it aloud while Grogan listened: "Filed Superior Court of the State of California, In and For the City and County of San Francisco. January 15, 2010. H. G. Thomas, Clerk... Screw them."

"Are you an idiot, McManus? Seriously," Grogan asked. "See what happens when you don't stop and check things out with me. Why did you kick the door and jump into that room."

"They were endangering a child," McManus said.

Grogan snickered. "CPS investigated and found the child was not underweight; it wasn't covered in filth. No bruises."

"I did the right thing. There was hardly any light; I could hear a baby screaming, I smelled marijuana, and I had an eyewitness for probable cause."

Grogan handed McManus a piece of paper with a phone number. "The *Chronicle* wants to do a story. Call them."

McManus shook his head. "The road to Hell is paved with good intentions. Screw them, too."

13

McManus stood in the pulpit at St. Anne Church, looking at the sparse gathering—only six mourners including himself. Every movement, cough, and sound echoed in the emptiness.

Years ago, hundreds of O'Connell's classmates had swooped down upon him at nearby Kezar Stadium on a bright and clear Thanksgiving afternoon. They'd carried him off the field in victory following his miraculous touchdown catch. Now, on just another overcast morning in the Sunset, his funeral attracted only a few cousins, a union rep, and one S. I. team-mate—me.

McManus had made the arrangements and paid for the funeral. He'd ordered a custom-designed floral football

helmet, made from red, white and blue carnations forming the number "82"—O'Connell's jersey number. It was
placed atop the high-gloss mahogany casket.

Clearing his throat, he began the eulogy with the words
O'Connell had longed for in life: "If you can hear me, Colin, we loved and appreciated you. I'll say that again. We
loved and appreciated you. Even in the worst of times,
we loved you because we knew what you were struggling
with. You punished yourself for not being as perfect as you
thought you should be, and you gave up."

He paused. *Shit, a eulogy is supposed to be about how
people remember you. I'm not going to lie. I'd like to talk about
the things you loved Colin, and how you touched people's lives...
But what did you love? You sure didn't love us. You were a selfish
asshole. And you deserved the shitty life you lead and how you
died... Maybe saying that truth here will make people laugh.*

"You were just too smart for your own good, Colin.
Always knowing that without really trying, you could beat
us at anything. But then you had to remind us of that."

The five other mourners chuckled.

McManus paused again to let the laughter subside. *This
isn't funny, O'Connell. You didn't give me much to work with
here, except how you got caught up in your own bullshit and
wouldn't do the things that really mattered.*

He drew in a deep breath to keep his voice from breaking. "What could I have done to help you, Colin? We grew
up together. We were teammates. We were brothers. If there's
one thing you don't do under any circumstance—it's let
your brother down."

McManus wiped his eyes, and then tightened his grip on the sides of the lectern. But his voice broke, and he stopped. *I'm no better than the man in the casket. I have nothing else to say.*

McManus returned home, loosened his tie, poured two fingers of Blanton's, and knocked the shot back in one gulp. The bourbon burned like lava down his throat before landing in his empty stomach. He blew out his breath, then walked to the bay window, and looked out at a gray afternoon. *Does God exist? Do we possess free will? Or is it all destiny and fate?*

He turned, grabbed his high school yearbook *Ignatian '67* from the bookshelf, and then settled down in the green beanbag chair. *With Cassidy and O'Connell both dying horrible deaths and me barely avoiding mine—Did we make some sort of pact with the Devil that's being called in now? Was it when Coach Paganini stuck his hand in the flame? I need to figure this shit out.*

McManus spread the yearbook across his knees, pulled out the faded clipping from the *San Francisco Chronicle,* and once again read the game story.

Late TD Gives S. I. 21-14 Win
To Take SF City Championship

Colin O'Connell snatched a desperation pass out of a mass of grabbing arms yesterday and raced in to score with 31 seconds left in the game, giving St. Ignatius a thrilling 21-14 victory over Lowell in the AAA championship play-off at Kezar Stadium.

O'Connell's dramatic score capped one of the finest exhibitions of football in the history of the Thanksgiving Day title game, threw cold water on what had been a fine Lowell second-half effort, and left the 17,000 fans either delirious or just plain stunned.

Even the most ardent S. I. rooters had about settled for a 14-14 tie when the Wildcats got the ball at the Lowell 45. Quarterback Pete Cassidy faded back and threw long toward the left sideline. There were three men at the 22 yard line, in a cluster—S. I. ends O'Connell and Phil McManus and Lowell's defensive back Alan Perper.

McManus and Perper leaped, both batted the ball, and it fell toward the goal. Then O'Connell made a half turn, grabbed it in the air, and set sail. Perper, the only defender near O'Connell, had no chance to recover and get him. The S. I. bench and rooting section went wild. Police managed to keep fans off the field while Lowell ran two plays after the kickoff.

I remember Perper had a sure game-ending interception until we collided and the ball came loose. As we fell, I lunged for it and managed to tip the ball with my fingertip, sending it spinning upwards. For an instant, the ball and the city championship hung in midair.

I'll never forget the amazed wide-eyed look I saw on O'Connell's face when he plucked the ball out of the air and headed for the end zone.

I fell on top of Perper, who slapped my helmet. "Get the fuck off me," his scream barely audible above the hysteria of the crowd. I rolled over onto the damp grass and watched O'Connell get smaller and smaller as he ran toward the end zone. I couldn't tell what was funnier—O'Connell's all-arms-and-legs running style or Perper crookedly trying to get up and chase him.

I remember O'Connell being carried off the field pointing his finger skyward and screaming, "Thank you, God. Thank you." The three of us felt like we were touched by the hand of God and destined for greatness. The play had bonded us for life, or so we'd thought.

When we returned to school the following Monday, the Jesuit faculty swooned all over the team. We knew it was because they saw the metaphysical nature of the win as exactly what they needed to steer our "innocent Catholic schoolboy minds" away from the sinful activities of the hippies. "Those Damn Hippies" resided a mere half mile from the school campus in the Haight-Ashbury where all inhibitions had been forsaken.

"Follow God's teachings of devotion, self-sacrifice, patience, and faith," the Jesuits preached to us that day. "And Believers

can expect their salvation… just like our football team did to win the city championship."

The three of us felt we were Golden—we could do anything. But then, when mom killed herself six months later, I knew that wasn't true. Cassidy would go on to experience the American Dream of fame, glory, money…and then be murdered. O'Connell would self-destruct in an ocean of booze and puddle of self-pity. And me?

14

A virulent strain of the "Blue Flu" swept through the San Francisco Police Department on Super Bowl Sunday. With SFPD staffing levels below normal, police supervisors scrambled to shift personnel around to cover the city. At Richmond Station, Grogan offered up McManus' name to replace the ailing cops at Ingleside Station to patrol some of San Francisco's most expensive real estate—and most crime-ridden neighborhoods.

When McManus arrived at Ingleside, he was paired with a rookie named Campbell, who knew the streets. He let Campbell drive and welcomed looking out at the change in scenery. *I hate working during the Super Bowl.*

Can't watch the game. Then after it's finished, we're guaranteed to catch a night of mayhem from the volatile mix of friends, alcohol and competition.

An alarm bell ringing from a residence in the affluent St. Francis Woods was their first run of the night. It drew a full response from the SFFD to the neighborhood of stately mansions set back from the street on spacious landscaped lots. When Campbell and McManus arrived, two huge aerial truck companies, three pumpers, an ambulance, and a fire chief's buggy blocked the street. The chief was talking to an elderly woman and didn't look happy.

He's probably pissed he's missing the game while the old lady's burning his ear. McManus and Campbell approached the pair.

The elderly woman made a beeline for the cops as soon as she saw them. "I think it's just terrible these wonderful firemen have to come out here all the time because of those people's blasted alarm," she said shaking her finger inches from McManus' face. "I wish their house would catch on fire—serve them right for disturbing our neighborhood all the time!"

McManus fought back a chuckle. *The chief's wearing a guilty look. Wonder if he kissed her off on us, telling her alarm bells were handled only by the cops. He just wants to get back to the station and watch the game.*

Campbell came forward to stand shoulder to shoulder with McManus. "What about us wonderful police officers?" The smiling rookie said to the woman.

Before she could answer, McManus stepped between the young officer and the woman. "We'll take care of it, ma'am," he said.

"Just make sure you do it sooner, rather than later," she snarled.

When they were out of earshot of everyone, McManus looked at the rookie and shrugged. "Kid, if you haven't figured this out yet, they fight fires—we fight people. San Francisco loves its firefighters. We're never going to win that popularity contest."

The rookie slumped. McManus patted him on the back. "Hey, just appreciate your freedom and autonomy. You're a cop. You get to drive around, wear a gun and make decisions. Those poor fuckers are locked up in a firehouse for twenty-four hours with a boss telling them everything to do. They're like leashed dogs begging to go out for a walk—we're tigers on the prowl," McManus said with a wink.

SUPER BOWL SUNDAY
JANUARY 31, 2010 • 2100 HRS.

McManus didn't hear the 219 call of a stabbing in the Sunnydale projects until the rookie activated the siren. Years of listening to radio calls conditioned him to tune out anything that wasn't in the Richmond district. Only when Campbell stomped on the accelerator snapping McManus' head back, did he realize they were heading into danger. McManus reached for the microphone and acknowledged, "Ten-four, responding."

Deceptively serene looking, the Sunnydale projects were located on tree-lined streets next to a golf course. When the fog rolled over the city, Sunnydale was often the only sunny spot in San Francisco...but it was the city's deadliest neighborhood.

Within minutes of the radio call, McManus and Campbell arrived at the intersection of Blythdale and Santos. From the car, they could see a large crowd of African-Americans gathered in front of a two-story concrete tenement apartment. McManus requested backup.

"Ingleside Four," the dispatcher advised, "Use caution. Repeat...USE CAUTION. We're trying to get you some-body...but you're going to be out there on your own for awhile. You do have Medic 43, two minutes out."

Campbell parked the radio car down the street from the aqua-colored housing project, and the two of them sat sizing up the crowd of about forty people.

"Let's sit tight 'til the ambulance is 97 on the scene," McManus said as a woman standing in the apartment doorway motioned frantically for them. Finally, when they heard the ambulance siren, McManus and the rookie exited the radio car and ran up a grassy knoll to the building.

"Oh, pray for him, Jesus. Pray for him," cried an anguished woman as they muscled their way through the crowd into the kitchen of a ground floor apartment. Two paramedics followed.

The room was hot and stuffy, packed with gawkers trying to catch a glimpse of a victim lying on the floor. The smell of pork ribs and barbeque sauce mixing with an intense body odor made McManus gag. As he pushed aside several young children, his foot slid out from under him. *Too sticky for shit…must be blood. Be careful.*

A male victim lay on his back next to the stove, his black skin turned ashen. An older woman knelt beside him holding a blood-soaked towel to the man's neck. McManus respectfully pulled her away to allow the paramedics to work. They applied a new pressure bandage to the man's wound and set up an oxygen mask for him. The victim reeked of the stale odor of alcohol. A bloody butcher knife lay on the floor near him. The crowd of onlookers pressed against McManus, who crouched in the sticky puddle of the victim's blood and picked up the knife.

"I know this guy's dead," McManus whispered in the paramedic's ear. "But keep working and get him out of here, so this crowd doesn't turn on us. We don't have any backup."

The medic gave a slight nod.

McManus stood, faced the crowd, and motioned for them to move back. "We need to clear this area people, so we can get this man to the hospital."

The crowd moved back, except for the older woman who had been holding the towel to the victim's neck. Her skirt and white blouse were stained with blood. She rose from the victim's side to help the paramedics lift the man onto a backboard. The crowd in the kitchen quickly thinned, but several gawkers followed the victim to watch him being loaded into the ambulance.

Nearby, McManus noticed a woman in her mid-20s slumped forward in a chair, weeping into her hands. She wore the same style skirt and blouse as the older woman. Her clothing was blood-stained as well. The young woman shrieked loudly as she heard the siren from the ambulance leaving Code 3 for San Francisco General Hospital. The older woman returned and immediately went over to console the younger woman. Tenderly, she stroked her hair and pulled her into an embrace.

They must have just come home from church. What do they think of God now? McManus radioed headquarters, requesting homicide inspectors to respond. Then he and Campbell shooed the remaining people outside. The house was now a murder scene and needed to be secured.

This is fucked up. You got 10-year old kids stepping in the blood and over there two women praying together. The sudden squawk of a portable police radio caught McManus' attention. Backup had finally arrived.

Oh, Fuck! Grogan! Welcome to the real world, Dipshit.

The Blue Flu had also affected the supervisory ranks. McManus smiled. The sergeant stood in the apartment's doorway and assumed his hands-on-hips "Patton Stance."

"What we got here?" he called out to McManus in a disdainful voice.

McManus didn't respond.

Grogan answered his own question. "Murder, hmm? They do it?" he asked, pointing to the ladies with the blood-stained blouses.

Grogan's question brought a scream from the younger woman. "You white mothafucka." She jumped up from her chair and rushed toward Grogan.

She was stopped by McManus and Campbell who grabbed her before she could reach Grogan. As they wrestled to handcuff her, a boy and a girl snuck back into the kitchen. McManus saw them open the refrigerator and grab the stubby necks of two stout malt liquors.

"Hey, you kids..." McManus screamed as the pair disappeared out the front door with the bottles.

"McManus, you secure this place by yourself," Grogan ordered, maintaining a safe distance from the struggling handcuffed woman.

"We'll take her back to Ingleside," he said following Campbell out the door.

You're a FUCKING coward, Grogan.

"Undetermined at this time," the radio dispatcher responded to McManus' inquiry about the ETA of the homicide inspectors. *This is going to be a long fucking wait. I'm starving. What's cookin'?*

McManus smelled ribs baking in the oven. *What the hell. The neighborhood knows they got a cop all by himself. This is off the chart... What if somebody with a hard-on for the cops decides to toss a Molotov cocktail or something in here. Then what? Fuck.*

McManus pulled the pan of blackened ribs out of the oven and let it cool. A tray of small red potatoes and cut vegetables rested on the kitchen counter. He picked a baby carrot off the plate, opened the refrigerator, and grabbed a stout malt. After draining his drink, he pulled out another to wash down some carrots. When that one was finished, he grabbed a third and carried the ribs to a table in the dining area. The two young sneak thieves were watching him through the kitchen window.

What the fuck. Let's do some Community Relations work here. "You kids eaten yet?" McManus yelled to them, holding up the ribs and beckoning them inside.

The kids opened the door and looked at each other. McManus sat down at the table, unfolded a napkin, and placed it on his lap. "You guys hungry? Let's eat." He pointed to chairs at the table.

They entered without speaking. McManus instructed them to sit down and showed them how to unfold and place their napkins in their laps. "You guys know how to say grace?"

The boy and girl remained silent. McManus brought his hands together in prayer. "Thank you for our food, and family, and friends. Amen." McManus smiled and looked at the kids. "Now, what did you guys do with that beer?"

Neither spoke. McManus chuckled, cut ribs from the slab, and flipped them onto the kids' plates. "Did you guys know David?"

A smart and talented Balboa High School senior had been shot in Sunnydale, days before Cassidy's Christmas Eve murder. The victim was David Harrington, a 17-year-old who could throw a baseball at 95 mph. Major league baseball teams had been ready to write him a check worth millions upon his June graduation. Instead, Sunnydale's vortex of poverty, jealousy and violence swallowed him. An execution style attack—two gunshots into his pitching shoulder and a third to his neck—had left Harrington "brain dead" and currently on life support at San Francisco General Hospital.

The boy looked at the girl, who shook her head.

"I'm not asking you to snitch nobody out."

The kids didn't respond.

"Whatever." McManus got up from the table and retrieved another beer. Out of the corner of his eye, he saw the two kids each grab another rib. McManus took a long pull on the bottle and sat down.

"It's good manners to ask," he said and cut more ribs off the slab and then passed them to the kids.

The boy looked at McManus. "How many people you shoot with yo' gun?" he asked as he ate.

McManus laughed and took another sip on his beer. "Never shot anyone." He arched his eyebrows to emphasize "never."

The boy remained silent.

"You guys see any of this go down?" McManus asked.

The kids silently looked down at their plates.

They don't have a fuckin' chance stuck in this cesspool. Do they belong to the two women? Where are they spending the night? This is totally fucked up. McManus shook his head.

He heard the faint sound of a car door closing outside. *Forget that, I'm liking these ribs.*

But the squawk of a PIC radio made him look up. Grogan was standing in the doorway. "Couple left, Sarge. Want one?"

Grogan stared at McManus. "You out of your fuckin' mind, McManus?"

McManus looked at the kids. "Guess you guys should go. I have to talk to the Sergeant."

SUPER BOWL SUNDAY
JANUARY 31, 2010 · 2300 HRS.

McManus slumped hard in his seat in the fifth-floor Hall of Justice conference room and stared across the large rectangular table at Homicide Inspector Arthur Lahey and four members of the department's Command Staff led by Deputy Chief Michael Turner. The brass all looked pissed off, having been called in on Super Bowl Sunday night to listen to some patrolman's B.S.

"So all you guys here to congratulate me on winning the department Super Bowl pool or something?" McManus joked. No one laughed as he'd just blown a .12 blood/alcohol test. Pending a further hearing, this was grounds for his termination. He decided not to wait for the arrival of legal counsel from the Police Officer's Association.

Why screw up their night? I'm done and I know it. At least I'll make them sweat to get me... But what's Lahey doing here?

Lahey placed a cassette tape recorder on the large mahogany table. He put on his glasses and read McManus his Miranda Rights. McManus started to sweat.

Without any pleasantries, Lahey began, "Phil, on Christmas night, we talked to you up at City Prison about why you were out at Lands End and what you were doing. We taped that discussion and I'm going to play it for you."

You kidding me! They're still barking up that tree? He fought back a chuckle as he listened to himself on the tape say: "You really think I'd kill a guy on-duty, pull his pants down to blow him, then hang around for you guys to investigate?"

The next voice on the tape was Frank Anderson, Lahey's partner. "Oh, one other thing we wanted to ask you. You lose anything out there?"

"Where?"

"Lands End."

"No."

When the tape ended, Lahey looked around the table, then eyed McManus.

"So, Phil, is there anything you'd like to add to that tape?" Lahey asked.

McManus shook his head.

Lahey drummed his fingers on the table, then reached into a brown paper bag. McManus remembered Lahey had carried a similar bag that night at the prison. The bag made a crinkling sound as he pulled out a battered SFPD hat and tossed it in front of McManus. The hat left a deposit of sand on the table.

"Oh yeah—my hat," McManus said.

"You just said you didn't lose anything. But here's your hat. It's got your star number inside. Looks like it's been in the Bay."

"Where did you get it?"

"A couple citizens found it washed up on Baker Beach," Lahey said.

"Oh, when I was walking around, it blew off."

"Where were you walking around?"

"Down by the Labyrinth Cliff."

"What were you doing down there?" Lahey smirked.

"Trying to find a barking dog," McManus scratched the back of his head.

"How close to the edge were you?"

"I wasn't close to the edge."

"Where were you, then?"

"I can't remember."

Lahey looked straight at McManus. "We got a 26-minute window of time we can't account for. From 0102 when you went out of service on an investigation, then you weren't heard from again until 0128. You had cuts and scrapes on your face. And you didn't make a report about losing your hat."

McManus' Irish face blushed fire-engine red. "I was looking for a dog, and the wind blew off my hat. It's just my hat. If it was my gun, I'd make a report. I had another hat in my locker. I forgot about it. It's just a hat, so I thought nothing of it."

Lahey looked around the table again, and then nodded at McManus with a sly wink. "This is what we think went down, Phil. You either were there to kill Cassidy, or you got something else going on. You haven't been acting right lately. You've been using up a lot of sick time. You were first on-scene with that big accident. You had that crazy arrest of all those women. And you haven't been too private about your drinking. It's been noticeable, Phil. You got your picture on the front page of the *Chronicle* dumping a guy. You were supposed to retire, but apparently you've called that off. And now this bullshit. We've known each other since St. Anne, Phil. Were you out on that cliff trying to kill yourself?"

"My fuckin' hat blew off. I wasn't trying to kill myself, and I didn't kill Cassidy. Fuck you."

Lahey reached into a manila envelope. "You write this, Phil?" He dropped a clear plastic evidence bag onto the table. Inside was a No. 10 white envelope addressed simply "San Francisco Homicide." The pencil-written large block letters looked like the work of a second-grader and were identical to those on the envelope McManus had received two weeks before.

"Zodiac?" McManus wiped his brow.

"I don't think so." Lahey sounded like he'd just watched McManus place more than ten items in the express lane check-out. He dropped a second evidence bag in front of McManus. It hit the table with a sharp splat. McManus saw a white sheet of multipurpose paper smudged with black fingerprint dust. The letters cut and pasted from a magazine spelled out:

McMANus Did it

Holy Fuck. McManus studied the envelope. *What's goin'
on here?*

"No prints," Lahey said. "Mailed from the Sunset district.
I don't want to waste the time and money on a DNA. You
found the body. Any idea who wrote this?"

McManus rolled his eyes. "Of course not. But I got one
of those, too. Except mine said, 'You will die.' I think you
should ask that little cocksucker, Grogan, next to you."

"That's enough, officer," Deputy Chief Turner said.

McManus looked at Grogan, who smirked back at him.
I'm done now, and I know it.

No one cracked a smile when the Deputy Chief—in a
tone so grave it sounded like he was kidding—said, "Officer
McManus, in accordance with department procedures and
pending a further hearing, you are going to be placed on
sixty days of unpaid administrative leave. And I'm directing
Dr. Rector, the department's psychologist sitting there at
the end of the table, to conduct an evaluation when we're
finished here."

Turner's eyes bored into McManus. "You have any
questions, Officer?"

McManus shook his head.

"I need to get your star."

15

McManus crouched behind the engine block of department vehicle 024 parked in the intersection of Geary and Arguello. He leveled the 12-gauge Remington shotgun at one of the approaching tripod-mounted Martian fighting machines. McManus guessed the weaponry was probably "higher than many houses." He saw heat rays coming off cameras mounted on tentacles reaching out from the fighting machines. One ray struck the Doggie Dinner, flattening it to look like a pile of hash browns cooking on a grill.

McManus jacked a round into the chamber of his shotgun and took aim. "Damn, this thing is going to be as effective as throwing spitballs at a battleship."

Suddenly articulated ropes of steel dropped from the fighting machines. McManus held his fire and watched as topless Dallas Cowboys cheerleaders repelled down the ropes. The sight of their bare breasts, panty-hosed thighs, and white boots aroused him.

"That's it. We're done, they're taking over. Women are in control now and will run the world." McManus stood up, threw down his weapon into the street, raised his hands, and surrendered.

"Aaaaaaaaaaaaagh!" McManus jerked awake. *Where am I? Great to be awake…or is it?*

He walked to the bathroom where he splashed cold water on his face and looked up at the mirror. *My God! What has life done to me? I look like Walter Matthau in* Grumpier Old Men.

He took a cup of coffee to the bay window to watch the city start its new week. The cold morning breeze had cleared the atmosphere, leaving a pristine view of the Bay Area. McManus picked up his binoculars and looked north toward Sonoma County. From 80 miles away, he could see the 4,300-foot snow-capped peak of Mt. St. Helena. *Wow, don't see that often. Looks like a postcard. It'd be a great shot to keep…*

Footsteps and the squawk from a police radio in the hallway drew his attention. An instant later, Carly erupted into a barking frenzy as someone knocked on the door.

He walked to the door, looked through the peephole, and saw the tall angular form of Sgt. Stan Murphy from Ingleside Station standing in the hallway. McManus opened the door.

"Morning, Phil. How ya doing?" Murphy beamed. McManus saw the effort it took for him to smile. *News travels fast. That debacle up on the Fifth floor last night has already reached the rank-and-file. Fuck!*

McManus stepped aside, allowing Murphy to enter.

"Got a call from Homicide to pick up a letter from you," Murphy said. Carly stopped barking and sniffed at Murphy's feet.

"Yeah, I'll get it for you." McManus went to his desk and opened a drawer while Murphy walked to the bay window to gaze out at the city.

"Wow, you're living the life up here, Phil." Murphy turned back from the window. "Must be sensational to watch the Blue Angels fly over during October's Fleet Week."

"Don't forget the fireworks on the Fourth of July," said McManus looking up from the desk. He returned to Murphy, holding the note with the pasted letters that read:

U will die

Murphy took the note and dropped it into the clear plastic evidence bag he had pulled from his coat pocket. "Thanks, Phil. You getting ready to pull-the-pin soon, aren't you?"

McManus shrugged. "Getting there."

After Murphy left, McManus felt betrayed.

He returned to his window to watch the morning commute on the Bay Bridge. *All those people going to work, and I'm not. The Department is deserting me, and soon all my friends will, too. That's the way it is. Nobody wants to be tainted by another cop's problems. Can't blame 'em, especially because of the way things are nowadays—with dipshits like Grogan scrambling for power.*

His eyes filled with tears, and anger rose in the pit of his stomach. *I can fight back. Appeal this thing. Raise a lot of hell...fuck 'em, they can't do this to me.*

MONDAY
FEBRUARY 1, 2010 · 0900 HRS.

Gina Cassidy peeked around the corner of her front door to see McManus. "Phil! What are you doing here?"

He looked her in the eye and nodded. "We need to talk."

Wearing a black and charcoal cowl wrap dress with large silver hoops in her earlobes, she led him upstairs to the Observation Floor of the Octagon House. *Wonder where she's going dressed like that this morning? She'd better have time to talk to me.*

In the room, she pointed to the same black wingback chair he'd taken on his previous visit. He scanned the room, taking in the skyline through the 270-degrees of un-obstructed floor-to-ceiling windows.

Something's different. Where's the Cassidy painting? Missing from the stark black and white room was its only source of color—the large abstract painting of Cassidy wearing his Oakland Raiders headgear and his white SFFD chief's helmet.

Something's up with her, more than me just barging in this morning. She sure looks scared. McManus watched Gina silently gazing out the windows down toward the streets.

"Did you tell Lahey that Pete asked you for a divorce?" McManus asked.

She flinched at the question. "No." Her eyes immediately began to moisten. She picked up a tissue from a box on a nearby table. "I'm worried something will come out about him that could be devastating for us, Phil."

That's exactly why I'm here—to find out what she knows that might tell me why Lahey is still after me. McManus stood up and walked to the windows. "Gina, let's be up-front here. You're dealing with San Francisco cops and firemen. If there's a rumor, it's not only out of the barn, it's already run the three legs of the Triple Crown. Personally, I haven't heard anything. But I am not always in the loop. What are you so afraid of?"

She turned and looked at McManus. The tears were now streaming down her face. Her eyes fiery with anger. "I don't want people to know I lost my husband to porn and prostitutes."

McManus backed away. "Whoa, what are you talking about? Porn and prostitutes?"

Gina looked back out at the city and continued to dab at her tears. "People admired and looked up to Pete. It was horrible enough he was murdered...but to have all this stuff come out would be devastating to me and the children. I've got to protect my kids, Phil...they don't know about any of this stuff."

McManus shook his head. "What are you talking about, Gina?"

She looked back at him over her shoulder. "Until about five years ago, I thought Pete and I were extraordinary lovers. He was sweet and very gentle. Then he began to hold back and, suddenly, he never came inside me again."

There it is. Did she really just tell me that? The great Pete Cassidy...The Alpha Male...Man among Men...This is unbelievable she's telling me all this. Why?

"It's almost unbelievable that I'm telling you all this," she said. "But therapy opened me up to acknowledge my feelings. There's this moment where you can be real with the other person... Where you're so vulnerable..." She stopped mid-sentence and stared out the window.

Most men wouldn't want to listen to this crap. But maybe I'll find out something important... Hey, why is Cassidy's picture missing? There's got to be a clue there. McManus put his hand on her shoulder.

"Pete would get into bed about 9:30. We'd cuddle and have this great chemistry thing, but no intercourse. A couple times, I tried to bring up the subject, but he just didn't want to go there." She sighed and touched his hand.

"So finally this one night, I just asked him, 'Why won't you come inside of me? What's going on?'" Her expression changed to one of disgust. "He just grunted and shrugged."

She took her fist and hit it into the palm of her hand. "I sat up in bed and detonated, 'YOU SON OF A BITCH!

Why can't we have a conversation about this!… Why can't you just tell me?'"

"So a couple nights later, he's wearing his Class A dress fire department uniform and tells me he's going to emcee a testimonial dinner. Then he says, 'Oh, by the way… Don't wait up. You know, the boys will be boys at these things and I'll just get a hotel room if I can't drive.' Those retirement dinners were a big thing for him and his friends."

They sure are. Testimonial dinners…the last vestige of the Ol' Boys Club. Good thing, women don't dare attend. No way they'd want to hear a bunch of guys bragging about how many broads they've banged. McManus watched a large yellow tabby cat enter the room and rub against Gina's leg.

"Archie, stop that." She kicked him away. "So I went to bed, but awoke some time in the middle of the night to sirens. We do hear a lot of that up here, so I quickly fell back to sleep. Then a couple hours later, about three in the morning, the doorbell rings. Now my heart stops. 'OH MY GOD.' I throw on a robe and I run downstairs thinking, 'Am I about to be told my husband has been killed in a fire?'

Do I dare stop her? I've heard a lot of stories about Cassidy, but not this one. McManus watched the cat jump up on the window frame.

"So I open the door and Pete's standing there with this guy. My heart just dropped. Pete had this gross look on his face. He just looked raunchy. And he's always looked so handsome in his black dress uniform with all the gold buttons…" Gina rubbed her arms as if to warm herself.

"He'd been picked up by the cops for soliciting an under-cover policewoman posing as a prostitute. The arresting officer was a guy he'd played football with at S.I.—Brannigan, who, instead of arresting him, brought him home to me."

You got to be kidding? Cassidy's out there trolling for whores in his uniform while she's home in bed asleep! "I'm so sorry, I never knew any of this." McManus pulled her in close and hugged her.

She gently pushed him away and looked up with tears in her eyes. "I mean the last time I saw him he was smiling and all dressed up for some gala affair. Now he's standing in our doorway with a cop telling me the story of how this all went down. And how I can find our family car parked in a Tenderloin back alley."

McManus gazed at the empty space on the wall where Cassidy's painting had been. *Okay I get it. She wants nothing more to do with the turd, let alone have a constant reminder in this room.*

Gina took a deep breath, held it, and then blew it out slowly. "So, Phil. You'd think that would have been enough excitement for him that night. Right?… But it wasn't. I usually sleep well, but not that Friday night. And I heard him get up."

You actually let that asshole back in the bed with you? How much in denial are you? McManus shook his head again.

"After about a half hour, he didn't come back to bed. And I think, 'Well, I'll just go downstairs.' I do, and he's locked in the bathroom with the lights on. So I just sit down on the couch… And I wait…and I wait…and I wait…and he comes out with his laptop and, of course, you know what he's been doing in there. I could hear him."

Oh my God! The guy was jerking off. McManus tried to stifle a grin.

Gina's face brightened and she laughed. "He comes out and he goes 'What the hell are you doing here?' I mean it's like… 'Good morning to you, too', I say. 'You were up, I wasn't sleeping, I thought I would join you.' So he quickly looked at his laptop and then shut it off and put it on the coffee table. He couldn't even talk to me, Phil. Then he walked away and looked back at the laptop. And I said… 'What are you angry about, now?' He said, 'I just like this time to myself.'"

I always thought Cassidy was an idiot. But this isn't normal asshole shit. This is Junkie Shit. He's got to be an addict. McManus looked at her. "Why in the world didn't you kick his ass out right then and there?"

"He walked away from me heading for the kitchen. I followed and saw him looking at a Cantonese paper left by our maid." Gina shook her head. "He was breathing hard. The whole night had unhinged him. He knew he'd gotten caught. He was masturbating in the bathroom, FOR GOD SAKES!"

McManus leaned forward and buried his face in his hands to prevent her from seeing him laugh. *Soliciting a prostitute in uniform. Getting arrested. Being dragged home to be embarrassed in front of your wife. The guy's a moron… or was.*

"So I went outside for the *Chronicle,* came back, and handed it to him. 'Here, Mr. Wonderful, you might be interested in today's paper. Then you can have something real to read instead of talking to me.'"

McManus chuckled. *So this is what love feels like in the end. Hey, if I'd married her, would I have wound up like Cassidy? No way.*

Gina took a breath, sat down in a wingback chair, and gazed toward McManus with a blank stare. "He actually said to me, 'It's nothing to do with you. You're beautiful and you've got an amazing body for your age.'"

"I wasn't fishing for compliments… I just wanted the truth. Once I realized what the issue was, it was a relief! I know this will sound absolutely bizarre, but he was an addict, Phil. A fuckin' sex addict! No wonder he wasn't interested in me. Now that I know this stuff, what am I supposed to do?"

McManus turned up his palms and shook his head. *You're asking me? What do I look like? Mr. Ann Landers?*

"Then two weeks later, Brannigan died of a heart attack. We went to his funeral and both of us sat in the church wondering, 'Did this secret about Pete die with him?' I didn't know. I suspect Pete knew more than I did. But for the last five years, he's barely even talked to me."

Gina paused. "They could have held Pete's funeral back then, for all I care." She dabbed at her moist eyes with a tissue.

McManus stood up, walked to the windows, and looked out. Due west out over the ocean, he watched a white 747 bank slowly, perhaps heading toward Europe. *Hearing this shit now, I figure Cassidy's killer's probably someone from that porn/prostitute world he'd lived in. Lahey will find this out ... if he doesn't know it already. But Cassidy was always a chameleon. Changing into what he needed to be. Charming on the outside, but dark and soul-less inside.*

McManus turned to look back at her. *She making up this whole story as a smoke screen for herself? If Cassidy'd been abusing her, she's got both a motive and an alibi. How do I tell Lahey this stuff without connecting myself as her accomplice? Jeez, this is fucked up.*

Gina pulled the cat onto her lap and started petting him. "I'm worried, Phil, something will come out about him that could destroy us."

No shit.

MONDAY

FEBRUARY 1, 2010 • 1300 HRS.

McManus found a box in the Richmond Station storage room to use for clearing out his locker. *Sixty days will be a long time away. Pretty ironic. I'm scheduled to come off suspension on April Fool's Day.*

After throwing his three dirty uniforms into the box, he unloaded the SIG P226. He'd never fired it—or any other weapon—in the line of duty. Next he cleaned out the amazing amount of miscellaneous junk a cop accumulates during the course of daily patrol: police association flyers, some firecrackers, a handful of Starbucks napkins, the menu from a Chinese restaurant that had closed three years ago, one of his business cards with Flo the waitress's phone number on the back, and the directions for installing wiper blades on his black Camry.

Mixed in with the junk he found the tattered butt of a marijuana cigarette. *Where'd this come from? Maybe I should fire it up to celebrate my suspension. Naw, Dipshit would probably bust me.*

Finally, all that remained was to sort through the file box at the bottom of his locker. It held at least twenty old notebooks with information from victims, witnesses and suspects for incident reports. *Let's just dump all this shit in the trash... No, wait a minute. Soon as I do that, I'm going to get subpoenaed for something I just tossed. What's the rush? The station's quiet. I'm the only one here. Let's take a look at this stuff.*

McManus sat down on the bench in front of his locker and scanned the pages, curious to see which incidents he could remember. One notebook dated "January-March 1993" contained his detailed notes from a strong-arm robbery on Thursday, January 22, 1993, at 0745 on the 2200 block of Clement Street. He raised his eyebrows reading the name of the victim: "James Michael Grogan, DOB March 31, 1980." *Holy fuck. Dipshit has kept this secret, and here it is—buried at the bottom of my locker for seventeen years.*

McManus' notes detailed how the "small-for-his-age" seventh-grader walked to St. Monica's School that morning, eyeing two older boys in front of him. When he caught up to the pair, Grogan found himself sandwiched between two eighth-graders from the Presidio Middle School. "Give us your lunch money," the bigger of the two demanded.

McManus' report further stated: "Grogan then reached into his pocket and pulled out a wadded-up dollar bill his mother had just given him with the admonishment, 'Don't lose it.' Grogan handed over his money, and then felt hands working at his belt bucket and zipper. He didn't resist. Victim was then pantsed by the below described suspects."

McManus read how he was "on routine patrol" when he observed "the victim Grogan in tears on the sidewalk trying to pull up his pants." He had put Grogan in the radio car and they soon spotted his alleged assailants.

The report went on to detail how Grogan appeared scared and refused to identify them. The suspects were then released. McManus remembered he'd contacted Grogan's mother and she'd met them at school, but the kid again refused to identify his assailants. McManus' notes contained a notation: "The mother scolded her son, 'Couldn't you at least have fought back?'"

I remember Grogan's mother later filed a complaint against me for being "rude" toward her son. McManus closed the notebook and tossed it back into the file box.

Good a reason as any to join the SFPD. To avenge getting pantsed and having your lunch money stolen when you were in the seventh grade. McManus rubbed his eyes and took a deep breath—he hadn't slept for almost thirty hours. He walked back to his car and drove out of the station parking lot without glancing back.

MONDAY
FEBRUARY 1, 2010 · 1500 HRS.

McManus tossed his mail on the kitchen table when he returned home. The letter with bold black type on the envelope caught his attention.

SallieMae – Private Credit
"Important Information About Your Student Loan"

Dear PHILLIP M. McMANUS:

The payment for the Sallie Mae student loan referenced above that you cosigned is at least 10 days past due. We want to take this opportunity to remind you to make your payment today. Your past due amount and your current monthly payment amount equal $116.58.

"Fuck," he said and went to slide open the condo's bay windows. The curtains swayed in the gentle breeze. *This is a refreshing change after our El Niño winter.* Almost seven inches of rain fell in January. But, now, according to the weatherman, it was supposed to stay dry. The sea wind that blew the morning haze into the Central Valley was the telltale sign that the storms of the past few weeks have moved north.

McManus stood at the window. *So what should I do now?*

He turned and stared at the three framed black and white photographs of the men who had inspired him: JFK, the idealist; Lombardi, the winner; Heffner, the man who was living the life he wanted to live. *Now all three make me feel inadequate. Maybe Grogan was right about my becoming a mall cop.*

"Don't ever get your hopes up, Phil," his mother always told him. "Soon as things go good, they go bad." Her advice hung over McManus like his own neurotic anticipation of the foghorns on a sunny afternoon.

I knew the fog was coming in, but when? I wanted to believe in something positive. I wanted to believe that sometimes it stayed sunny all afternoon, and the fog didn't come in. That's why I never let go of the memory of the Turkey Day game. Things had looked hopeless that day, but that game turned out far different than anyone at halftime could ever have envisioned.

Why did that game turn out the way it did? Was it Paganini's words—"Is your will to win stronger than your pain?" or was it divine intervention? The years have slipped by and I still don't know. Maybe this is why I'm going crazy. I like to think of myself as the romantic underdog—the Comeback Kid. That hopeful and inspiring figure whom people loved and admired. Shit. What am I talking about? That was Dan White's problem.

McManus had witnessed first-hand how his friend, ex-cop and firefighter Dan White had gotten himself elected to the Board of Supervisors. Then White drove himself insane trying to be something he wasn't. His dreams of glory twisted into a garish nightmare of gun smoke and blood in City Hall when he shot to death Mayor George Moscone and Supervisor Harvey Milk in 1978.

How do we define evil? White believed he was acting with honor when he killed them. Why'd that happen? Destiny and fate? Divine Intervention as some believed? Are we allowed to hate in the name of righteousness? Maybe I need to stop fighting against the world, stop trying to figure out all this shit, and just smoke a joint like everyone else. Get high, dude. Mellow out. Makes as much sense as anything else right now.

McManus reached in his pocket and found the joint from his locker. He rolled it between his fingers. It felt fragile, ready to crumble from age. He walked away from the window. *I've never smoked pot before. Wonder if the effects from my first joint will bring me enlightenment—or the start of my slide into drug addiction? Am I just a hypocrite? I busted a lot of pot smokers.*

McManus' fingers spun the dial on his iPod, looking for some bittersweet music. He slipped on his ear buds and found an Al Stewart song about a mysterious woman "running out of the sun in a silk dress." He put the joint to his lips and lit it. The smoke snaked upwards, and a skunky odor filled the condo. *Whenever I smell this shit, I immediately think of rundown apartments in the Haight and hippies in torn clothes sitting in the park getting high.*

After a brief pause, he made the sucking sound that had always annoyed him. *Fuck. Now I'm one of them!*

He held a mouthfull of marijuana smoke that scratched and seared his lungs. He coughed once, and then started to gag. As McManus jerked the joint from his lips, Carly looked up from her bed next to the fireplace and crept over to him. She sat at his feet looking as if she were worried about him.

"Shit." He coughed again, and as his lungs cleared, McManus stood up and fanned the air with his hand. *Sure don't need the neighbors knowing the cop next door is getting high.*

He spit, then threw the joint into the sink and washed it all down the drain. *Enlightenment's going to have to come from someplace else. Maybe I should just grow a beard…and look like a shit-bum.*

McManus sat down at the kitchen table, folded his hands in front of him, and sat trance-like. *I just need some sleep. But I feel so uptight. A bulldozer couldn't pull a pin out of my ass.*

He stood up, opened a bottle of Blanton's, took a swig and swished it around to get rid of the taste of the marijuana. Then he swallowed the booze.

This feels so weird. After a lifetime living under the restraints of the San Francisco Police Department, I'm free. How about that? For the time being, I don't have the burden of walking around with the power of life and death holstered to my hip. Gone also is the need to be hyper-vigilant. This is bizarre. People used to call me for help. But now, it's MY life in crisis, and I don't know what the fuck to do.

McManus got up, went to the hall closet, and grabbed a bucket. With a sponge and a bottle of Mr. Clean, he went to work scrubbing the kitchen floor. *Mom used to do this every time she got depressed. Our floors were usually spotless.*

Margaret O'Malley McManus might have been a curvaceous Irish woman with coiffed auburn hair, but she wasn't afraid to get down on her hands and knees to keep her house clean. Appearance was paramount to her.

A dental hygienist, she worked downtown in the 450 Sutter Building. Then she'd come home to the foggy Sunset district. That fog messed with her mind. She'd complain how she hadn't seen the sun all day. Said she felt trapped by it and the 50-degree gloom that kept her bundled in sweaters all year round.

The deaths in the same year of my father and her beloved Irish Catholic President Kennedy left her deeper in darkness. After work, she would often pour a drink and scrub her floors by hand, singing the Mr. Clean song to chase away the blues. I learned to judge Mom's moods by what she was drinking. Jameson Triple Distilled Irish whiskey was her favorite. One night, in a good Jameson mood, she called me downstairs. Together, we scrubbed the kitchen floor, singing: "Mr. Clean will clean your whole house and everything that's in it..."

That was the happiest I ever saw her. And my favorite memory of Mom.

Other nights, she'd call to me, "Red sky in the morning, sailors take warning." Then she'd make a Tequila Sunrise. I was too young to know the drink's name, but knew to avoid her when she held the orange and yellow high-ball glass.

Never knew what made her happy or sad...but dealing with Mom was sure good training for becoming a cop.

After an hour of cleaning, McManus' sweat-soaked T-shirt clung to his back. He stripped down and got into the shower where his body finally relaxed. The water carried away the dirt and grime of the last 36 hours. When it became lukewarm, he got out and wrapped a towel around his waist. Standing in front of the mirror, he wiped away the condensation and stared at his reflection. *Something's got to change. This is not the life I'm supposed to live.*

McManus went to his clothes drawer and found a small black velvet drawstring bag. He emptied the contents into his palm, ran his finger over a penny-sized silver medallion, and untangled the chain.

Walking back to the mirror, he studied himself again and removed the St. Michael medallion from around his neck, dropping it into the velvet bag. *I'm no longer a cop. No need for the patron saint of police officers.*

From his palm, McManus took out the other medallion: "St. Christopher Protect Us." He raised it over his head and placed it around his neck. *Mom would be happy.*

16

The victim lay sprawled on his back atop a pile of fallen eucalyptus bark. His nearly severed head awash in a black mess of dried goop was cocked at an unnatural angle on his shoulders. A knife to the kidneys followed by a throat slash. The best way to kill a man when you want to do it quietly— learned that in basic training at Ft. Lewis.

Oh, Fuck! McManus bolted upright in a panic. The nightmare left him nauseous.

Wow! These dreams are getting too real. What time is it, anyway? He rubbed his eyes and looked at Carly sleeping peacefully next to the fireplace. Then he glanced at the clock.

Shit, it's after midnight. I'm late for work. McManus reached for his cell phone to call Richmond Station. Then he collapsed back onto the bed when he remembered his life had changed...

My God! What did I do? "Aaaaaaaaaaaaagh!" He pounded his fist into the bed, then stared at the fireplace flames dancing on the wood-beamed ceiling.

No way I'm going to be able to fall back to sleep, now. Might as well get up. He rolled out of bed to pour a shot of Blanton's.

Where did THAT dream come from? I don't remember a knife wound to Cassidy's kidneys, but his throat sure was slashed. That mean anything? Like maybe, the killer didn't have military training in close-quarter knife work? Maybe the killer's an amateur? That would explain the overkill and mutilation of Cassidy's body. Somebody was really pissed at him.

McManus stood up and stretched until he could feel the disks in his back pop into place. He walked to the bay window with his glass. *The fog's back in. Time for a consultation with Foggy.*

He slid open the window. "Hey, Fog, guess what? I got suspended today and tried to smoke a joint."

McManus waited for a response but nothing happened. He ran his fingers through his thinning hair. "Foggy...I am scared. If I had this whole thing to do over again, I don't think I would have done this."

He could almost hear the fog asking him, "Done this? What *this* is *this?*"

This? So if I were to answer Foggy, I'd list a dozen things I've screwed up since the year started. McManus leaned against the window frame and shrugged. Then he shut the window and walked to the kitchen.

He was suddenly very hungry. He oiled a frying pan, poured in half a bag of hash browns, lay down three strips of bacon, and grabbed a spatula. Then he diced some onions and tossed a fistful of shredded cheddar cheese on everything. When it melted, he emptied the pan onto a plate, salted the potatoes, and sat down. *Saved myself ten bucks. Maybe I can come back as a short-order cook.*

After finishing his meal and rinsing the pan and plate, he stretched his arms above his head and burped. Then he walked to the bookshelf next to the fireplace to scan his personal library. The titles ranged from the mind-boggling *Critique of Pure Reason* by Kant (which he had begun reading at S.I. over 45 years ago and had yet to finish) to the nostalgic, *A Flag for San Francisco: The Story of the 1961 San Francisco Giants.*

The latest addition to this collection was a curious used book he'd purchased a few weeks before at the Green Apple on Clement Street called *Voodoo in New Orleans.* All told, McManus' book collection contained 127 titles with a San Francisco theme; *The Natural World of San Francisco* was his all-time favorite book.

He pulled *Critique of Pure Reason* off the shelf and slid down into the beanbag chair to give it another go. Like all his books, the pages were marked with yellow highlights and red notes written in the margins. *This was Denny Wayland's favorite book. Wayland was one of my all-time favorite people. Thirty-five years ago, we worked together.*

He was the sanest, most stable man I ever met in the SFPD. A couple years older than me, he was the big brother I never had.

Denny always carried a copy of Kant's book in his briefcase. During our lunch breaks, amidst the hustle and bustle of Zim's or the Copper Penny, he'd pull out this 700-page monster and study it. I was blown away by his concentration in the middle of a busy restaurant. I'd watch him read and then highlight important ideas in yellow. With a red pen he'd write comments in the margin. That's where I got the idea to do that with my books.

McManus pulled off his slippers to warm his bare feet in front of the fireplace. Carly rested her head on his thigh and fell asleep.

Denny had a favorite saying he'd gotten from reading Kant: "Happiness is having something to do, someone to love and something to look forward to." The father of four, he was stricken with testicular cancer at age 33.

I went to see him as he lay dying in a hospital bed. He told me: "There is nothing more tangible than the present moment." Then he tapped his heart with his fist and looked me straight in the eye. "What you're hoping to find 'out there,' Phil, is already within you."

Thirty-five years later and the search goes on...

TUESDAY
FEBRUARY 2, 2010 • 0143 HRS.

McManus put the book down when the sound of sirens woke Carly, who sat up, looked around, and howled.

"Quiet, you'll wake up the whole building." He marked his place next to a paragraph entitled, "The Fourth Paralogism of Ideality (With Regard to Outer Relations)." *I don't know what the fuck this thing's saying anyway.*

Carly stopped howling and dropped her head. After a moment, she looked up at McManus and gave him a sideways glance that said, "Hey, Mr. Anti-social. When somebody talks to me, I talk to them." Then she darted to the window, stood up on her hind legs, pressed her front paws against the glass, and looked out. Her head whip-sawed back and forth like she was watching a tennis match.

McManus took off his glasses and rolled out of the beanbag chair to join Carly at the window. The view resembled the inside of a cotton ball. He saw nothing, so he slid open the window and felt a blast of cold night air. Shivering, he listened to the moan of foghorns and the wail of fire engines responding from all over the city. Like a junkie in need of a fix, he felt his heart pounding while his body craved the adrenaline rush of an emergency. He turned on the police scanner next to the window.

"…Repeating Third Alarm…Box 4533…Cole and Page…Units due…"

"Come on Carly, let's go for a ride." McManus got out his brown bomber jacket from the closet, pulled his Giants cap tight, and grabbed Carly's leash. Hearing the leash's metal clip jingle in his hand, the dog jumped up and down.

"Relax." McManus searched through his CD collection for his Fog Mix.

"Got it. Let's go." He took the stairs down to the street as Carly rode the steps like she was bouncing on a pogo stick. Outside, McManus took a deep breath and filled his lungs with the foggy air. *Aw, that feels better.*

He walked to the Camry, and Carly jumped in as soon as the door opened. Looping her leash around the brake release handle, McManus started the engine. Seeing his breath waft like puffs of smoke into the air, he rubbed his hands together. *It's warmer outside than it is in the car.*

After turning up the defroster, he went outside to clear the dew from the front windshield with a Squeegee. He glanced down Red Rock Way. *Can't see the end of the street, and it's only a hundred feet away. Don't think cleaning the window is gonna make much difference… Just like most of the shit I've been doing lately.*

When he finished, McManus got back into the warmed up car. *Let's go to Twin Peaks. I gotta feeling we might see something spectacular. Don't ask me why. Just Foggy talking to me.*

Slowly he navigated through the narrow winding streets before stopping for the light at the intersection of Clipper, Portola and Burnett. He pushed his Fog Mix CD into the player and selected track four. With the sound of a harp filling the car, the Mancini orchestra played the theme from the San Francisco film noir thriller, *Experiment in Terror.*

A white Audi A4 stopped at the light next to him. McManus saw the driver pull his attractive young woman passenger closer for a kiss. *Ah, to be young, rich, and in love in San Francisco at four in the morning. You want to change places, pal?*

On the green turn signal, he went left onto Portola, leaving the couple in the Audi still embracing at the light. A half mile down the road, he turned right onto Twin Peaks Boulevard and ascended the switchbacks toward the top, the fog thinning as they climbed. Rounding a bend near the top, the Camry suddenly burst out of the fog and into the clear. *I've seen this happen before. It's like a landscape painting lit by a full moon at the DeYoung.*

McManus' heart beat faster as he drove and parked next to the police radio transmitter at the top of one of San Francisco's famous seven hills. The Camry was the only car in the lot. When he rolled down his windows, Carly stuck her head out and looked around.

Below them, the fog reminded him of a huge white living room carpet. *It's spread out in all directions and looks so thick and inviting, I want to take off my shoes and walk on it all the way across the Bay to Oakland.*

Except for the occasional distant moan of a foghorn, all was as silent as a reflection. The tops of the skyscrapers poked through the fog. Their silhouettes, lit by the full moon, cast long shadows across the city. *Jeez, I feel like a voyeur watching a beautiful woman asleep in her bed.*

McManus closed his eyes and remembered the nights in high school he parked here exploring the mysteries under a girl's skirt. The moment was perfect until an obese raccoon waddled in front of the car from a nearby garbage can. Carly went into a barking frenzy. The coon shot a "fuck you" look back at the little Yorkie. *Fuck you, too, you fat piece of shit.*

Just as McManus brought out his cell phone camera to take a picture, Carly jumped through the window to run after the raccoon. "Whoa, Carly," McManus yelled. He got out of the car fast enough to grab her as the raccoon disappeared.

"Way to go, partner. That's how you jack-up a shit-bum to get him moving off the street." He held Carly tight to his chest as they marveled at the foggy landscape beneath them.

"Just you and me, little girl. I love you." He petted her head as she panted heavily with eyes bright and tongue out. "Thanks for coming into my life… Now, let's go home and get some sleep."

17

Today's jam-up of golfers waiting at the fourth tee of the Lincoln Park course annoyed McManus. He wasn't comfortable standing around the spot where a few weeks before he'd almost ended his life.

I used to love standing on this tee, looking out at the ocean. Now the place feels haunted. Well shit, a hundred years ago before they built the course, it was a cemetery. Then they dug up all the bodies and moved them out to Colma. Let's hurry up and get the fuck out of here.

"Remember, Kid, loosen the grip. Don't strangle it," Guido Donatelli said to McManus, who smiled at his former police partner now retired one year. They kept in touch on the phone from time to time, and when Donatelli heard about the suspension, he suggested the golf date.

The pair had worked together to arrest a psychotic creep who had pointed a shotgun at McManus several years before. Responding to a noise complaint on a Saturday night, McManus was climbing the stairs of an apartment house on Turk Street when he looked up and saw a naked man standing at the top of the stairwell grinning with a shotgun leveled at the officers.

Instead of immediately drawing his weapon and shooting the man as he was trained to do, McManus froze and couldn't react. However, his hesitation allowed the gunman to throw down his weapon. A miracle had saved both of their lives. Only Guido following McManus up the stairwell knew the whole truth.

Guido kept my secret. He could have ruined me. Not too many guys would have covered for me, but he understood what happened. I just couldn't react. The last thing I was thinking about walking up those stairs was running into some fuckin' guy with a shotgun. And, despite all the years of training and mental preparation preparing for that moment of truth, when it finally happened, I was so shocked I couldn't react. I was that sure we were both dead men.

Later, the story came out that the man had been attempting suicide-by-cop. Therefore, instead of receiving the usual Gold Medal of Valor for facing down an armed suspect, McManus and Guido received only Silver Medals of Valor. The incident was quietly swept under the carpet to avoid publicity, which might have inspired similar cases of police-assisted suicide. As a result, McManus' Medal of Valor always seemed tainted to him.

"You're up, Kid," said Guido as he saw the all-clear signal from the players on the green. Guido had started calling him "Kid" twenty years before when McManus began to lose his hair. The nickname was an example of Guido trying to make his friend feel good—like helping a pal forget a sign of aging. Not everyone saw Guido's upbeat personality as real. Some more cynical cops thought he was naïve and preferred to call him "Father Guido."

McManus took a couple practice swings, inhaled a deep breath of cool ocean air to calm himself, and addressed the ball. *It's been six weeks now since I parked the radio car over there and put the gun in my mouth.*

He licked his lips, drew his club back, and swung. The ball exploded off the tee. He looked up to watch as it sliced wild to the right.

Thunk... The sound of the ball hitting a cypress tree echoed like a gunshot over the course. It ricocheted back onto the fairway and rolled down into a dale, disappearing from view. By the time the ball came into view, it had lost most of its momentum and stopped atop a brown knoll about 125 yards from the pin.

"Nice shot, Kid," Guido laughed.

"Just the way I planned it." McManus nodded and put his hands in his pants pockets ready to do his Tiger Woods "Aw Shucks" walk.

Guido hit his ball just short of the green. Then the former partners walked down the sloping fairway for their next shots. McManus felt a chill and looked up. A tell-tale whiff of fog drifted overhead having broken off from a huge bank waiting offshore. "We're in San Francisco. Here comes the fog again." He looked at his watch, then back up at Guido. "Expect the fog in twenty minutes."

When he reached his ball, McManus saw that the lie was an easy, straight-ahead shot. "I'm going to do a punch-and-run with a five-iron," he said, waiting for the green to clear.

"Sounds good. Keep it down, out of the wind, and let it roll to the hole," Guido gave him the OK sign. "By the way, Kid, nice beard."

"It's only two day's growth, but I'm gonna shave when I get home. I'm starting a job, and I don't want to look like a shit-bum. Mambo hired me to work on his tour buses again."

Vic Mallamo, nicknamed, "Mambo," was a retired SFPD officer, former classmate of McManus at St. Anne and S.I., and owned Silvano's City-Sights tour bus company. The previous summer, he'd given McManus a tryout to see if working as a tour bus guide was something he might enjoy doing in retirement.

"Mambo's got a good heart," Guido said with a nod. "He never forgets his roots and always finds ways to help the rank-and-file. When do you start?"

"Next week. Gotta get out of the house and do something." McManus took a practice swing.

"Just like that, Kid." Guido smiled and gave him a thumbs up.

McManus smiled back and addressed his ball. Using a short backswing, he punched at the ball and sent it straight and low toward the hole. The ball cleared the dale and landed just short of the putting green when it struck a pebble and caromed wildly away from the hole, landing on a steep hillside next to the putting green.

Shit. McManus threw his club in the air.

But, after the ball paused for a moment, it rolled down the incline picking up speed.

"Hey, that's got a chance," Guido yelled.

McManus watched the ball approach the cup. "Come on, baby. Get in the hole!" His heart jumped into his throat as the ball hit the flag stick, dropped straight down, and disappeared.

"Oh, Baby. Eagle two! Ya did it, Kid." Guido hooted.

McManus grinned like a schoolboy getting a star on his spelling paper as he walked to the hole to retrieve his ball. He kissed it and shook his head. "That makes my day."

18

The open-topped Silvano's City-Sights tour bus idled as it sat parked along Jefferson Street in Fisherman's Wharf. Up on the bus's top level, McManus rested against the guard-rail and looked down at the crowd of tourists waiting to board. He'd forgotten how physically demanding the job was from when he tried it on for size last summer.

His lower back and quads ached from all the walking he'd done during four 90-minute tours yesterday and on Monday. And his throat felt raspy—not from all the talking he was doing — but breathing in the exhaust fumes from the traffic. He did enjoy the job, working outside and being surrounded by people. But he missed the ego gratification of wearing a star, carrying a gun, and being the center of attention.

"You'll get used to it," Mambo had told him after watching McManus rubbing his calves the day before. Vic Mallamo had been one of the most popular Deputy Chiefs in SFPD history. But last year, when a new Chief of Police brought in his own people, he forced Mambo to retire. Without breaking stride, the following Monday Mambo went to work running the family-owned bus company he had inherited from his Uncle Silvano.

Mambo called McManus when he heard about his suspension, asking if he wanted to work for him again. He liked to hire ex-cops as tour guides, reasoning they had years of experience dealing with the public, came complete with highly entertaining stories, and knew the city's history. Most importantly, he saw his bus company as providing a "soft landing" for recently retired police officers who were tired of the life-and-death responsibilities of being a cop—but missed the energy of the street.

McManus wondered if his time to pull-the-pin had finally arrived as he watched Mambo walk through the crowd carrying a red company parka and then enter the bus.

"The training wheels come off today—you got the mike for this one," Mambo said after coming up the steps and handing him the red jacket.

"You sure I'm ready?" McManus swung the jacket over his shoulders. "What? You're not going to help me put it on like they do with the green jacket at the Masters?"

Mambo blew out his breath, turned, and walked back downstairs to take tickets. McManus took a sip from his water bottle. *I guess I'm ready. That's Mambo's way of saying things without saying things.*

McManus slipped into the jacket and watched an elderly couple approach. They moved one by one up the narrow winding steps like two dump trucks struggling up the Waldo Grade. But before the man reached the top step, four young children ducked around him and claimed the prized seats in the first row. The children's action angered the couple. The elderly woman looked at McManus and said, "The man downstairs let us on first, so we could get those seats because they'd be out of the wind."

Before McManus could say anything, one of the kids' mothers appeared behind the elderly couple. Dressed in a stylish poppy-color double-breasted cashmere trench coat, she spoke up, "Ah, I think I heard the man downstairs say, 'Sit anywhere.'"

Oh shit. Here...we go. McManus nodded. "In most cases that's true. But we like to accommodate older passengers who may have problems with the wind and the cold. Do you think two of the kids can sit somewhere else—perhaps in the last row? They'd have a clear view there also."

"No," the other mom said. "We promised the kids they could sit in the front row. Can't you accommodate us?"

Fuck me. First passengers of the day...and I'm arguing with them. Always dealing with some unyielding citizen. Only now I'm not wearing the persuasive power of a 7-pointed silver star and a SIG P226 semi-automatic pistol. "Can't you accommodate me here, lady, and show a little respect for older people—someday that's going to be us." McManus tilted his head and gave her a wry smile.

"Fine," the annoyed mother said. "Give us our money back—we'll just find another bus company."

"You don't have to leave," McManus said turning up his palms toward the woman. "Just sit in different seats."

She glared at him as she gathered her disappointed children. "The *man* says we have to leave."

McManus blew out his breath and watched the mothers lead their kids off the bus.

Soon, the thirty-eight rows of gray plastic seats on the open top level were filled. McManus went downstairs and reported to Mambo they were ready to leave. He nodded, and together they started back up the stairs. Halfway up, Mambo stopped and looked back at McManus. "I know you can do this, Phil. Don't let me down." McManus saw his sincerity and drew in a deep breath to calm himself.

"No problem," he said to Mambo, who made his way to the back of the bus to watch. McManus stood in the stairwell out of view and checked to make sure the pockets of his khaki cargo pants were stuffed with tour pamphlets and city maps. Then he made the sign of the cross, drew another deep breath, and put on a comedian's mischievous smile.

With his arms pumping like they were pistons in a high-powered engine, he ran up the stairs and burst into the daylight where he faced the passengers. He thrust his arms above his head in a victory V: "With apologies to any

New Yorkers aboard, WELCOME TO THE GREATEST CITY IN THE WORLD!"

McManus immediately felt the floor jerk out from under him as the bus pulled away from the curb. His smile turned to shock as he fell forward, having to grab a seat handle to steady himself. As the bus picked up speed, the wind pushed his wide-brimmed hat down over his face, blinding him.

"You better be careful what you say there, pal," a passenger with a thick New York accent called out as McManus struggled to regain his balance. "You're talking about New York—to New Yorkers, here. And you're already off to the worst start since President William Henry Harrison caught pneumonia at his Inaugural and died 31 days later." The New Yorker's wife elbowed him in the ribs to be quiet.

McManus' eyes lit up like high beams on a car. "That's a great line, my friend. Can I borrow it?"

The New Yorker laughed. "Forget about it."

McManus watched Mambo grit his teeth, sitting in the last row. *Shit, He looks like I just fumbled away the opening kickoff on the five-yard line. Regroup. Time starts now.*

McManus stood, picked up the microphone, and started again.

"So…you're in San Francisco, and on this bus you can be whomever you want to be. As long as you don't stand up, you don't bother anybody, and you don't smoke anything. Even if you have a prescription Medical Marijuana card. And that, people, is what's called tolerance and is the spirit of San Francisco…except on smoke-free buses."

McManus smiled back at Mambo, who sat with his arms crossed and nodded. Mambo had taught him that the first three minutes of the tour were critical when it came to connecting with the passengers.

Walking down the aisle holding the microphone, he canvased passengers about where they were from, if there were any newlyweds aboard, and how many were visiting San Francisco for the first time. He learned from "New Yorkers" Dick and Dot that they weren't really New Yorkers, but from River Edge, New Jersey, "right next to Hackensack." They both wore blue San Francisco-logoed fleece tops, an emergency purchase from a street vendor because San Francisco was "colder than friggin' Jersey," they had told him.

McManus described the sights as the bus drove along the waterfront. "Up ahead on the left, the building with the clock tower is the Ferry Building." He pointed toward the Bay while sweeping his eyes across the passengers.

"Yo, Phil…" Dick called from his seat. "Is that the same building the big friggin' octopus pulled down?" Dick smiled at himself when his comment drew laughs from the other riders.

What fucking octopus? McManus paused for a moment, trying to figure out what Dick was talking about. Then his face brightened.

"Great memory, Dick, *It Came From Beneath the Sea*… 1955. Yes! That is the same building."

With a straight face, Dick asked, "How long did it take to rebuild the friggin' place?"

McManus took a dramatic pause and smiled. "Quite a while…You gotta remember that octopus also pulled down the Golden Gate Bridge. And when they started rebuilding everything, they gave the Bridge priority."

McManus saw Mambo roll his eyes and chuckle.

"So as long as we're talking about disasters, let's talk about earthquakes," McManus said. "Most of you can probably remember the Loma Prieta quake, which is also called the World Series earthquake—because it happened just before the start of Game Three over at Candlestick Park. It lasted 15 seconds and measured 6.9 on the Richter scale." McManus noticed he had the full attention of the passengers.

"By contrast, the great earthquake of 1906 measured 8.0, and lasted 48 seconds. Can you imagine how long those 48 seconds must have seemed?"

"Yeah," Dot, seated next to Dick, yelled out. "That's about how long Dick can last." All eyes turned to look at the New Yorkers from River Edge as nervous laughter trickled through the bus. Dick turned toward Dot with a pained expression. "What did you have to friggin' say that for, Dot?"

The bus turned onto Market Street and stopped in front of the Hyatt Regency Hotel. Dick and Dot got off before a dozen women and six men, all wearing convention badges, came aboard from a line outside.

Mambo got up and went downstairs to collect tickets. Within minutes, the bus was underway again, rolling past City Hall and along Van Ness Avenue. McManus talked more about the 1906 earthquake, describing how the city caught fire and burned for three days and nights.

"Only by dynamiting all the beautiful Victorian mansions that had once lined Van Ness Avenue here, to create a fire break, were firefighters able to stop the spreading flames," he said. "And someday—maybe even tonight—that's all going to happen here again."

A few minutes later, the bus arrived at the Golden Gate Bridge and stopped to take on new passengers. The wind blowing in from the Pacific whipped over the open deck and buffeted the passengers. But when the bus started again, heavy traffic on the Bridge brought it to a complete stop. During this break, McManus walked up and down the aisle quizzing the new passengers about their home states. When he came to a young Latino couple, the man sitting on the aisle asked if he could take the mike and ask a question of the woman beside him.

"Just as long as you don't say something that the government can use to shut us down." McManus handed over the mike.

The passenger nodded his acceptance as he took the mike. Squeezing himself out of his seat, he got down on one knee in the aisle. The bus began crawling along slowly near mid-span. McManus watched the man reach into his jacket pocket and pull out a small box. Beaming broadly, he faced the woman, opened the box, and revealed a simple quarter-carat diamond on a narrow silver band.

"Oh, my God," the woman gasped as she brought her hands to her cheeks.

"Ellie, will you marry me," he asked, taking the ring out of the box.

Cheers and applause quickly drowned out the sound of the wind and traffic. The woman squealed her acceptance and leaned across the bench seat throwing her arms around her future husband's neck. McManus took the microphone back from the man and smiled like a kid in a candy story.

"First time for everything. First time I've ever seen that," McManus said as he patted the man on the back. "That's pretty classy. Right here at the mid-span of the Golden Gate Bridge…Wow. I hope you guys have a great life together."

McManus laughed again. Then in a voice sounding slightly better than fingernails on a blackboard, he began to sing:

"At last…my love has come along…"

19

McManus was starving. He'd only had a hot dog at the ball park in Scottsdale a few hours before flying back to San Francisco. Now, trying to find parking near the Shinge Yagura Zen Restaurant at 41st Avenue and Balboa, he felt as frustrated as if he was trying to find a gold chain dropped in the sand at Ocean Beach. He made two more trips around the block before giving up and parking in the crosswalk. McManus hoped he still had some department juice left if he needed the ticket pulled. He walked to the restaurant in the wind, cold and fog.

After a weekend wearing shorts and watching the Giants Spring Training in Arizona, I was getting used to working on my tan. But I needed a change of scenery before coming off suspension next week. I haven't been working much on the bus because of the poor weather. Now that I'll be back to work, maybe I'll feel like looking up Fratelli. But then again, why start something I can't consummate if she isn't interested in men.

McManus entered the restaurant and was greeted by the aroma of tempura and beef teriyaki. Roy, the 70-year-old owner, sushi chef, and Japanese Renaissance man, nodded when he saw him and asked, "You park in the crosswalk again, McManus?"

McManus smiled.

"Fuckin' cops." Roy smiled and shooed away two hangers-on from the sushi counter, so McManus could sit down. A waitress placed a steaming cup of green tea in front of him. Shinge Yagura Zen was one of McManus' favorite restaurants. He enjoyed Roy's quirky Zen outlook of "right mind, right posture" mixed with a prankster's charm and wit.

"So, how'd the Giants look, so far?" Roy asked from his grill.

McManus shrugged. "I think this is the year, Roy. Lincecum's throwing well and this kid Posey, the rookie catcher they signed for six million bucks, he can play—he's going to be great."

"Stupid," said Roy shaking his head. "Six million bucks for a rookie! I'll believe it when I see it. Those fuckin' guys are torture to watch. They always break your heart!"

McManus shrugged and sipped his tea while studying the chart on the wall behind the sushi counter:

Roy's Rules to Live By
- **Choose to Care**
- **Leave No Trace**
- **Be Responsible**
- **Acknowledge Feelings**
- **Participate**
- **Be Vulnerable**
- **Accept Criticism**
- **Be Accountable**

"Okay, Roy," McManus said. "How about number two tonight? 'Leave no trace.' That's some sort of an environmental idea, right?"

"It could be," Roy smiled.

As was their custom, McManus chose the evening's topic for Roy to preach about. "It goes back to when I was a kid," Roy said. "We made sure we used up and didn't waste a thing. We left no trace." He made eye contact with McManus. "It also refers to cleaning up your messes, so no one else has to."

Roy's a wise old soul, and I like some of his beliefs, particularly when he talks about reincarnation. I've always thought I had a previous life as a 19-year-old gunner on a B17 bomber during World War II, and I was killed on a mission over Germany.

Shit, better not go there. People'll think I'm really nuts if I start talking about that stuff. But the bomber crews stationed in England suffered the most casualties. Over 56,000 guys in just two and a half years. What a slaughter! That's a lot of souls floating around Purgatory.

Hey, here's a crazy thought. Maybe I DID die in a B17 and THIS is Purgatory.

An approaching siren interrupted his thoughts. He looked out the front windows and saw red lights reflected on the buildings across the street.

"Your grease flue goin' up again, Roy?" The sushi chef shook his head.

"Somethin's going on," McManus said and went to investigate.

Outside, the acrid odor of smoke overpowered the smell of teriyaki. A frightening orange glow came from the lower flat of a building on the corner. "Oh, shit!" *This is definitely what they mean by an Oh Shit Fire.*

Flames had exploded the glass out of the front windows, lighting up the foggy night sky. McManus ran to the engine parked in front and found the driver Rich Falkenburg attaching a hose to a hydrant.

"Kids in the building," yelled an older Asian man with his hair and eyebrows singed.

"You sure?" Falkenburg shouted above the roar of the fire engine.

"Mother went shopping," the man cried.

"How many?" asked Lieutenant Rich Ames, the officer in charge of Engine 34.

"Two," said the old man beginning to shiver. He grabbed his arms and shook his head.

"Oh, shit." Ames reached for a microphone hanging from his shoulder and radioed for an immediate second alarm. McManus stood next to the engine and looked up.

This one's going to be a real burner.

Falkenberg yelled the information about the kids to the rest of the crew. "This is bad," he said turning back to McManus, who helped him to unkink the hose line.

"It's just us. The fuckin' truck company and second-due engine are on the other side of the district workin' an auto accident."

McManus caught sight of Trish Fratelli as she flipped the yellow cylinder of a Scott air pack over her head. She glanced back at him, and then her eyes disappeared behind the face piece of her breathing mask. She secured her black leather helmet and pulled on her gloves.

Ames grabbed a forcible entry tool called the Chicago Door Opener off the rig. "Let's go," he said to her.

McManus watched Fratelli pull a hose line and follow Ames up the front steps. At the door, Ames slammed the forcible entry tool into the wooden doorjamb with the same picture-perfect swing that had won him All-City baseball honors at St. Ignatius High School. A Christmas wreath fell off the door. Fratelli crouched low behind Ames, ready to attack the flames with the hose line. Ames then popped open the door, unleashing a torrent of black smoke and sending a rodent scurrying over their feet and down the steps.

On the street, McManus could feel the heat radiating out of the building. *If it's this hot out here, what is it like for them inside?*

The flames mesmerized him. Fratelli and Ames disappeared into the churning smoke while water filled the hose line, making a whooshing sound as it ran up the stairs and into the house. A moment later, a blast of water blew flaming debris through the front windows and down onto the street.

McManus heard sirens in the distance. A lump caught in his throat. *Hurry up and get here. They need help. Shit. This is hard to watch. I can't do a thing. They've only been in there a couple seconds, but it seems like an hour. Much too long.*

"Oh, my God," came a cry from the gathering crowd behind the fire engine.

McManus looked back at the smoky doorway and saw Fratelli appear with a limp young boy cradled in her arms. The child's limbs flopped about like a rag doll as she carried him down the front steps.

Another engine company arrived and parked in front of Engine 34. A firefighter jumped down from the rig and grabbed the kid from her at the bottom of the steps. Fratelli turned around, followed the hose line back into the smoke, and disappeared again.

The volume and color of the smoke lightened as more firefighters entered the building, attacking the flames with a second hose line. Another collective groan came from the crowd when Fratelli reappeared in the doorway and carried the second little boy down the steps. Several pairs of hands reached for the limp body to carry him to the waiting paramedics.

Fratelli then knelt on the sidewalk and pulled off her breathing mask. Her face was awash in beads of perspiration with strands of hair matted against her forehead. She caught her breath and looked back up at the flat. White-gray smoke now replaced the orange flames rolling out the windows.

A crew of arriving firefighters relieved Ames, who joined Fratelli on the sidewalk. He ripped off his mask and glanced at a gray blanket already covering the first child's body. Nearby, paramedics were performing CPR on the second child whose lifeless body was clad in a pair of blackened SpongeBob Square Pants pajamas.

Above the din of Engine 34's pump, a woman's shriek cut into the foggy night air. "My babies!"

McManus turned and looked back toward the voice. A woman carrying two bags of groceries dropped them in the street. McManus felt his heart drop. *Where did the love of God go?*

He watched the woman run toward the paramedics and the unresponsive children. "My babies," she wailed.

Ames reached out to keep her from interfering with the paramedics, but she fought Ames's restraint and spit into his face. "Give me my babies!"

Fratelli got to her feet and rushed to help Ames control the woman. A cop jumped into the struggle, and together they pulled her away. Ames wiped the spit from his face while Fratelli walked behind the engine. McManus followed her to see if she was all right. He watched as she stopped, leaned forward, held her hair in place, and vomited.

Ames stood next to her. His smoke smudged face reflected the horror he'd witnessed inside the burning building. Traumatized, his Irish temper flashed as he looked up at the smoldering ruins. "Un-fuckin' believable," he screamed. "Who has their fuckin' Christmas tree still up in March?"

20

Heavy rain and high winds pelted the windows of McManus' condominium when he returned home. He lit the fireplace and settled into the beanbag chair. His nerves were rattled by what he'd witnessed, but he didn't want alcohol to numb his feelings.

Fratelli showed a lot of balls going into that fire. Wonder if I could still do something like that? He sighed and leaned forward, putting his head in his hands.

What bugs me is I'm jealous of her. I envy the resolve on her face. Her look said, "This is who I am, what I do, and why I'm here." I have nothing like that in my life anymore. I'm a suspended cop, and my life is so fucked up I don't want to retire. But if I go back to work, am I going to wind up sitting in a radio car sucking on the barrel of my gun, again? What the fuck is wrong with me?

THURSDAY
MARCH 25, 2010 · 0500 HRS.

Kezar Stadium exploded in riotous cheers as McManus lay on the damp turf. He watched from forty yards away as Colin O'Connell fell to the ground after scoring the Turkey Day championship-winning touchdown for St. Ignatius. In an instant, players came off the bench, and fans scaled the fences to charge the field in celebration. McManus got up and leapt into the air, not knowing if he was going to cry or scream.

"Thank you, thank you, thank you," he bellowed.

"No, no, no," a female voice whispered to McManus in the darkness. "The play is no good." Lowell players were standing about politely clapping. "See the penalty marker? Five-yard penalty—backfield in motion."

No.

"Now, Phillip, you know I've warned you to never get your hopes up. Soon as things go good they go bad."

No.

"Now, watch this," the female voice said.

Pete Cassidy, upon seeing the penalty flag, ran up and pushed O'Connell to the ground. From the thigh pad inside his football pants, he produced a fluorescent-colored scuba diver's knife and slashed at O'Connell's neck.

"You stupid shit," he screamed as a torrent of blood sprayed into the air and soaked O'Connell's white football uniform. "You cost us the championship!"

McManus gasped and hastily looked away. Overhead, a flock of seagulls swooped and screeched, impatiently waiting for the game to end so they could have lunch. One seagull broke away from the flock, making a bombing run toward McManus. It pulled up and glided to a landing. The seagull stared at McManus. Then it pecked at the ground and walked to his feet.

"You should be watching this," the seagull said.

Why?

"You're going to learn something about your future."

McManus looked down the field to see O'Connell clutching at his throat. Cassidy pulled O'Connell's blood-stained white football pants down to his ankles and then swung wildly with the knife. The blade slid through O'Connell's groin, ripping his testicles from his scrotum.

"Wow. You see that?" the seagull laughed.

McManus instinctively brought his hand down to his groin and there on the 20-yard line, before 20,000 people, he embarrassedly searched between his own legs. They were still there. He looked up and watched the macabre scene playing out in the end zone.

With O'Connell's bloody testicles hanging from the blade, Cassidy held the knife over his own head like a sword in triumph. The celebratory crowd on the field froze and watched in horror.

"Let this be a lesson to you," Cassidy screamed at them. "You don't fuck with me." Cassidy thrust his other arm over his head as a sign of victory, causing the testicles to fall to the ground.

Meanwhile, right tackle #78 Arthur "Baby Huey" Lahey scrambled up to Cassidy and patted him on the back. "Way to go to Cassidy. I never did like that little cocksucker," he snickered and reached down to pick up the bloody testicles. "Hey, McManus. Now you can finally have some balls." Lahey hooted as he threw the testicles at McManus.

"You are indeed Prince Hamlet," the female voice said to McManus. "For you were born with ragged claws to scuttle across the floors of silent seas with self-preservation your only goal."

Holding his balls in the palm of his hand, McManus looked down at the seagull. "So what future lessons am I supposed to be learning from this fiasco?"

The gull pecked at the grass again and looked up. "I have a friend named Jon, and he always says, "Don't believe your eyes.""

"Huh?"

McManus pushed himself up in bed feeling his heart pounding, glad to be awake. *Why am I always thinking about that game?*

The rain sounded like gravel hitting the windows. He gazed out at the city. The wild storm he'd fallen asleep to was still in progress. He got out of bed and pulled the curtains closed, fearful the high winds might shatter the windows.

Walking into the kitchen, he grabbed a handful of Oreos and stood over the sink to eat them. A white flash lit up the darkness inside the condo. An instant later, a loud rolling crash rocked the walls. Frightened, Carly barked and ran into the kitchen. McManus bent over and picked up the quivering dog.

"It's just lightning, sweetie. It's pretty rare around here." He held her tightly against his chest and sighed. "Like getting unconditional love."

THURSDAY
MARCH 25, 2010 · 0630 HRS.

The stormy night gave way to a peaceful morning. A golden beam of sunlight peeked through the split in the curtains and stretched across the carpet to where Carly lay sleeping next to the fireplace. McManus awoke and studied her. *Wish I could sleep like that.*

He rolled onto his back causing the bedsprings to squeak. Carly lifted her head and perked up her ears. Seeing him, she snapped wide-awake and scampered across the room, leaping onto his bed to greet him with a "good morning" wet tongue across his face.

"Stop it," he protested lifting her tiny body off him. He held her at arm's length above his head as her legs ran furiously trying to find traction.

How can a foot-tall dog jump onto a two-foot high bed? That's like a six-foot man high-jumping twelve feet! McManus set her down, and she snuggled next to him atop the comforter.

Carly, you need a haircut. I can barely see your eyes, anymore. McManus yawned and asked, "So where do you get your hair done?"

He got up, stretched, and pulled open the curtains. The brilliant sunlight made him squint as he watched the conveyer belt of traffic on the Bay Bridge flowing into the city. He went into the kitchen, opened a bag of Carly's favorite jerky dog treats, and then tossed one to her. She caught it on the fly.

McManus' mind drifted back to last night. *God, I can still hear Fratelli gagging and the sound of her puke splattering on the sidewalk. She did all she could to save those kids. They didn't have a chance.*

THURSDAY

MARCH 25, 2010 · 1030 HRS.

This was uncharted territory. McManus walked down Sacramento Street in Laurel Heights with a leashed Yorkie in one hand and a vibrant colored bouquet of orange tulips mixed with blue and grape hyacinths in the other. *Jeez, I look like Jimmy the flaming gay blade. What the hell am I doing here?*

McManus watched a dark blue SUV pull to the curb in front of him and park. On the back glass of the vehicle was a large crayon drawing of words surrounded by clusters of hearts and flowers:

DEAR LIFE, I WILL LIVE YOU TO MY FULLEST ABILITIES.
LOVE, ROZZI
P.S. I HAVE THE GREATEST BEST FRIENDS EVER
IN THE WHOLE WORLD

Wow, haven't seen something like that since the "Flower Power" days of the "Summer of Love." McManus watched the SUV passenger door open and a teenaged girl step out without looking up from her cell phone. *Texting her latest minutia to the world? Can't believe how fast that girl's fingers can move over the keyboard.*

Then the driver jumped out to help guide her texting friend into a fashion boutique whose window display featured boots, belts and purses.

Fratelli lived in a corner Queen Anne-style apartment house surrounded by an eclectic mix of trendy boutiques and pre-earthquake San Francisco architecture. The building had a secluded alcove entrance. McManus entered and noticed two large trellises of jasmine vines. *That's smart. All the drunks probably pee in here at night after leaving the bars down the street. Nothing better than jasmine to mask the odor of piss.*

McManus ran his finger down the list of tenants' names next to the doorbells. His stomach dropped. Apartment #105 listed two names: Fratelli/Buckholtz.

Fuck me. Why didn't I call ahead? I don't want to face her roommate. Gotta get out of here. But what about these flowers? He glanced at Carly. She took her sit pose and looked for his approval.

OK, you're right, Carly. We need to stay and I gotta man-up. McManus pressed the buzzer and waited.

"Yeah."

It wasn't Fratelli's voice. *Shit, the roommate's home.*

McManus caught himself and didn't automatically respond "San Francisco Police." Instead, he cleared his throat, pressed the intercom button, and answered. "Hi, this is Phil McManus. I'm a friend of Trish's. May I speak to her, please?"

The amused and condescending voice retorted. "She's not here, PHIL. Workin' a trade. Be back tomorrow morning."

He reached forward and pressed the intercom button again. "I got something for her."

"Hold on," came an even more annoyed response and then silence.

Is she going to come...should I wait?

In a few minutes, though, Carly barked. *She must hear footsteps.* "Quiet," said McManus as he pulled her leash tight.

Wonder if this is going to be the same blonde Fratelli was with at the funeral? What made me think they lived apart?

McManus recognized her when she opened the door. Barefoot and wearing a pair of faded blue sweatpants with "SFFD" printed on one leg, her yellow polo shirt smelled like she'd just pulled it out of the dirty clothes hamper.

Bad timing. Let's just make the best of an awkward situation and get the hell outta Dodge. McManus smiled and raised the bouquet of flowers toward her. "Hi, I was at the fire last night and was worried about Trish. Would you see that she gets these?" McManus handed her the bouquet.

She stared at him with the same put-upon expression he used to see whenever a woman wanted the police to get a man out of her house.

"I'll see that she gets them." She smirked.

McManus smiled back at her. "Thank you, I would appreciate that." *Is she gonna do it for me? Her look sure says otherwise.*

Then she pointed down at Carly. "Is that your dog?"

Carly pulled on the leash and growled. McManus nodded. *Why the fuck is she asking that?*

"Where did you get her?" She asked putting her hands on her hips.

"SPCA."

The blonde bent down to look more closely at Carly's face, and the dog went into a barking frenzy.

"Hmm, not very friendly, is she?" The woman stood back up and looked at McManus curiously. "Now I can see why a Yorkie like that was waiting for adoption at the pound the last two times I visited. You sure you got her there?"

McManus shrugged and smiled. "Guess I just had good timing. Not to change the subject or anything, but are you Trish's roommate? You look familiar."

"Bailey," she said without extending her hand. "I'm the night social worker at the General. You're the cop, right? I heard about you. We've probably crossed paths."

"I heard about you." Jeez, that's what the nuns used to tell you in grammar school just before they pulled out the ruler to hit you.

He saw her studying his face as she twirled a finger through a blonde curl in her hair. "Trish and I have a committed relationship, you know. Occasionally she does find a stray dog on the street," she said, cocking her head to the side. "I guess she feels sorry for 'em. But she's not going to be anybody's love interest, if you know what I mean."

Fuck you, Bitch. I got the perfect comeback line for that. To match her arrogance, McManus mimicked her pose, leaning his head, and lifting his nose to the air. He frowned and turned his palms up. "Whatever," he said in his best raspy Godfather voice.

It took a while before she spoke. Then she nodded her approval, looked straight into his eyes, and said with exaggerated confidence, "So tell me, McManus. Who is that you're trying to be?"

THURSDAY
MARCH 25, 2010 · 1420 HRS.

Thursday afternoon was an unusual time for his neighbors to be at home and knocking on his door. Carly barked and sniffed under the entryway. McManus went to the door to look through the peephole. He got a fish-eyed view of two big guys standing in the hallway dressed in sport coats and ties.

Oh, shit. Joe Grasso, an inspector in the General Works detail, stood next to a younger man in his 30s McManus didn't recognize. Grasso had come into the department a couple years after McManus and was known as a guy you didn't want to fool around with.

Carly barked again when McManus opened the door. "Quiet," McManus said. "Joe, how you doing? Long time, no see."

"Afternoon, Phil. This is Brad Hansen, my partner." Grasso glanced down at the dog. "And I imagine this is Carly."

I'm done. He's knows. This is not good. "Come on in guys," McManus said motioning for them to come in.

"Wow. She looks just like Toto from the *Wizard of Oz.* Long, silky hair and small black eyes, twinkling merrily, on both sides of her funny wee nose," Grasso said.

Carly growled and Grasso looked back at McManus. "This isn't a social call, Phil, so let's make this easy. We're working on a felony grand-theft dog case, and this sure looks like the dog. You know what I'm talking about, right, Phil?"

Signed, sealed, and delivered. Well, one thing I've learned from 37 years of police work is don't make spontaneous statements. He's waiting for a response. McManus looked away trying to avoid making eye contact. He said nothing.

Grasso reached into his coat pocket, retrieved his notes, and read them aloud: "Okay, here's the deal. Carly is owned by Gabriella Sutherland, whose father is Stanford Sutherland, who resides on the 3000 block of Broadway. Right up there on the Gold Coast. You know what we're talking about here, right? People who have way too much time, money, and influence. People you don't want to fuck with."

McManus rocked back on his heels and almost lost his balance.

Grasso continued, "Ms. Sutherland has all the dog's papers. It's pretty clear to us this is the dog. According to Ms. Sutherland, she's worth about $2,500 a pop for every puppy she can hatch. So that makes it grand theft, which is a felony. And Ms. Sutherland wants the dog back."

Grasso paused. McManus remained silent.

"So this is how we know you have her. The Sutherland's hired a private dick to sniff around at the Cliff House where Ms. Sutherland claims the dog got loose and ran away on Friday, January 8." Grasso paused for dramatic effect then said, "The private dick found Tyrone."

McManus' heart dropped. *That must have been a good payday for him to rat me out.*

"Tyrone gave you up. And I'm sure it won't take too many C-notes to keep him loyal to the Sutherland family. After checking the radio logs for Richmond cars on the evening of January 8, we discovered you were "Seven-M" at the Cliff House. That's about the same time Tyrone said you talked with him when you were parked in front of the fire hydrant."

The edge to Grasso's voice softened as McManus' eyes began to glisten.

"Tyrone says he saw you with the dog in the car, Phil." Grasso pulled out a couple small professional-looking portraits of Carly. "Take a look. This sure looks like the dog at your feet."

Grasso bit the edge of his lip and said, "I think we need to take her, Phil. I'm sorry."

McManus could no longer contain his anger. "Do you know why the dog got loose?"

"No, Phil, tell us."

McManus put his fist in his hand. "The dog shit in her purse, and she grabbed the dog by the collar and threw it on the ground and it ran away."

"Did you see this? Because we didn't see any police report from you concerning a dog on January 8."

McManus' body slumped.

"Here's what we're trying to do for you, Phil. Ms. Sutherland wants you arrested. But I'm sure if she can get her dog back, and the dog is still fertile, and she's in decent shape, which she appears to be, the incident will be forgotten. You didn't get her fixed, did you?"

McManus shook his head.

"I don't know what you were thinking that night," Grasso said. "But I understand you got involved in that big accident they had out there. So I think we can save your ass from going to jail and having all that media coverage. You know what I mean?"

McManus said nothing.

"They got ya, Phil. Give her up. Dogs are a dime a dozen. You can get a new one in two hours. In fact, while you're at it, get yourself a man's dog—not some wussy shit like this one that some chick carries around in her purse."

McManus had no fight left in him.

Carly sniffed at Grasso's shoes, then looked up at him like she knew what he'd said. McManus reached down and picked up Carly, letting her lick his face. From a nearby table, he retrieved Carly's leash and hooked it to her collar. He kissed her on the head and handed her to Hansen.

"Done," McManus said, trying to hold back his tears.

"You did the right thing, Phil. I think you're going to be OK," Grasso said. "We'll try to calm down the Sutherlands."

The pair of Inspectors turned toward the door. McManus looked away, refusing to watch them leave. When the door closed, Carly started to bark, the sound echoing in the hallway until it went silent.

21

The brown-and-black Yorkshire terrier ran full speed toward the N-Judah street car stop at 23rd Avenue. Responding with red lights ablaze, siren screaming and air horns blaring, a fire engine with Pete Cassidy at the wheel roared down Judah and struck the dog. Carly sailed through the air, looking like a football spinning end over end.

McManus bolted awake from his dream shaking with anger as if he'd been struck by a cattle prod. "Fuck you guys," he screamed, not caring if he woke up the whole building. "I loved that little dog."

Why? Tell me why that had to happen? McManus collapsed back onto his pillow and stared at the wood beam ceiling.

He knew the answer.

"Just when things go good, they go bad." His mother was right, again.

FRIDAY
MARCH 26, 2010 · 0040 HRS.

The lane dividers on Ninth Avenue came at McManus like bullet tracers as he drove toward the Richmond district. He blinked and reached toward his chest to feel the reassurance of his star. It was gone. McManus cut through the park and drove past the Japanese Tea Garden. At 6th Avenue and Geary, he thought about stopping at Richmond Station. *Just to say hello and let everyone know I'm coming back.*

He turned right onto 6th Avenue, drove past the station, and saw his old radio car, department vehicle 024, parked in the white zone in front. McManus kept his eyes straight ahead and gripped the steering wheel tighter. *Hope no one saw me. If I go in there, they'll think I'm just another pathetic cop stopping by to visit because he has no other place to go.*

McManus rolled down the window and felt the cold air on his cheek. *This all could have been avoided if everything had gone right at the Labyrinth Cliff. Wonder if that Voodoo curse has made things worse?*

McManus arrived at the four-way stop at 6th Avenue and Balboa at the same instant as a maroon Cadillac Escalade. The Escalade lurched forward, and McManus locked his brakes to avoid a collision. The Escalade's driver, who was talking on his cell phone, took his free hand off the wheel to flip McManus off.

Well fuck you, too. McManus checked the Escalade's license plate. "Union-Nora-William-Seven-Two-Two. OK, asshole, you just got a $100 ticket for parking in front of the fire hydrant at 10th and Clement," he said aloud as the Escalade disappeared from view.

McManus shifted in the seat, wanting to feel the comforting weight of the SIG P226 on his hip. But it was gone, along with his ability to avenge traffic slights by writing a "flyer." The victim would have a hard time trying to figure out and deal with a ticket written for a parking violation he didn't commit.

McManus circled the block. At 7th Avenue, he turned left onto Geary and headed out toward Ocean Beach. About a mile from the ocean, San Francisco Fire Station 34 protected the northwestern corner of the city. Like from a scene in an old noir movie, it was a quaint 1928-era brick structure located at the intersection of 41st Avenue and Point Lobos.

The station's lights were on when McManus parked in the driveway at 0045. He got out of his car, stood under a Gothic arch that framed the large red bay door, and knocked. After a short wait, he heard footsteps echoing inside as someone wearing hard-soled shoes walked across the concrete apparatus floor. The door creaked open slightly, revealing a thick-shouldered Latino firefighter.

"Hi, Fratelli still up?" McManus asked. The man ran his fingers over his thick black mustache.

"I think she's asleep. Can I help you?"

"Just tell her McManus from Richmond Station needs to talk to her."

"You got a badge?" he asked.

McManus reached for his back pocket. "Oh, shit, left it at home. Night off. Sorry, don't have it with me."

"No way man I'm waking her up," he said and began to close the door.

"Look, I'm a cop, McManus, Star 1125. Call Richmond Station Five, five …"

The firefighter cut him off with an amused smile. "McManus, huh? Heard about you. I know who you are. Listen…man to man…don't get involved with her. She's got a real jealous girlfriend. Those flowers you gave her wound up getting thrown all over the street here." The firefighter turned and walked back into the station.

Oh, fuck! I knew that bitch would do something like that. This is great. Fratelli's probably already pissed. Now she's going to be furious, having me show up here at one in the morning.

He was right. Fratelli didn't look happy as she rubbed sleep from her eyes when she appeared in the doorway. "Hi, what are you doing here?"

"I need to talk to you." He held up his palms and looked into her eyes.

Fratelli shrugged, then motioned him to come in.

"Can we talk out here? It's important."

Gone was the warmth and intimacy of their coffee date two months before. Wearing heavy firefighting turnout pants held up by red suspenders atop a blue T-shirt, Fratelli rubbed her bare arms as she stepped out into the foggy night air.

"The department suspended me," he said without hesitation. "Sixty days."

"Yeah, I heard."

McManus searched her face for sympathy. He needed it like a drowning man needed a preserver. Instead, he saw only a dismissive look of contempt. The coldness in her voice made his heart drop.

"How did you hear?" he asked, putting a hand to his head.

Fratelli was wide awake now. "You're kidding me," she said, shaking her head. "Shit, you're like the Hindenburg, McManus. You can't immolate like that and not expect it to go viral. What were you thinking?"

McManus' body slumped as if someone had pulled the disks out of his spine.

Fratelli rubbed her bare arms again. "McManus, it's uncomfortable talking to you here. I'm at work. You look like you've been drinkin'. I'll talk to you later."

Fratelli turned and walked back into the station. Before closing the door, she stopped and said, "By the way, thanks for the flowers."

Yeah, right. But I'm a complete moron. McManus watched her close the door.

Before it shut, though, Fratelli stopped and peeped out around the edge. Her face softened slightly as she looked at him. "When's the last time you had a home-cooked meal, McManus?"

The question took him by surprise. "Why are you asking?"

"Let's try this again. I'm off tonight. I guess you know where I live, right? Come by about seven." Fratelli looked McManus in the eyes and then said, "You do eat things besides meat and potatoes, right?"

FRIDAY
MARCH 26, 2010 · 0240 HRS.

McManus stood high atop Turtle Hill on a stunningly clear September night. In a beer-induced glow, he and a dozen of his victorious St. Ignatius teammates watched the lights of the Sunset district twinkle below in celebration. A few hours before, S.I. had defeated the Lincoln Mustangs, 21-6.

Behind him, the senior girls from Presentation giggled their way up the concrete stairs that climbed the hill. Leading the pack was the gorgeous Homecoming Queen and Student Body President Gina Fratelli, who was the property of quarterback Pete Cassidy.

Some girls carried six-packs of Olympia beer, stolen from home to celebrate with the victorious football players. And all had shed their Catholic school uniforms—blue pleated plaid skirts and white blouses—for torn jeans, patched jackets and hooded sweatshirts.

"Where's Pete?" Gina demanded when she reached the crest.

Cassidy was below at the base of the hill, busy atop a step-ladder painting on the block-long retaining wall. His huge red, white and blue "S.I." letters would be seen for miles. The afternoon's victory was sweet payback for the 30-0 playoff loss to the Mike Holmgren-led Sunset district Mustangs the previous season.

"Who's that?" Colin O'Connell asked McManus, pointing to one of the Prez girls holding a can of Oly.

"Fratelli's sister. She's only a sophomore."

"Doesn't matter, she's mine."

A few moments later, McManus watched O'Connell's bare white ass glow in the darkness as he humped furiously between the sophomore's legs.

"OH MY GOD," Gina Fratelli cried when she spotted her sister. "Where's Pete, I need him to stop that guy."

Cassidy appeared behind her, his face and hair covered in red paint. "The fuckin ladder slipped."

"Make him stop, Pete!" Gina cried.

"Aw, let 'em fuck. She's doing it a lot better than you."

Bailey Buckholtz heard Gina's screams for help and ran toward the copulating couple. She reached down and grabbed a handful of dune tansies and sand to throw at O'Connell's ass. When the sand hit him, O'Connell shot up off Fratelli like a kangaroo. Buckholtz then kicked him in the balls, and he crumpled in agony.

McManus jerked awake.

FRIDAY
MARCH 26, 2010 • 1858 HRS.

Stars and a three-quarters moon reclaimed the sky above Trish Fratelli's Sacramento Street flat when McManus arrived. She greeted him at the door him wearing a dark coral sweater, form fitting blue jeans, and a fresh pedicure.

He gazed at Fratelli's ass held snug in her jeans. *Shit, looks like she's not wearing any panties and she's supposed to be a dyke? I don't know how I'm going to get through tonight without touching her.* "Sorry I'm early," he said looking down at his watch and sneaking a peek at her candy-apple red toes.

"No problem," Fratelli said in a husky voice and motioned him inside.

The well-polished hardwood floor creaked as McManus followed her into the kitchen. He looked around the flat as clouds of steam billowed toward the ceiling from the stainless steel stove.

Stark is the best word to describe this place. Must be a hundred years old, but it makes the institutional showrooms of IKEA look homey and lived-in. Not a single piece of art anywhere. "Nice place," McManus said.

"I got lucky," she said standing over the sink tearing a head of romaine lettuce into bite-sized pieces. "Three guys from the crew on Engine 10 own the building. A couple years ago, they responded here on a resuscitation for the 92-year-old owner. The guy died, but his grieving widow was so appreciative of their efforts, she sold them the place dirt-cheap."

"You're shitting me," he said looking around.

"Nope." She slid the lettuce wedges into a bowl. "Then they set about remodeling, and after they finished, offered me this unit with a three-year, below-market lease."

"So how often do the Jakeys stop by to see how you're doing?"

Fratelli stood barefoot on the terracotta tile floor and smiled. "Not as often as they did at first."

Sure. She's unbelievably hot, getting a huge break in the rent, and those guys don't think they're entitled to come over here anytime and try and bang her? I would.

"Can I help you with something?" he asked. *Hope she says no. The extent of my Italian cooking experience is opening a can of Chef Boyardee.*

"Just pour me a glass of wine and make yourself comfortable," she said. "There's a bottle of 2002 Oak Knoll Willamette Valley over there." She pointed to the wine rack on the counter. "Do you like Pinot Noir?"

"You got any Blanton's?"

"No, but the Pinot will knock your socks off."

Is she coming on to me? Wow. First that dream this morning, now this. There's only so much teasing a man can take, you know. McManus found the opener and, with a few quick twists and a strong pull, popped the cork. He poured the wine, and they clinked the glasses.

"Thank you."

"For what?" she said with a mischievous smile.

"This."

Fratelli said nothing and went back to chopping vegetables.

I've seen "fag hags" in action, women who find safety and excitement in the effervescent company of flamboyant gay men who can talk about food, sex and fashion, This some sort of lesbian trick? Does she just want to hang around a guy in order to talk fishing, fucking and football? No, that doesn't make any sense. Fratelli works in a firehouse full of guys. What does she need me for? What's going on here?

McManus spotted a fading color snapshot in a broken gold frame on a sideboard. Since he wasn't wearing his glasses, he squinted to identify the two young girls in the picture, both wearing fluffy chiffon mid-'60s prom dresses. *My God that is a really young looking Trish and Gina standing alongside a tuxedoed Pete Cassidy. Wonder what cracked the picture glass between the sisters?*

"Sure I can't help you with something?" he offered again.

Fratelli shook her head. "I got twenty years of firehouse cooking, McManus. I don't need help."

He started to nod his head and then laughed under his breath. He enjoyed the moment and comfort of her presence until an alarm bell went off in his head. "Bailey working tonight?"

A strange expression came across her face. "She left. Moved out." Her voice sounded anxious.

"What?"

"Was gone when I got home this morning. Weird. Just left a note saying she was going home and all her stuff was gone." Fratelli flipped her hair to the side and returned to fixing their salads. "I called the hospital, and they said she just up and quit her job. Departed, just like that." Fratelli turned her hand up in frustration, "Good riddance."

McManus hesitated. *Something's not right here. You don't just up and leave like that.* "What happened?"

Without looking up, Fratelli said, "I'm sorry about what she did with your flowers. Her former husband abused her when they found out she couldn't have kids. She came to San Francisco sure she must be gay—one of her many issues."

Fratelli shook her head and looked over at McManus. "Every gay friend I have ever had has told me they knew they were gay when they were kids. It's been really awkward for both of us. I think it's just never occurred to her that she was straight. Quite frankly, I was going to throw her out. She was weird. Too much baggage."

So what does all this mean? It was hard to picture those two together anyway, because of the age difference. But, what the hell do I know about lesbians? Be careful here. Don't say something stupid. I think I gotta chance. "Sorry" he shrugged as he swirled the wine in his glass.

"No worries, shit happens." She poured Italian dressing on the salads. "Bailey was having a tough time at the hospital. It was that high school pitcher who got shot in Sunnydale. He's brain dead and on life support. You heard about that, right?"

"Oh! Horrific story," McManus said. "I saw where dozens of kids from his school were picketing the other day down at the General. They had a bunch of signs all reading, 'Don't Pull the Plug.'"

Fratelli carried the salad bowl to the table. "Bailey was in the middle of it, getting grinded by the kid's mother. She just can't accept he's brain dead. And then there's the heartless hospital administration that just wants her to pull the plug and get the kid out of there."

"Yeah, bad scene. I can see her throwing her arms up in frustration and just leaving." McManus finished his wine.

"Where's Bailey from?" he asked.

"Akron, Ohio," Fratelli said, then chuckled. "Maybe one of her problems was her father named her after his favorite baseball player."

McManus' eyes lit up. "Ed Bailey? He played for the Reds, then was catcher for the Giants. I had an Ed Bailey model catcher's mitt when I was a kid."

"Really?" Fratelli rolled her eyes and snickered.

"Fuckin' Cassidy broke the webbing on it one day when he was pitching and I was the catcher for St. Anne in the Midget League. I even got Ed Bailey's autograph on it—but he had signed it with a ballpoint pen, and the name got rubbed off."

Fratelli chuckled again. "I never asked her the player's name." She reached over to spin the dial on her iPod. A pounding techno-beat reverberated through the flat. Fratelli's hips began rocking back and forth.

"What's that song?" he asked.

"'Jump,' by Madonna. My theme song."

"Never heard it before."

Fratelli rolled her eyes again.

McManus shrugged.

Fratelli stopped swaying to dry her hands on a towel.

"Saw another good reason to never have children."

"How's that?"

"We had a run for an auto accident in the park the other night. Some kid from Washington High loaded the family car with all his friends after his parents went to bed. At 3:30 in the morning, he wrapped it around a tree."

"Anybody hurt?"

"Not at the scene, only when the kids got home." Fratelli reached up to get a bowl from an upper shelf.

"Can I help you get that down?" McManus asked.

"Okay, but be careful, it's the only thing I have left from my marriage."

"So, you had a husband? *Wow, the list of things I don't know about her is growing. Wonder if a woman's story's any different from those of the pissed off ex-husbands I listen to every night?*

Fratelli hesitated. She poured ravioli from the stove into the bowl and carried it to the table. "Yeah, I had one. My marriage was just more fallout from the relationship with my sister. She was 'Daddy's Girl,' and I was, 'The Other Daughter.'"

McManus heard the anguish in her voice and suddenly felt guilty about his sarcastic mindset. *This is something important she wants to tell me, and I need to listen.*

Fratelli laid out plates and silverware around the table. "Gina got the big May church wedding from my father, and I felt left out. Three months later, I married a guy I worked with at UPS. He was older than me. He thought he'd won the Super Bowl. I don't know what I was think-ing. Just glad I didn't get pregnant. It wouldn't have been a child conceived in love."

McManus looked at her intently. "So, what kind of wed-ding ceremony did your father throw you?"

She laughed cynically. "Let's just say Daddy figured my marriage probably wouldn't last eighteen months. It certainly wasn't the majestic event he gave Gina."

McManus' eyes never left Fratelli. "That was no excuse for him to do that."

Fratelli took a loaf of sourdough from a brown paper bag, placed it on the cutting board, and looked up at him. "That wasn't one of my better chapters. Let's eat."

McManus nodded, and they sat down across from each other. Fratelli reached for the half-empty bottle of wine, refilled his glass and emptied what was left into hers. "Here's to your eventual retirement, Big Guy." They clinked glasses.

"So what did you do, next?" He smiled at her.

"I quit UPS after I divorced him. Then I traveled. When I came back, I took over the night shift running the family bar on Taraval Street. I was wild and crazy," she laughed. "Cynical of everything. But I played soccer and softball. And I surfed and kayaked. When the fire department opened up to women, I was 35. But I was in great shape and got in."

"You still look great."

They ate slowly with McManus savoring the moments. *I can't remember the last time I had a home-cooked meal with a woman at her place.* "You know, your sister Gina called me a couple weeks ago."

Surprised, Fratelli looked up at him curiously. "Really?"

That's an interesting expression on her face. Wonder what she's thinking? "Gina wanted to talk about the investigation. Didn't like how it was going. Thinks the Russians did it."

"So do I. How could they have Pete's badge if they didn't kill him?"

"Good question…You did know Cassidy wanted to divorce her?"

Fratelli stopped her fork inches from her mouth and stared at him. "She said that? When was this going to happen?"

McManus took his napkin and wiped his mouth. *Whoa. She didn't know! Let's see where this is going.* "That's the thing," he said chewing on his food. "It hadn't happened, yet. But it sounded to me like she was in big-time denial. She told me she hadn't even notified Homicide."

Fratelli arched her eyebrows, looked down, and resumed eating.

She's pissed. Wonder what's goin' on in her head? Maybe she's primed to dish some information about that asshole Cassidy? Let's see if one more question might do it. "Did you ever suspect…"

"What?" Fratelli snapped.

"That maybe, he… Maybe, Cassidy played both sides of the ball?"

Fratelli studied him in the dim glow of the pendant light above the table. "Pete was a politician. You should eat now."

FRIDAY
MARCH 26, 2010 · 2158 HRS.

Two hours later they had emptied their second bottle of Pinot over small talk about San Francisco politics and sports. When the subject of "what the hell was wrong with the 49ers" came up, Fratelli became so animated she spilled a full glass of wine in her lap.

"Shit, I'm a clumsy firetruck...no, not that. I'm, I'm on the en-engine. That's what I'm, I'm talkin' 'bout. There's an ENORMOUS d-difference, and everybody knows it," she slurred. Giggling, she headed to the bedroom.

While McManus cleared the table, he heard the shower running. Then he stretched out on her couch, crossed his ankles, and stared at the flames flickering in the fireplace. *Hmmm. I can still smell her, the aroma of a woman. There's time. This evening could go in many different ways.*

His heart was pounding in his chest when he heard a door open. She came into view dragging something long and white.

"Glad you're still here," she said softly as she appeared in a fresh pair of tight jeans and a blue SFFD T-shirt—minus bra. "I need some help here, Mister."

He saw what looked like a white comforter in one hand, and in her other, she dangled the pump of a body oil bottle on her index finger.

Wow. I think I like the way this is going. That coy smile alone is getting me hard. She's gotta be able to hear my heart;

it's pounding so loud. Thought my days of getting an erection without the blue pill were over. Guess not, thank heavens.

McManus got up and helped her lay the comforter in front of the fireplace. Fratelli poured them both glasses of Pinot Noir from a new bottle. She took a long sip, then sat on the comforter, curling her legs underneath.

He stood above her. "You okay?"

She paused for a second and gave him a serious look. "You ever think about the Good Life and what it is, McManus?"

Where's she going with this? How am I supposed to answer that? "Well, frankly, Fratelli," he chuckled. "That's something I've never even thought about. If I had to guess, I'd say that comes from a fear of disappointment. My mom always used to say, 'Don't ever get your hopes up. Soon as things go good, they go bad.'"

She looked up at him empathetically. "My mom used to say stuff like that a lot, too. One of her issues was money. Things were always tight. She told us never to ask for anything. It got to be absurd. I remember wearing shoes I'd outgrown that made my feet bleed. Mom just told me to put Band-Aids on the blisters." She frowned.

"Mom was even more terrified of my violent father. He physically abused both me and mom, but never touched Gina because she was the apple of his eye. She could do no wrong." Fratelli dropped her eyes.

"Oh come on, really." McManus crossed his arms and took a seat on the couch in front of her.

"I'm serious," Fratelli stamped her fist into the floor. "My parents tried to scare us into being perfect little girls…

it worked with Gina. She did everything right, good grades, she was pretty. I was a fuck-up. My parents were always on me. After I got kicked out of Prez, mom was mortified. I wasn't as good as Gina. My sister was going to USF to be a nurse. 'You're not even going to be able to find a husband,' she'd say to me."

"Why did she think that?

"My mother believed in order to find a 'Good Man' like our father, for instance…" She smiled sarcastically. "I needed to look, walk and dress a certain way. And if I didn't, I was never going to be loved. Or have the security of a man."

"That's pretty Old School," McManus said as he leaned back into the sofa cushions and shook his head.

"Well, it was the '50s and the '60s, McManus. They were Old School Italian Catholics. So when Gina married Pete, it freaked me out. And I hooked up with a guy just to have a husband. It was gruesome, I couldn't take it very long, and I divorced him and left." She shook her head and said, "Yuk."

"Then I traveled around Europe for awhile before coming back to The States. My first job was in New York City, but it didn't work out, so I dragged my ass home to San Francisco. I had no money. No job. And I was back living in my parents' house, like I was 16 again."

"Then what happened?" McManus sat forward and caught her gaze.

"Worked nights and closed up the family bar." Fratelli snorted and sipped her wine.

Where do I fit in this story? Does she think I've got any answers? I know one I could give her, but I'm not sure she's ready for it, yet.

"So is it normal to confess all this stuff to you?" Fratelli asked.

"If it matters to you, it matters to me. I'm here. I'm listening."

She gave him a skeptical look. "You serious?" She looked shocked.

"Yeah." *I'm trying to connect with you.*

Fratelli shrugged and smiled weakly. "On Friday nights, my father stayed late supposedly to manage the crowds and help shut the bar down. But I knew he was seeing other women. He'd leave early and then some female customer, who'd been by herself all night, would get up, pay her bill and walk out the front door. I knew what was going down. Mom would call sometimes, and I'd cover for him. I don't know why I did. Fear maybe. But, I did."

Fratelli's expression softened and she looked over at the fireplace. "My father and I never talked about it, but I noticed he started to give me more space." She laughed beneath her breath and finished her glass of wine. "That's how I coped. It was about as close as my father and I ever got. I learned to speak my truth, by not speaking, if that makes sense."

McManus sucked in his breath, leaned back, and slung his arms across the back of the couch. "So why the sudden question 'What's a Good Life?'"

She looked thoughtfully at him for a moment, and then said, "Because Pete's murder and those kids dying the other night is starting to scare me. I'm just tired of all the pain and tragedy. You ever get tired of this shit, Phil, I mean really tired of it?" Her voice trailed off.

"That's why bourbon's my friend," he laughed.

Fratelli gave him a look that said she expected more of an answer.

"Sorry." McManus closed his eyes. *The good life? Hmmm… What did Denny Wayland say it was? "Something to do, something to dream about, and someone to love."*

He opened his eyes. "What's a good life—or, do you mean THE good life?" he asked, nodding his head. "Good question, Fratelli. How's this?"

He stood up from the couch and extended his hand. After pulling her up, he hugged her, lifted her off her feet and swung her around in a circle. "Here's to enjoying being alive," he said. "Remember saying that at Starbucks?"

"Yeah," she nuzzled her head into his shoulder.

She likes it. And I do, too. He stopped and put her down.

Then she glided down to the floor and sat cross-legged in front of him.

I remembered hearing once that the biggest regrets in life are the opportunities not seized. He sat down next to her on the floor and placed his hand on her thigh. She looked down at it with an amused smile. He met her eyes, and then let his hand slide around her leg.

"You're off-the-chart beautiful, lady," he whispered and covered her mouth with a gentle kiss. Fratelli didn't resist.

"I've heard that one before, I like it," she smiled and kissed him back.

He reached under her T-shirt. She purred and didn't pull away.

"So, what does that say about my life—that I go out with a guy I met while we were standing over a corpse?" she asked wide-eyed.

"I don't know, but let's find out." He pulled his sweater over his head.

She touched his chest, pulling a little bit on his hair.

Unbelievable. We're gonna fuck. I want to please this woman. If I ever did anything right in my life, it would be to please this woman right now. McManus took her shoulders and gently moved her onto her stomach. He then poured a small amount of body oil into his palm and warmed it by rubbing his hands together. He leaned forward and kissed the back of her neck. She shuttered with delight as her mouth and lips formed a silent "O" of pleasure.

She likes that. Think I'll file that spot away for future activity. His thumbs kneaded the muscles of her shoulders and worked their way to the curves of her ass.

Soon, the firelight glistened on her entire body.

McManus' breath became shallow with excitement. He strained to contain himself as she rolled onto her back, and he used his lips and tongue to explore the rest of her body.

"Some women don't like that. But I'm not one of them."

Then he worked his hands up her thighs and pushed her legs apart. Two oily fingers played with her clit and then went deeper into her.

She whimpered and started to breathe very hard.

McManus raised himself up on his elbows and pushed forward, sliding easily into her. He rocked gently back and forth, exploring her, marveling at how perfectly he fit inside her. He felt Fratelli wrap her strong legs around his hips and pull him in.

A guttural sound escaped her throat. "I want to ride you," she gasped.

She brushed a stray hair out of her face and mounted him as they flipped over. Closing her eyes, she slid down onto him. He heard her moan and felt the waves of pleasure roll through her body again. He watched her breasts bounce in rhythm as she rode him furiously until she gave a short scream.

They continued to make love with a desperate passion felt only by people who knew that at any moment, their lives could end with one misplaced step or a capricious turn of fate.

Wow! That's the look I've always wanted to get from a woman. Maybe it's a little late in life coming, but I finally got it. I'm a man in love for the first time. And the World is perfect...

22

McManus turned right from Clayton Street onto Upper Market and crept home through the fog, thinking about Fratelli. *She's not gay. Maybe goes both ways. But, definitely knows her way around a dick. I really wonder why she did me. Jeez, love's like being on drugs. Makes you feel alive, and then comes the crash, and I wind up floating in the toilet waiting to be flushed.*

The fog became so thick at Clipper and Portola that he could have used a foghorn to navigate the left turn.

Her sister Gina was the one against whom all other women were judged. I would have married her. I could see myself being in love with her and our two kids living in Novato or Pacifica and being really, really happy. But then she just vaporized. That worries me. Trish going to do the same thing her sister did to me 35 years ago?

Once home, McManus collapsed onto the beanbag chair after looking out his bay window. He sat head in hands. *Boy am I fucked up. My car's out on the street, not in the garage where I thought I parked it.*

He blew out his breath in frustration. *That's the sure sign I'm in love. All I can remember is being inside Fratelli. I'm so tired I can barely move. I can't even get up to move the car. She's so awesome…thank you, whoever sent her into my life.*

He rolled off the beanbag and got two Tylenols. He swallowed the pills, poured a shot of Blanton's, and threw it down. His head shook like a wet dog as he felt the alcohol burn down his throat. He returned to the chair and plopped down, sending a couple small white pellets flying out from a seam. *There've been other women, but I just thought relationships were too painful and required too much energy. I've never had that Great Love Affair.*

McManus laid his head back and let the afterglow of sex and alcohol play out in his mind. *Maybe I'll be that heroic romantic figure who slays the dragons in Fratelli's life. Has anyone ever loved her? She's not gay, is she? I don't get what's going on with that. But I want to see her again. Like right now.*

He went to the refrigerator where he saw the card with her name, address, and phone number stuck to the door. Removing the card, he cradled it in the palms of his hands. *She wrote that for me. Her DNA is on that card, a piece of her lives in this house. God, I'd forgotten how good a kiss could feel. Still has that same surreal, fantastic quality of a dream. I liked how she flirted with me. I want to make her laugh and I've never wanted that before.*

He pulled a cold bottle of water from the refrigerator and drank it without stopping to take a breath. Then he went back to the beanbag, sat down, and stared out into the abyss of the fog: "I haven't talk to you in a while, Foggy, how ya doing? Got a question for you. I'm interested in another woman named Fratelli. I think I'm in love with her. She's Gina's sister. Remember her from 35 years ago?"

McManus stood up, slid open the window, and stuck his head out. He felt the wind ruffle his hair. *Ah, the wind's blowing so the answer is going to be yes.* "Yeah, Foggy, Gina was pretty unforgettable."

"Foggy, do you think I should pursue a relationship with her sister, Trish?" Suddenly the breeze stopped, and there was no sound.

Son of a bitch. Disappointed, McManus closed the window and went to bed.

SATURDAY
MARCH 27, 2010 · 0300 HRS.

The sound of the foghorns announced the end of a week-long October heat wave.

McManus walked out of the field house, pulled on his helmet, and jogged across the old St. Ignatius High School practice field. Grateful for the cooling afternoon breeze pushing the fog in from the ocean, he hoped it would dampen the coming fireworks from Coach Sal Paganini. Losing the Homecoming Game to Sacred Heart had enraged the coach.

On the bus returning after the game from Kezar Stadium, Paganini had warned the team to expect a punitive Monday afternoon practice filled with tackling and conditioning drills.

Soon, the fog transformed the S.I. practice field into a scene from the "Hound of the Baskervilles." Paganini's condemnation was brutal and non-stop.

"That's NOT GOOD ENOUGH, young man," he yelled at Sullivan, the middle linebacker. "You're killing our football team. DO IT AGAIN… GET UP… How dare you lie down on my football field and feel sorry for yourselves!"

Paganini drove his hand into his fist and stopped practice. He called everyone to circle around him. McManus stood grimly with the team and listened.

"Out of a student body of a thousand, only forty guys are good enough to be on this team," he said…and then raised his voice: "You all are supposed to be special. You represent this school: How we Look, How we Play…EVERYTHING reflects back on this school…on me…the faculty…the administration…the student body…and your parents!

"If you're not willing to work…if you're not willing to sacrifice…if you're not willing to give all you've got…"

Paganini caught sight of the team's charismatic leader quarterback, Pete Cassidy, stifling a laugh in the back row of the players.

"CASSIDY, DAMN YOU," Paganini screamed. He took off his baseball cap and threw it into the ground.

"You're supposed to be the leader. You're the fuckin' problem here, Mister. You were more interested last Friday in escorting that snotty-nosed little girlfriend of yours to Homecoming— than playing football for us."

Paganini saw McManus standing nearby. The practice session had reopened the angry-looking cut McManus had suffered on his nose during the game. Paganini turned to him, ordering him to remove his helmet and hand it to him. McManus complied. A smile came to Paganini's face when he saw the sight of dried blood on McManus' face and jersey, and the coach tousled his hair.

"You seniors should be ashamed. Biggest game of the year... Homecoming... Sacred Heart...and a junior's the only guy who showed up to play." Paganini then spat on the ground. He turned toward Cassidy and threw McManus' helmet right into his stomach. Cassidy doubled over and collapsed to the ground. The shocked team watched in silence as Paganini's eyes grew wild with contempt at the sound of Cassidy's groaning.

"If you guys aren't willing to bleed like McManus here— then, I don't want you!.... GET THE FUCK OFF MY FIELD!"

S.I. Homecoming Queen Gina Fratelli appeared behind Cassidy. She was the "snotty nosed little girl" whom Cassidy had escorted to the dance. She wore a red brocade suit and her tiara. Her white high heels were covered with dirt. "What's wrong with all you guys?" she yelled.

Her voice stunned Paganini, McManus, and the rest of the players.

"I can yell and scream and throw things just like a guy," she said.

Gina reached up, pulled the tiara from her head, and then threw it at Paganini, striking and cutting his nose open. "Hey Coach, I'm glad you're willing to bleed for me."

Then stepping out of her high heels, she reached down and pulled them out of the soft ground. McManus' moment of glory ended when she threw both her shoes at him.

No one spoke. The stench from forty sweaty and dirt-covered football players hung in the air. Fratelli looked around at all the white boys' faces.

"You guys are all dinosaurs. This 'Gentlemen of S.I.' ole boy entitlement IS BULLSHIT," she hissed. "Guess what? Thirty years from now, my daughter will not only be going to this school—she'll be the best athlete. And what's more, if any of you think you're going to wind up Chief of the San Francisco Police Department someday... Forget about it. A woman's going to be in charge. And get this! She's going to be Chinese..."

The football players dropped their heads and stared at the ground, refusing to make eye contact with her.

"Oh, and you guys who want to join the San Francisco Fire Department...good news. You're still going to have an Irish chief. But...she's also going to be a woman."

Cassidy whimpered in the background.

"Oh yeah, and one last thing," Gina Fratelli said. "The President of the United States of America...he's going to be black."

SATURDAY
MARCH 27, 2010 · 0330 HRS.

Holy Fuck! What kind of dream was that? McManus sat up in his bed, rubbed his eyes, and looked out the bay window. The fog was still in.

Where the fuck is my Camry? GOD DAMN IT! It's gone. Never should have gotten a car that everybody wants to steal. McManus pulled on a pair of jeans, his slippers, a fleece, and ran down the stairs and out onto Red Rock Way.

They stole my car from right under my fucking window. Can't believe I didn't hear them break the windows or drive away. Wait a minute. There's no broken glass. I did park here, didn't I?

McManus walked back into his building and entered the garage. *There's my car. What the fuck!... This is a bad combination. Being in love and drinking too much.*

SATURDAY
MARCH 27, 2010 · 1630 HRS.

That afternoon, McManus knew for sure the knock on the door was Inspector Arthur Lahey; he'd never learned to use his knuckles to tap a polite, "I hate to bother you."

Instead, he used the beefy side of his fist to pummel the door with a knock that shouted, "Open up! I know you're fuckin' in there."

McManus could taste bile in his mouth. He got up from the beanbag chair and opened the door.

"Hey, Phil, we were just in the neighborhood," Lahey greeted him in mock sincerity. "Heard you had a great place…thought we'd stop by and see it." He entered without an invite and immediately walked to the bay window.

"The taxpayers paying for this visit?" McManus asked.

Lahey gave the city view a once-over, and then walked back to join his partner Anderson standing with McManus in the kitchen.

"Quite a place, Phil. You must get a lot of pussy up here." A large grin came across Lahey's face as he noticed the card with Fratelli's name and phone number hanging from the refrigerator door. "Glad you guys took my advice," he chuckled. "Guess you didn't need to get a room after all."

"What do you want?" McManus asked in a flat tone to mask his anger. Lahey smirked, reached into his coat pocket, and pulled out his notes.

"We're still working the Cassidy murder and we ran across Eddie Rodriguez—the bondsman and process server. You know Eddie, right?"

Oh fuck. I knew this was going to happen.

"Eddie said he saw you hanging out at Cassidy's house with the widow."

McManus rolled his eyes. "She called me. I saw her at the funeral and I gave her my condolences and my card in case I could do anything for her." *Okay. Let's drop all the bullshit, asshole.* "She's upset with your investigation."

Lahey sneered back at McManus. "Well, that's the reason we're here, Phil. We're hoping you're not out there freelancing on your own, getting information you won't share with us."

He's giving me that baleful stare to intimidate me. Have at it, Lahey. McManus just smiled back.

"You're under suspension; you're just a civilian, now. Not one of us. Besides, you never worked any investigations. We try to keep what we do under the radar. And we sure don't want you giving information back to the family because we don't know who's involved here."

McManus' face tightened. "I'm not freelancin'… his wife's pissed at you guys because she thinks you're incompetent. She didn't like the way you roughed her up with some of your questions."

"She's pissed at us?" Anger burned in Lahey's eyes as if he'd just been kicked in the balls. "We know how to do our fuckin' jobs, pal," he bristled.

You arrogant asshole. We'll see. "Did you guys know Cassidy wanted to divorce her?"

Aaaaaaaaaaaaaagh! That was stupid. Why'd I say that…?

Lahey's face glowed red, like it did when he'd squished his head into a white S.I. football helmet. "There're no divorce papers on file. We checked that. So, what's the deal McManus? You trying to fuck BOTH of 'em? The sister's a dykie, you know?"

Anderson stepped between the two men.

McManus heeded Lahey's warning shot. "Okay, I'm done talking to you. Next time, it's with my lawyer."

"All right, everybody calm down here," Anderson said, guiding Lahey toward the door, but Lahey pushed him back.

"You were always a fuckin' pussy, McManus. Truth be told, I loved it when Cassidy kicked your ass that day at St. Anne. You couldn't handle your shit then, and now you're a fuckin' embarrassment to this department. I mean…just what've you ever done on this job—besides work at the ball park and bum free coffee from the Doggie Diner?"

Anderson opened the door and pulled Lahey into the hallway.

"You're a sick fuck, Lahey. You don't have shit on me," McManus yelled back.

Anderson released his grip on Lahey, who turned back toward McManus. "How do you know I don't have shit on those sisters, Phil?"

McManus froze.

"Oh, and I forgot," Lahey said. "The coroner called us after going through O'Connell's house. Said they found a bunch of cut-up magazines. Also said they matched the cuttings to that letter: 'YOU KILLED CASSIDY.' Know why your best friend would do that to you?"

Then Lahey leaned forward and took a final look inside McManus' condo. "Nice place, Phil. Enjoy it while you can."

23

MONDAY
MARCH 29, 2010 · 1150 HRS.

Frustrated as he circled through the Cow Hollow district looking for an on-street parking spot, McManus gave up and pulled into a $15-per-hour garage on Union Street. *I've only got ten minutes before Fratelli's yoga class begins. Fuck, I don't want to be late. I need to see her—not piss her off.*

Wearing a pair of black swim trunks, which contrasted with his pale legs, he walked upstairs to the second-floor studio at the corner of Laguna and Union Street. He paid for the class, asked for a mat, and looked embarrassed when only pink ones were available. *Welcome to Chick City. It is what it is. I guess, I need to show I'm willing to step outside my comfort zone for her.*

The hardwood floor squeaked as he entered the yoga studio where a dozen women sat cross-legged atop their mats with their eyes closed. A grayish light filtered through the leaves and branches of several large magnolia trees visible through the studio's floor-to-ceiling French windows.

It was 11:59. *I made it on time and it feels pretty cool in here.*

Fratelli sat on her mat in front of the class wearing a black-and-orange San Francisco Giants tank top. Her face brightened when she saw him. *She looks like a little girl in a pet store seeing a new puppy.*

McManus mouthed the word "parking."

Fratelli got up and grabbed two gray blankets and foam yoga blocks. She led him to an open space at the back of the class and helped unroll his mat.

"This is a good spot for you to watch what's going on," she whispered. "Just sit cross-legged like they're doing." Her hand touched his elbow to help him sit down on the mat. "This isn't the SI /SH game for the Bruce Mahoney Trophy, McManus. Listen to your body. Don't stretch beyond what's comfortable for you. Just let go…to open up. Got it?"

"Got it." McManus struggled to find a comfortable spot. *Shit, I'm the only guy here. All these women remind me of how much I want Fratelli.*

He watched her walk back to the front. *Jeez, how am I going to focus on anything except ravishing her?*

"Good morning, everyone, I'm Trish. Before we get started here, is there anyone working with injuries I should know about? Anyone pregnant?"

Should I raise my hand to be cute? No, that'll just make me look like an asshole. How long we gonna sit like this? Don't know if my hips can take it. McManus shifted his weight on the mat and looked around to see if anyone else looked uncomfortable.

"OK," Fratelli said, "Let's come to a seated position with our palms together in front of our hearts and get started."

During the next hour, McManus contorted his body in ways he hadn't experienced since his football days at S.I. He heard a strange new lexicon of words like "lion's breath," "child's pose," "down-dog," "*chaturanga*," and "mindfulness."

A little after 1:00, Fratelli said, "Let's bring our mats to the wall, so we can do a final stretch and get ready for *savasana*."

Stiff and sore, McManus stood up and dragged his pink mat toward where two young women were already lying with their legs up the wall. When they saw McManus looking for an opening, they each rolled out of their poses and moved their mats. *Wonder if a guy would have done that? No way, unless, of course, he was part of this unique yoga world.*

Ten minutes later, Fratelli thanked her class, and then walked towards him. "So how are you feeling, Big Guy?"

"Okay," he nodded. "I'm sure this is going to be a three-Advil-afternoon when I get home."

"I'm very proud of you," she said. "Think we'll ever see you in here, again?"

He nodded. *I want to tell her I miss her. It's only been three days, but I need her to know I mean it.* "I care about you,

Trish. I don't want to lose that feeling we shared on Friday."

Fratelli looked up at him.

He leaned forward and kissed her with all the feelings he'd pent up since Friday night.

She had closed her eyes, then opened them and smiled coyly, "Let's just say the other night woke up some feelings in me, as well."

24

TUESDAY
MARCH 30, 2010 · 0515 HRS.

Sergeant Jack Grogan sat with San Francisco's Gen-X mayor on an overstuffed couch in his City Hall office. The police sergeant had the mayor shedding tears of laughter with his bullshit stories. This time, how he'd hung out with Mick Jagger and the Rolling Stones while leading the SFPD security detail during the Stones 2002 concerts at Pac-Bell Park.

"You know how Mick is," Grogan winked.

"Oh, yeah!" agreed the mayor as he poured Grogan a glass of the Napa Valley 2004 Spottswoode Cabernet Sauvignon.

"A glass of 'The King' for the new Chief of the San Francisco Police Department," the mayor toasted. Grogan nodded smugly and they clinked glasses.

McManus jerked awake. *That little cocksucker! Now I'm having fucking nightmares about HIM.*

Groggy and puffy-eyed, McManus wobbled out of bed to make coffee. Then he stood in the window and watched the usual conveyor belt of traffic flowing into San Francisco on the Bay Bridge. He looked to the left and saw the morning fog hanging over Twin Peaks.

"Morning, Foggy. Should I retire?" he said sliding open the window. The fog answered in the affirmative by blowing a gentle ocean breeze that ruffled his hair and cooled his face.

Maybe it's time to just accept the inevitable. What can I do about Grogan, anyway? No one is going to be in my corner when I return. Who's going to listen to a 37-year veteran complain how a little shit like Grogan can intimidate me?

TUESDAY
MARCH 30, 2010 · 1000 HRS.

Filled with trepidation, McManus arrived to file his retirement papers at the Van Ness Avenue office of the San Francisco Employees' Retirement System. In less than 48 hours, he was scheduled to return to duty from his 60-day suspension. *Thinking about Grogan just sucks the energy right out of me. If I go back, it's going to be the same shit.*

He sat down at the desk of his caseworker, Shawnika.

"You're at the Pearly Gates now, McManus," she winked at him typing his name into her computer to retrieve his retirement file. "I'm St. Shawnika, and this is the 'Keyboard to your Heaven.'"

McManus shook his head and silently chuckled. *Jeez, avoiding this moment was why I was standing out there on the edge of a cliff ready to jump on Christmas morning. Someone's easy manner and laugh is not what I expected. Maybe all will be okay...Hmmm.*

The only sound in the room was the clicking sound generated by Shawnika's fingers racing over the keyboard.

Do I have the courage to walk away and give up this cop identity? It's been my whole life? Can I survive without the job? Or am I going to just drown myself in bourbon and go off that cliff again? There was only one way to find out.

The clicking rhythm stopped abruptly. "Wow, I was a mere three days old when you joined the police department, McManus," she said. "You want to surrender the deposit you paid in 1972 for your star—to keep it?"

McManus laughed. "How much was it?"

"Seven dollars."

"I don't have the star with me," he said.

"Oh," Shawnika said in a low tone. She looked up and cast a sideways glance at McManus that said she knew he'd been suspended. The caseworker then printed out several pages and handed them to McManus to initial and sign.

"I'll go make your retired SFPD identification card for you," she said and stood up.

"Don't bother," he said. "I won't need it."

"What?" Shawnika asked. She stopped and looked back at McManus. "You'll need it to carry a concealed weapon."

"I've done that all my life. I need to start a new life and not hide behind a gun and star."

Shawnika looked McManus in the eye. "I've worked here for over five years and I ain't never seen one of you guys come in here and refuse his star and retirement ID."

McManus shrugged.

"Good for you, McManus. You just turn in your police equipment to the property clerk at the Hall of Justice, and I'll personally make sure you get your first retirement check within thirty days. I just got one more form for you to sign," Shawnika said and left the room.

McManus sighed and stared at the floor. *So this is how it ends? Pretty uneventful. Sure looks like the world is still spinning. Hey, Everybody, I'm retiring.*

He leaned forward to see where Shawnika had gone. He couldn't see her. *God, I got that mouthful of pennies taste, again.*

McManus sat down and his ears began to ring. He reached into his pants and pulled out his wallet and counted his cash. Two fifty-dollar bills, four twenties, and three ones. $183.00. He laid all the bills on Shawnika's desk as she returned.

"What's this?" she asked giving him a quizzical look.

"I really apologize for making you do all this work, Shawnika. Can you just forget I came here?"

25

The irony that it was April Fool's Day was not lost on McManus. *This is a joke. What am I doing here?*

Grogan grunted and shut the door as McManus sat down in his office at Richmond Station. *That's not a 'Welcome Back' greeting. Guess he wants to make sure no one overhears what he's gonna say.*

McManus watched Grogan bow his head and fold his hands in front of him. *We going to pray together?*

Grogan looked up and smiled at him.

That jerk's smile gives me the creeps.

"Just so you know," Grogan began. "The department is down almost 400 men. That's the only reason you're still here. They had no choice, McManus. They need bodies," Grogan shook his head. "And a body is about all the city's getting from you—unless you quit."

Grogan's eyes turned evil, sending a chill through McManus. "And I'm making it my job to ensure that happens."

McManus sat back in his seat and blew his breath out. *I'm not surprised to hear Grogan say that. At least he's honest. But what the fuck am I doing here, then?*

"Some things have happened since you left," Grogan continued. "Juan up at the Doggie Diner is pissed at all of us. Apparently, he wasn't too impressed with that drunken friend you begged him to hire. So thanks to you, no more free coffee or hot dogs. ... You're not too popular around here."

McManus bit on his lower lip to keep from saying something.

"And you and I are going to become very intimate, Officer," Grogan continued. "Every hour on the hour we're going to 904 to make sure you're squared away. Any questions?"

McManus' eyes narrowed. "Why not nail my hands and feet to the cross, then?" he said.

Grogan's eyes bore down on McManus like a shotgun barrel. "That's not a bad idea."

THURSDAY
APRIL 1, 2010 · 1430 HRS.

McManus sat behind the wheel of department vehicle 024 waiting for the light at Sixth Avenue and Geary. *Why didn't I file my papers, Tuesday? I knew this was going to happen.*

The light changed, and the radio car entered the intersection. McManus noticed a silver streak out of the corner of his eye. He slammed on the brakes to avoid being t-boned by a Mercedes SLK 350 convertible driven by a young blonde woman, whose hair trailed behind her wildly.

"Oh, thank you, sweetie." He hung a quick right, activated the light bar and caught up to the Mercedes when it stopped for the red light at Fourth Avenue. McManus blipped the siren and watched the woman flush with anger as she looked up in her mirror. *Sometimes the gods just work this way. I get my ass kicked. Now I kick some ass. Pull it over sweetie.*

The driver stopped a block later in the bus zone at Third and Geary.

McManus got out of the radio car and approached the Mercedes.

The driver, her boobs aided by a push-up bra, looked no more than nineteen years old. "Really, you're giving me a ticket?" she whined.

McManus noticed her left eyelash was coming loose and flapped around as she talked. He laughed. *Look at that thing, that's funny. Feels good to laugh.* "Do you know why I pulled you over?"

The young woman tilted her head back. Her bleached hair needed another dose of chemicals to cover about ¾-inch of dark roots. She didn't answer McManus' question.

Okay, fun's over. "I need to see your driver's license, vehicle registration and proof of insurance, please."

The color drained from her salon-tanned face, and her eyes widened with disbelief. "You don't understand. I can't get another ticket," she said.

Oh, yeah. Here comes the rich-bitch routine. "When was your last ticket?"

"About two weeks ago."

"For what?"

"Speeding on Geary."

"You need to slow down and stop for red lights, little girl."

"You don't understand the stresses in my life, officer. I'm stressed out. Really…" The loose eyelash continued to flap up and down as she talked.

"I can understand why you're stressed," McManus said pointing at her eyelash. "Doesn't that thing bother you?"

The woman ignored him.

So are the gods fucking with me now. This is a righteous and redemptive ticket, and it's turning into an Amy Poehler comedy scene with me playing the straight man. The smile left McManus' face. "How stressed can you be?"

The woman quickly checked her blindingly white capped teeth in the mirror for lipstick smears, and then looked back at McManus. "I go to college. And I've got student loans. My dad expects me to get good grades."

McManus backed away from the car and rolled his

eyes to the sky. Then he lost it. "You have no idea what stress is about. You wanna know what stress is? I just got off a suspension. My boss told me the only reason I'm still here is because they're so short of cops. He said it's his goal to get me fired. DON'T TALK TO ME ABOUT STRESS."

The young woman's voice became hysterical. "You don't understand. I can't get another ticket."

"No, no. I need your license and registration."

McManus watched the young woman reach down and shimmy up her skirt to reveal a pair of green panties. She smiled. "I…I…I will do anything…anything, not to get another ticket." She raised her pleading eyes toward him to see his reaction.

That eyelash is defining the laws of physics staying attached to her eyelid. McManus stared at her and said nothing.

"But…you don't understand, officer," she cooed. "I'll do anything…anything…sir…not to get another ticket."

"Slow down, then, and stop for red lights," McManus said.

"Okay, I'll do that," she said in a relieved tone of voice and reached toward the key to restart the car.

"Hey! I need to see your license, your registration, and your proof of insurance."

"NO, NO, NO, I'll do anything." She pleaded.

"NO, you're getting a ticket."

Her eyes grew moist and she dropped her gaze to her chest and held it a moment. McManus said nothing. Reluctantly, she reached into her purse and gave McManus her information. When he returned to her car, he handed his ticket book to her. "Sign this."

"You're giving me a ticket?"

"You blew the red light. I told you you're getting a ticket."

"You don't understand, I will do anything in this world not to get a ticket."

"You need to shut up," McManus said. "Because right now I just wrote you up for running the red light. If you continue down this path, I'm going to bust you for propositioning an officer, and solicitation of prostitution. Would you like those?"

A tear trickled down her cheek. She stopped and wiped at it, then sat up tall. "I thought you guys didn't give cute girls tickets."

"We don't," McManus said. "Press hard so we can read your signature on all copies."

THURSDAY
APRIL 1, 2010 · 1700 HRS.

McManus stopped for coffee at Mz. Brown's on California Street, but Flo wasn't working. He downed a quick cup and made his first 904 meeting with Grogan at Masonic and Geary. After that, he resumed routine patrol. Near Palm Avenue, he watched a white truck blow through the stop sign without even slowing down. McManus caught up to the driver when he pulled into a school parking lot.

The Latino male driver, wearing a dirty red work shirt and jeans, jumped out of the cab and approached the radio car.

"You're pulling me over here?" he said spreading his arms wide.

"Well, this is where you stopped," McManus said as he got out of the car.

"I'm running late to the AA meeting," the man pleaded.

McManus again rolled his eyes toward the sky. *What's going on today?* "You haven't been drinking, right?" he asked. "Because what's going to be really bad is if I have to balance you out here in the parking lot of your AA meeting, and make a DUI arrest with all your friends watching."

The man shook his head and said, "No, man. I'm not drinkin'. I'm not drinkin'."

"Okay," McManus said. "I'm going to write you a ticket for running the stop sign. You know you gotta stop, right?"

"All right, man, all right." He looked around as McManus wrote the ticket. "Can you make it fast?" he said as cars arrived. "I'm going to be the talk of the meeting."

McManus shrugged and continued to write while the man pleaded his case. "The reason I'm late is I'm the dessert guy tonight. I had to pick up all tonight's fresh warm cookies," he said.

McManus looked up.

"I'll give you a cookie if you don't give me a ticket."

McManus looked at him for a moment, and then laughed, "About an hour ago, some 19-year-old chick offered me sex...and she still got a ticket. Sorry, pal. Your warm cookies ain't gonna do it."

The man looked sadly at McManus, "Yeah, I can't top that. Go ahead and give me the ticket."

26

It was a mistake to come back to the force—this job steals your soul. McManus sat in department vehicle 024 as he looked out the windshield into the darkness that was the fourth hole of the Lincoln Park golf course. He reached toward his right hip, unsnapped his service weapon, and pulled the black gun from its leather holster. He tightened his grip on the handle and ran his fingers over the barrel, admiring the weapon's precise construction and balance.

I wonder if I was too sensitive to be a cop. This can be a dehumanizing business. I never liked being Officer Hard-Ass. Not my nature to hurt people's feelings or make them think I didn't trust them or thought they were lying. But I don't have a lot of faith in the goodness of people, either.

The job popped my cherry. Make a traffic stop with a friendly attitude and I might get my head blown off. Make a traffic stop with a chip on my shoulder, I'll be talking to Internal Affairs about my lousy attitude. Holding both attitudes at the same time is impossible. Hiding behind the uniform and letting it do the talking just hasn't worked.

"Protect and Serve" is a nice concept, but the reality is I'm just trying to do the best I can to stay alive. I've had enough.

Grogan's radio call brought him out of his daze: "Richmond 61 to Richmond Six,"

McManus took a deep breath and sighed. *Fuck that little cocksucker. I should kick his ass, once and for all.* McManus re-holstered the weapon and reached for the radio. So far, McManus had been prompt in meeting Grogan's check-in times.

This is getting old. "Richmond Six," he responded.

"Richmond Six, what's your 10-20?"

"Lincoln Park."

"10-4. 904 me at the gas station at Stanyan and Geary in five minutes."

Fuck me. That's on the other side of the district. McManus hesitated before he answered, then said. "Richmond 61, that's 3 miles from my current 10-20 location. Are you requesting a Code Three response?"

"Negative, Officer. I'm requesting you meet me at Stanyan and Geary in five minutes. Do you copy?"

Grogan sounds like he's getting himself revved up to take another bite out of my ass. Fuck you, you little bitch. "Negative, 10-9. Say again, I can't copy you, Richmond 61."

Grogan repeated his message.

McManus hesitated, and then said, "Headquarters, can you relay for Richmond 61. He's breaking badly."

"We copy both of you, 10-2, no problem, Richmond Six," Headquarters responded. "He says he wants you to 904 at the gas station at Stanyan and Geary in five minutes."

McManus sighed. "10-4."

He got out of the car and heard the wind whistling through the eucalyptus trees as he took a piss in the dark. Back in the car he drove as slowly as he could to meet Grogan at Stanyan and Geary. When he arrived, he saw Grogan slumped in the seat of his car, his head barely visible above the steering wheel.

Then Grogan sat up quickly when McManus arrived.

He's gonna be pissed I took so long to get here. To McManus' surprise, however, Grogan said nothing. His silence emboldened McManus. "Well, I've made all our meetings tonight, Sergeant. Can we just get past this little game you're playing, now?"

Grogan's eyes ignited like napalm and burned into McManus. "You don't get it, do you?"

"Get what?"

"How short a leash you're on, Officer."

"Why?" McManus shrugged.

Grogan dismissed his question by pursing his lips and drawing in a deep breath through his wrinkled nose. "I guess, we can't even trust you driving a radio car any more. Tomorrow night you report to the police stable as the night guard."

McManus got upset and raised his leg like he'd just stepped in wet dog shit. "Oh fuck you," he said turning his palms up.

Grogan cocked his head to the side and smirked. "…And this reassignment comes directly from Captain Lagomarsino."

"You can't do this, I'm going to the Police Officer's Association."

A smile crept across Grogan's face as he looked up at McManus.

"The trouble with you, McManus, is you don't have any friends. The Captain is concerned about your well-being out here on the street. He's not sure you're up to the job, anymore."

"Bullshit," McManus said, wishing he had a better word.

"You're in denial, McManus. What's your production been around here lately? You think the city's getting its money's worth out of you?

"That's total crap…I've only been back eight hours," McManus protested.

"How many tickets did you write tonight?" Grogan asked.

"Two."

Grogan rolled his eyes and said, "Just two. You've been out here all night. What have you been doing?"

McManus put his hands on his hips. "They're righteous tickets."

"If you say so," Grogan said looking at him suspiciously.

"Well, I say so, Dipshit." McManus nodded.

Grogan pursed his lips again. "I'm sorry, Officer. But I'm going to have to report your attitude back to Captain

Lagomarsino. He's not going to be happy."

"Fuck you."

"Excuse me, Officer."

"You heard me… Fuck you."

Grogan smiled and reached into his coat pocket. He removed a small recording device and pointed to a microphone pinned to the outside of his coat.

"The latest in technology the department is trying out," Grogan said as he pressed rewind, and played the muffled sound of McManus' voice saying, "You heard me… Fuck you."

Grogan placed the device back in his coat pocket and looked up at McManus. His grin reminded McManus of O'Connell's face the day he plucked the ball out of the air and ran for the championship-winning touchdown.

This time, McManus wasn't laughing. *The end of my career is near.*

"Un-officer-like-conduct and insubordination," Grogan chuckled and added, "You might not have to show up at the police stable tomorrow night after all, McManus." He started his engine and drove away.

McManus stood watching Grogan's car disappear in the traffic on Geary Boulevard. *This has gone far enough.*

The rain began to fall. McManus got back into his car and spun the tires out of the parking lot. He rolled down the window and stuck his head out. Driving one-handed down the middle lane of Geary Boulevard, he let the raindrops whip against his face.

So, if I shoot Dipshit? Cop Murder/Suicide…that'll make the news. Mom killed herself. So, it's in the family genes… Makes sense.

McManus returned to the fourth tee at Lincoln Park and got out of the car in the rain. He turned on his Kel-Lite to illuminate the path and, without notifying headquarters, he started the long walk down to the Labyrinth Cliff.

A furious squall moved in as he arrived at the promontory. Wet, shivering, and frustrated, McManus pulled his hat tight. He lowered his head and struggled against the driving wind to continue toward the Labyrinth. Once there, he picked up a handful of rocks and, one by one, threw them with all his might into the darkness and over the edge. Tears mixing with raindrops ran down his cheeks.

Why Mom? Fuckin' razor blades. What a horrible way to die. You're so pissed off at the world you cut your hands off! Give me a fuckin' break.

She was sprawled on the bathroom floor when I came home after school one afternoon. She was supposed to have been at work but, instead, she'd held razor blades in her teeth and thrust her wrists back and forth. She bled to death naked on the powder blue tile, encircled by a black pool of goo that had streamed from her severed hands. Her skin was ashen-gray, her eyes open and locked in a death stare.

As it turned out, it was to be good training for being a cop. Learned to put it all in a box, bury it deep in my soul, and leave it there.

Below McManus, the waves crashed onto the rocks with a muffled thud that reverberated in his chest and ears. Standing there, he bent forward, rested his palms on his knees, and looked down at the water.

I want to hear a voice. I want to see an image... something... What am I supposed to do? Please. Give me some guidance.

Silence.

After a few moments, he stood up and turned around. Deliberately, he lifted his foot over the rocky edge of the Labyrinth and stepped inside. Taking a deep breath, he followed the serpentine path to the Labyrinth's center— one cautious step at a time.

"Let go to open up," Fratelli had said in her yoga class. *Time to forget about mom's suicide and move on...but where?*

Fratelli's working tonight...that means she'd be the one to go down onto the rocks and pick up my pieces. What a relief to no longer be a cop. But can I really do that to her?

At the center of the Labyrinth, McManus felt an uncontrollable urge to rid himself of everything evil. And, then, as suddenly as the squall had started, it moved on.

He forced his fingers against his chest. *Okay, I know what to do. I can feel my breastbone splitting apart.*

His thumbs and fingers plunged deep into the muscles, searching... *I can feel it, the actual substance that contains everything bad in my life.*

McManus heard a "pop," like a knuckle cracking. *I can pull myself free. I can smell and see that piece of burnt wood exposed to the air, smoldering and hot to the touch. I can juggle it back and forth in my hands. Ain't nothing but a thing. No way it's gonna hurt me anymore.*

He used a two-hand chest pass as if to toss an object over the promontory's edge. Then he fumbled in the darkness for the clasp of the star attached to his jacket. Finally pulling the pin free, he held the star in his palm and squeezed it until his fingers bled.

So be it—it is done. And then he placed the star in his pants pocket.

The Kel-Lite cut a beacon through the darkness as he left the Labyrinth and headed back up the hill to his radio car. He started the engine and turned on the headlights, which illuminated a cluster of orange California poppies growing at the base of a nearby tree.

He got out of his car and picked a dozen of them. *The first sign of spring…and my first act as a retired cop, I'm committing a crime. The law says no one can remove flowers from publicly-owned land. Curious, I once cited two tourists for that very offense. Mine, however, is an act of love.*

He placed the poppies inside his jacket pocket. *Time starts right now, and Trish Fratelli is the light at the end of my tunnel.*

Paper and debris blew along Geary Boulevard as McManus left Lincoln Park and drove west toward the brick firehouse at 41st Avenue. He parked the radio car in the firehouse driveway. *Another violation of the law, 22500d.*

After knocking on the large wooden door, he heard footsteps echoing across the concrete apparatus floor in the firehouse.

Fratelli opened a side door, saw the radio car, and smiled. She was wearing her black turn-out pants held up by red suspenders over a blue T-shirt. "You can get a ticket for parking there," she said.

McManus nodded. "I know the cop who works this area; he's a friend of mine."

Fratelli stepped outside and took a deep breath through her nose. "Feels like a Pineapple Express is coming in."

McManus smiled in agreement. "So how are things going?"

"Glad you're here, was about to call the police. Bailey's back."

"What?" McManus threw up his hands in surprise.

"She's upset about something. Came to the door about an hour ago, with this pathetic pleading voice, telling me she loved me and couldn't leave San Francisco without me. Wants me to go back to Ohio with her. Can you imagine?"

"Where is she now," he asked putting his hands on his hips.

"I had to push her out the door. She kicked it and started screaming and carrying on. Saw her get in her car and drive off."

"What kind of car?"

"A black Camry—just like yours."

Bailey drives a Camry? "Really… I'll run a DMV check for the license and keep an eye out for her."

McManus reached into his jacket pocket and pulled out the poppies. "I got you something. Sorry all the flower shops were closed, so I had to break the law for these—384a of the Penal Code—you can look it up."

As he handed her the flowers, she smiled. The wind tousled her hair, and she pushed it behind her ears. "How sweet."

"They're from Lands End, but I'm going to start calling it 'Lands Beginning' from now on. And here's something else for you." His heart pounded as he reached into his pocket and pulled out the seven-pointed star. Its surface glistened from the reflection of the street lights.

"I've outgrown the need for this thing. It's time to pull the pin. Time to retire and start enjoying the world." He watched for her reaction.

She stared at him in shock as he handed her the star.

"It's just like you said in yoga, 'You got to let go to open up.' I want to do that. And I want to be there for you, Trish. But I'm going to need your help to get through this thing."

The 38 Geary bus thundered past them. Fratelli waited for the roar to fade as she crossed her arms and pulled them tight across her chest.

Are the arms across her chest for warmth or a sign of her rebuff? Quitting the business is terrifying. But her rejection now would be even worse.

"You don't look like you've been drinking," she said smiling.

Just then, the be-bop alarm tone rang inside the firehouse, and all the lights flashed on.

"Unit dispatch, Engine 34," a voice blasted over a loudspeaker.

"Shit," Fratelli said. "Terrible timing. I'm sorry, McManus. Better move the car. We gotta a run."

Fratelli placed the star and poppies in the pocket of her pants, leaned forward, and kissed him on the cheek.

"Let's talk this afternoon when I get off," she said and ran back inside the firehouse.

27

SATURDAY
APRIL 3, 2010 • 1200 HRS.

It had rained hard Friday night. McManus called in sick. *Fuck Grogan. I'm not about to guard the stables for him. Fratelli hadn't called either. She said we'd talk yesterday afternoon. What am I supposed to do now?*

McManus heard scratching on his door and then a knock. *Hey, that whine sure sounds a lot like Carly.*

His heart raced, and he rose quickly from the beanbag chair. At the door, he looked through the peephole and saw a man in a blue blazer with white close-cropped hair staring back at him. The scratching grew desperate. McManus grasped the knob and opened the door just a crack. Just enough to allow a small brown-and-black Yorkie to wiggle through and run inside like she was making a jail break.

"Carly!"

The dog leapt at his knees.

"Officer McManus?" the man in the hallway asked.

"Yes," he said looking down at the dog.

The man extended his hand. "Peter Guichard, I'm an attorney representing Gabriella Sutherland, whose father is Stanford Sutherland. May I come in?"

McManus glared at Guichard with the look he used for pimps, child molesters, and litigation attorneys. *What's this asshole doing with Carly?* "You know what... I'd rather come out there."

Guichard hesitated and pulled back his hand. "As you wish. I do have some great news for you, though. It seems Ms. Sutherland has received an exciting opportunity in New York City, but, unfortunately, she's not able to take Carly with her."

You're so full of shit, I can smell you. I don't like you no matter what you say. McManus stepped outside the door without shutting it. The dog followed him.

"She was grateful for the condition in which the dog was returned to her, which, I might add, was the reason she declined to press legal action against you. She wished me to contact you and offer you the first right of refusal regarding the dog."

"How much?" McManus put on a look like he was interested.

"Five thousand dollars."

McManus chuckled. "Whoa, pal, use that shit on somebody that doesn't know any better."

"I'm sorry you feel that way," Guichard said as he pulled back on Carly's leash.

"Hey, I got an idea of what's going on with Ms. Sutherland," McManus said. "I probably could show up at the SPCA tomorrow morning and adopt her for a hundred bucks and the cost of a dog license…which I see she still doesn't have."

Guichard didn't respond. He tightened his grip on the leash. Carly barked and whined at McManus. When McManus said nothing, Guichard turned and pulled Carly down the hallway. She struggled against the leash, taking it in her mouth and shaking it.

McManus grabbed the leash and jerked it out of Guichard's hand. He reached into his pocket and found some change and flipped the coins at Guichard. They fell onto the carpet.

"All sales are final. Get the fuck out of here."

Carly's ears and tail stood straight up, and like she was shot out of a canon, she scampered away from Guichard and disappeared into the condo. McManus slammed the door. Carly dragged her leash to the bay window and jumped up against the glass.

McManus smiled at her and found his iPod. *I know the perfect song.*

The pounding beat and Huey Lewis' driving voice soon vibrated through the condo.

"The power of love is a curious thing…"

He reached down, picked up Carly, and held her in his arms. They rocked together—side to side—in front of the bay window looking out at San Francisco. "This is going to be our song, sweetie," he said as tears welled up in his eyes. "OK, so here's the deal. No conditions, no expectations. Love only. I love you, you love me..."

McManus reached into a kitchen cabinet and retrieved a bag of chicken jerky dog treats, Carly's favorite. He hadn't had the heart to throw them out.

SATURDAY
APRIL 3, 2010 · 1600 HRS.

McManus and Carly sat together in the beanbag chair the rest of the afternoon looking out at the city. Despite being a month into spring, the El Niño winter didn't want to leave San Francisco. By late afternoon, three-quarters of an inch of rain had fallen in San Francisco, but now the sky was clearing.

"I hope you're a Giants fan, Carly. We got something to look forward to this season. We got the pitching and we got the Panda Sandoval. Let's take a walk along the waterfront and go to the ball park.

SATURDAY
APRIL 3, 2010 · 1630 HRS.

McManus and Carly drove to the Embarcadero. He parked at a meter and used his credit card to pay. *I remember when parking was only a penny.*

He flipped up the collar on his bomber jacket against the cold wind coming off the Bay and attached Carly's leash. They headed off along the Embarcadero promenade toward AT&T Park.

Around him, McManus heard the sound of laughter. He watched people walking, jogging, riding their bikes and just taking in the splendor of the San Francisco skyline and waterfront.

Off in the distance, McManus heard a collective groan from the ball park. *Things don't sound like they're going well.*

He tried to pick up their pace, but Carly stopped to smell every parking meter. *What's the rush? I got my dog back. Just want to enjoy her.*

The promenade bent to the right, and the ballpark came into sight. The sun made a brief appearance before hiding again behind ominous clouds out over the Bay. Carly stopped again to smell another parking meter.

Come on, Carly, let's go. McManus pulled impatiently on her leash. She dipped her head and the collar and leash slid off her neck.

Oh, shit. Carly bolted into the street running full speed toward the oncoming traffic. Faster than a Google search,

McManus' brain processed the scene and saw the irony.

I first laid eyes on Carly when she bolted in and out of traffic near the Cliff House, and she lived. Now, she's on the other side of town, and she's going to die. The most foolish thing I can do is think she won't. That's how my life has always worked.

He saw Carly freeze in her tracks as a white Escalade bore down on her. McManus closed his eyes an instant before the impact and heard multiple vehicles also skidding to a stop. *That's the sound of death. I can't look at that little dog lying bloodied in the street.*

He kept his eyes closed as the unmistakable smell of burning rubbed assailed his nose. But when he opened his eyes, a small object moving through the smoke caught his attention.

She's still alive!

Terrified, Carly ran down the street into approaching traffic. McManus ran out into the street after her. He waved his arms above his head to warn the oncoming traffic.

"Carly, stop!"

Her ears perked up at the sound of her name. She turned around, looked back at McManus, and stopped. When he reached her, he scooped her up and without breaking stride made it back safely to the sidewalk.

SATURDAY
APRIL 3, 2010 · 1800 HRS.

When McManus and Carly arrived home on Red Rock Way, he spotted a motorcyclist wearing a tight one-piece black leather riding suit. At the sound of their approach, the rider worked loose the straps on the crash helmet. McManus recognized the shape of the rider's hips and ass. *Is that Fratelli?*

He stopped the car and rolled down his window. In the black visor of her helmet, he saw his reflection. "Jeez, you ride one of these things?"

"Yup, just like the song. 'Tank is full, the switch is on... rocket-bike is all her own.'"

McManus nodded. *I know those lyrics. "Eye of the Huricane." David Wilcox.* "But does she want to run away somwhere the pain won't come again?" he asked.

Fratelli pulled off her helmet and gave him a concerned look. "Bailey followed me up here. I thought it was you, 'til I saw her face."

"Me! What?"

"She drives a black Camry just like this one," she said pointing to his car.

"Where's she now?"

"Gone. When I spotted her, she stopped and backed down the street."

"What the fuck is she doing?"

"I don't know. I've called her cell, but she doesn't pick up."

Wait a minute. That black Camry I thought was mine parked below the window when I came home from Fratelli's…

Carly jumped up on McManus' lap and looked at Fratelli.

"Who's that?" she asked.

"Carly. My new partner."

Fratelli nodded. "You want this back, don't you," she asked as she reached into her leather riding jacket and handed McManus' his star.

"I called in sick last night. I'm not going to need it anymore. I'm done."

"Yeah, that's the other thing I wanted to talk to you about." Fratelli said haltingly. She lifted her head and stared up at the gray clouds. Then blew out her breath.

Oh shit here it comes. I've learned her expressions. And I don't like the look on her face. McManus shook his head.

She closed her troubled eyes for a moment, then spoke, "I don't know if I can help you, McManus. I'm not good at relationships."

"Well, neither am I. But how long you gonna sit out here in the rain?"

Fratelli looked at him with a sheepish grin.

"Come on in. I'll show you the view and we can get you out of those wet clothes."

SATURDAY
APRIL 3, 2010 · 1915 HRS.

McManus lay on the beanbag chair, listening to Fratelli shower. *She's been in there a long time. Wonder if she's waiting for me to go in and pin her against the wall and fuck her right there?*

Carly sniffed under the bathroom door and then returned to sit next to him just as the shower turned off. McManus waited and listened. Fratelli emerged from the shadows in the hallway wrapped in a white towel. Again, from her index finger dangled the pump of a bottle of body oil she'd found in the medicine cabinet.

"Need some help here, Mister," she smiled.

"I think I've seen this movie before," McManus laughed.

"Oh, you think so, huh," she said sitting down on the shag rug in front of the fireplace. "I want to tell you about my dream last night."

He slid out of the beanbag chair and joined her, then smiled and hugged her. "This should be interesting."

"I thought so. Here ya go. It's a bright, moonlit night. And I've left the door to my flat open for you to check on my well-being."

"That'll get you in trouble every time," he chuckled.

"Shut up." Fratelli smiled and pulled the towel tighter around her breasts. "It's 4:20 in the morning. You park your radio car on the corner in front of the fire hydrant. Nobody will notice. You've been here before. Silently, you open the front door."

She hiked her eyebrows and in a seductive voice said, "You know where I am. You make your way to my bedroom, where you find me asleep on the bed. It's a warm evening, so I've kicked off the covers, and I'm lying on my side. My pink silk negligee is pushed up around my waist, and you can see my ass silhouetted in the moonlight. You smile at the sight and your cock stirs…"

McManus leaned forward, breathed in her scent, and kissed her neck. In mid-sentence, she stopped talking as her mouth and lips formed an O. Her eyes gleamed with pleasure.

When he looked up, she turned around and kissed him. "Do you want to hear the rest…or…"

"Okay. No more distractions," he said and with a heavy sigh, got up, and sat back into the beanbag chair.

"You take off your gun belt and lay it quietly on the floor, trying not to wake me. Your pants and shirt come off and finally your body armor. You hover over me. What to do first? So many choices, and you know they all bring me pleasure…"

SATURDAY
APRIL 3, 2010 • 2230 HRS.

"I gotta surprise for you," McManus said as he held up a bottle of Oak Knoll Pinot before uncorking it. "I started drinking this stuff last week to remind me of you."

He poured the wine and carried a glass to Fratelli, who lay naked on the shag rug. She pushed herself up and sat

Indian-style. They clinked glasses and took a sip.

"You still thinking much about death and dying?" he asked.

Fratelli coughed on her wine and looked up at him, amused. "That's a strange post-coital question, McManus. What the hell do you think I am, a Praying Mantis that kills her partner after sex?"

McManus shrugged. "Last week you were talking about how you were scared because of Pete's death and those kids who died in the fire. It's been on my mind, that's all."

The fireplace crackled and cast an orange glow on the side of her face. She stood up and, being careful not to spill her wine, planted a long hard kiss on his lips. "Why would you want to talk about that?" she asked as she grabbed a blanket lying nearby.

Is that why this woman has such a hold over me? She kisses me and I feel sparks. There's something happening here. My stomach is actually doing flip-flops. But it feels right. Is this what love feels like? Tell her. See what happens.

McManus laid his wine glass on the bricks next to the fireplace and sat up. She looked at him curiously.

"Maybe this is a little quick for you, Fratelli, and you're going to think it's just pillow talk. But I'm in love with you."

Fratelli's expression changed from interest to a look of concern. "Why do you say that? Because I'm an easy lay?"

McManus crawled next to her in front of the fireplace. "You've touched my heart. And I like it." He tilted her head up with his finger, paused, and gave her another long kiss. "I think kissing is one of the most intimate acts two people can do."

"So you really mean that, or are you just trying to impress me?" She gave him a sweet smile.

McManus shook his head. "I do mean it, but I need to tell you something…it was what was happening just before I found Cassidy's body."

"Do I want to hear this? Sounds like a mood spoiler to me," she responded sounding annoyed.

He shook his head again. "I haven't told anyone this. But I was going to eat my gun in the radio car, that night."

She flinched at his words and looked at him with hardened eyes.

"Then I realized everyone would know it was a suicide. So I walked down to the Labyrinth Cliff to jump off."

"That's pretty sick, McManus." She pulled the blanket tighter around her, grabbed her glass of wine, got up, and walked to the window.

He stood and joined her. He reached his arm around her shoulder. "That's why I want to talk to you about death."

Fratelli took a sip of her wine and then lifted his fingers off her shoulder. She turned toward him. "Go ahead. Everybody in our generation thinks they're never going to grow old and die. Let's hear what you've gotta say."

We're standing inches from each other, but all of a sudden it feels like miles. He ran his hand through his hair. "I've been scared I could die without ever having had a great love affair. Things are so different now. That's exactly what I want to have with you, Trish."

She rolled her eyes. "You still feel like killing yourself?"

"No. That was a bad moment, but I got past it. Now,

though, everything seems so much brighter."

"Well, then … What about what I want? What's in this great love affair for me? Are you expecting me to throw my arms around you now and say 'Yes, Darling, yes, please sweep me away'"?

She looked at him with contemptuous amusement. "This 'I love you' stuff is very easy to say. But are you really ready to start making plans with me? You know, McManus, it's not just all about you. How are you going to make me feel fulfilled?"

McManus frowned and looked away from her.

Fratelli raised her voice. "And besides getting laid, what else do you want? Because, believe me, I got some stuff in my life you don't want to know about."

McManus turned back toward her. "I don't care. I can give you whatever you need."

Fratelli shook her head. "Guys just don't change, McManus. You've lived in isolation all your life. You got your routines and habits. You really think you're going to change all that just to have me around all the time?"

She drained her wine glass and set it on the window sill. Then she turned and looked him in the eyes. "You're too selfish. Too set in your ways. I'd want to change a lot things about you."

Fratelli started to walk around the room studying his pictures on the wall. "These would all have to go. But, actually…I'd move you out of this place."

McManus squinted and put his thumb under his chin. "Hmm."

"You ready to work your ass off doing things that would be just for me?" Fratelli returned to the window and looked out into the distance. "I want to go climb Mt. Everest—you ready to do that? It's a real ball-buster of a trip. Couple weeks out on the trail at altitude in sub-zero temperatures. You'd have to take your shits out in the open and watch me dump out, too. Could you handle that?"

"Then I want to ride my bike around Ireland for a couple weeks. You think you could get out of your comfort zone to do that with me? How about China? I want to do that, too. You gonna sit on an airplane for 24 hours full of ethnic Chinese coughing and spitting on the floors—just to spend a couple minutes with me walking on the Great Wall? Would you do that with me?"

McManus took a deep breath and hiked his shoulders to say he didn't know.

Fratelli looked down at her hands. Her voice and tone softened. "Point is, McManus, you've always taken the safe road. Personally, I believe you're capable of doing some truly great things, but you've always let your ego and your fears get in the way."

McManus turned up his palms apologetically. "Are you angry with me? Was I moving too fast...or is it you?"

Fratelli threw her hair back and laughed. Her eyes twinkled in amusement. "I'm all over the place," she said. "I change every day. You're like the beach, and I'm the waves. You think we can handle that?" She looked at him as if expecting an answer.

The beach and the waves? I'm getting a little lost here. What's going on ...?

After a moment, she tightened her lips and nodded to herself. "See, that's what we're talking about here. You've got to accept who I am. And you gotta find out who you really are."

McManus listened in silence.

Fratelli's voice grew frustrated. "You guys are so clueless," she shook her head. "Any wonder why I hang out with lesbians?"

"I could guess?" he smiled.

Fratelli laughed. "The answer is I want to be the one in charge. I want to make the decisions about who approaches me. I know men, McManus. I've lived with you guys 24 hours a day for over 20 years. I know how you think."

She walked toward the kitchen and looked back at him. "Mind if I have another drink?"

"No problem, I'll open a new bottle and get another glass for both of us."

Fratelli sat down on the rug and leaned back against the beanbag chair watching him go into the kitchen. "You guys are so cocksure of yourselves."

"Yeah?" he asked bringing in the two glasses.

She took her glass and sipped without making an effort to clink with him. "You all think you know women, but what you really don't know...or at least don't acknowledge, is that we own your dicks. We call the shots; you guys just respond."

She took another sip and lowered the blanket exposing her breasts. McManus' eyes reflexively dropped to her bare chest.

"See, think I'm kidding. We go braless, wear tight jeans, and you guys are toast. All we gotta do is make you think you have a shot at us. It's all very flattering, but after awhile…it's nothing more than a distraction."

He watched her study him.

"I want something real, McManus." She looked into his confused eyes and laughed. "Do you know why I'm here right now?"

I'm too stunned to answer.

"Because I want to be here," she said.

28

EASTER SUNDAY
APRIL 4, 2010 · 0735 HRS.

McManus awoke Easter morning, stretched his toes, and rolled over. The unfamiliar weight on the bed beside him was a surprise, and he shuddered. His movement caused Fratelli to open her eyes, and without speaking, she nestled her body closer to his. The luxurious warmth of a woman's body under the covers aroused him. He nudged her legs apart with his knee. She rolled onto her back, he climbed on top, and they kissed.

After they made love for a half hour, Fratelli rested her head on McManus' chest and they looked out at the city. Easter Sunday in San Francisco was going to be rainy and gloomy. Carly jumped up on the bed and looked at McManus.

"Okay, I get the message," he laughed, and then kissed Fratelli. "Back in a minute," he said.

He got out of bed and pulled on his jeans and a blue fleece. "Don't go anywhere," he said as he blew her a kiss.

"Wow, two intimate acts in thirty seconds. I won't be going anywhere," she smiled. Then with a deep sigh, she closed her eyes and snuggled into the pillow.

When McManus returned, he heard the water running in the shower and wandered into the steamy bathroom. Through the shower doors, he saw her turn toward him.

"Save water, shower together?" she asked.

He smiled. "I think I've got something you might enjoy even more."

Fratelli made a pouty face and said, "Suit yourself." She turned away from him.

McManus went into the kitchen and dug a frying pan out of a cupboard. He poured in a couple drops of oil and turned on a burner. From the refrigerator, he took out a package of hash browns, and then poured them into the heated oil. They crackled and popped while he placed strips of bacon and four eggs into a second frying pan.

Wonder what she'll think of my cooking? He brewed coffee then set the table. When the smell of sizzling bacon and brewing coffee wafted into the bathroom a few minutes later, it brought a scream of delight from Fratelli.

"Are you really cooking breakfast?" she yelled.

"Come and find out."

"I got to see this," Fratelli said. She wrapped a towel around herself and trailing water, padded barefoot into the kitchen. McManus stepped back from his frying pans.

She looked at him with interest. "Eggs, bacon, and hash browns," she said, turning up her palms. "So where are the strawberries, bananas and peaches?"

His smile dissolved.

"You've gotta at least have blueberries. They're the healthiest thing you can eat—plenty of antioxidants."

"I eat blueberry muffins," he said as he scrambled the eggs.

Fratelli put her hands on her hips. Water dripped from her hair. "That doesn't work, pal." She took off the towel and dried her hair.

I could get used to a naked body at breakfast every morning. She'll love this, blueberries or no. He turned over the bacon.

"Well, here's another thing I'd change. Give me a month and with a little tweaking of your diet, you could lose 10 pounds without even trying."

McManus slid the frying pan off the burner and hiked his shoulders. *Shit, she's starting to make too big a deal out of this. We need to talk.* "I heard everything you said last night. And I can't argue with you because you're right."

I wonder how convincing that sounds to her. "I've obviously never given any thought to a lot of things you talked about, simply because I haven't had to. Maybe that's why my life's a mess. I acknowledge that, and I know I'm lucky to even be alive."

He could see her face relax. "I'm tired of being alone and waking up in an empty bed, Fratelli. I'm getting older and I can feel it."

McManus' face and lips tightened and reflected his resolve to change. Neither of them said anything. He reached out, pulled her into him, and searching for confirmation of his feelings, he kissed her long and hard.

"This is Easter Sunday," he said when he released her. "The day of rebirth through the resurrection of Jesus."

Fratelli looked surprised. "You have heart, McManus. Remember I told you that at Starbucks when we had coffee? I expected you to be like your buddies Cassidy and O'Connell."

Water still dripped from her hair onto the floor as she reached into the frying pan, pulled out a crisp piece of bacon, and began to chew. "This is what I want for you, McManus. You have choices. You can change. I want you to be a man who's guided by love, not fear."

McManus shrugged. "I am willing to take some risks, Fratelli. I've wanted a real relationship for a long time. Just hasn't happened… I want to make it happen, now."

He looked at her and smiled. "It's time. I can start this morning by sharing a special place with you. Let's go out to the Labyrinth at Lands End. We can have our own personal Easter service," he said.

McManus reached into the frying pan and picked up a strip of bacon. "Stuff's good, huh?" He smiled. "And you know, what?" he said as he chewed. "Let's stop at Safeway and get some blueberries."

EASTER SUNDAY
APRIL 4, 2010 · 1000 HRS.

McManus watched Fratelli pull her ponytail through the back of one of his old Giants caps. They walked down the cart path next to the fourth hole at the Lincoln Park golf course, heading toward the Labyrinth. He zipped his brown bomber jacket and turned up the collar to cut the bite from the cold ocean breeze blowing off the Pacific.

Carrying a small paper bag full of blueberries they'd stopped for at the Diamond Heights Safeway, he popped a couple berries into his mouth and exaggerated his chewing motion. "They're okay, but not as good as a blueberry muffin."

Fratelli shook her head and buried her hands deep into the pockets of her motorcycle jacket as she kept stride with him. "They're more than okay," she said. "They're a natural food that's good for you."

McManus laughed. It felt good to laugh. "So you really think it's possible to change and start all over again." He watched her take a deep breath of the brisk ocean air.

"Yes, I do," she said and grabbed a handful of berries.

Guess I'd better clean the slate and tell her before she finds out on her own. McManus reached down and picked up one of the ubiquitous eucalyptus pods littering the cart path. He flipped it to the side. "You know if we're treating this as our Easter Service, I probably should go to confession."

Fratelli gave him a questioning look. "What do you mean?"

"If it gets back to your sister that we are hooking up, I don't want you to be surprised."

"I still don't understand what you're talking about." She grabbed his shoulder and stopped walking.

"Remember my admission to you at Starbucks. I mentioned the woman who ruined me for sex 35 years ago?"

"You're shitting me," she said.

"I confess…," he smiled. "You're a better lover than she was. You've healed me."

Fratelli's face tightened in anger, and her eyes burned into him. "This isn't funny, McManus."

"It was 35 years ago."

"You're an asshole. What did you gain by telling me that?"

"Honesty. Transparency. I care about you and want us to have a serious relationship."

She continued to stare at him.

Honesty is overrated…apparently. Why did I tell her? What on earth was I trying to prove?

"Was this when she was working at the Franciscan Treatment Room?"

McManus nodded.

"Well, spoiler alert. She'd just gotten dumped by a French intern named John Paul. She'd really had the hots for him and to get her revenge, she was grudge-fucking every guy in sight. I can guarantee one thing, McManus. You didn't ruin sex for her."

McManus turned up his palms. "Sorry, I pissed you off."

They resumed walking as darkness enveloped them under a canopy of eucalyptus and Monterrey cypress trees near the spot where Cassidy had been found.

"His memorial of flowers and remembrances is still there," McManus pointed to the spot, but Fratelli stared straight ahead as if she wanted to ignore it.

Neither spoke for awhile as the wind wailed like a siren. *We couldn't hear one another even if we wanted to talk now.*

They reached the Lands End Coastal Trail and turned right. After another twenty yards, McManus stepped in front of Fratelli to lead her down the wooden stairway to the Labyrinth Cliff. "The wind should lessen once we start going down those steep stairs," he said and then heard Fratelli gasp behind him. At the same time, the sound of shoes skidding on the loose gravel made him think Fratelli had slipped.

Twisting around, he caught a glimpse of an insane-looking woman coming straight at them. She had a knife. It was aimed at the back of his neck. An instant before she reached him, McManus raised his forearm. He deflected the weapon and knocked the attacker off balance. The woman screamed as she stumbled past McManus and Fratelli with the knife still in her hand. Its blade sliced through the top of his bomber jacket, cutting into his shoulder like a bolt of electricity. Blood spurted through the tear in his jacket.

Fratelli jumped onto the woman's back and pile-drove her face into the ground. The knife fell from the attacker's hand. With his arm dangling at his side, McManus kicked the weapon away and then dropped his knees hard into the woman's head and neck, knocking her unconscious. Only

Fratelli's pushing him off had kept his knee from crushing the attacker's windpipe.

"Motherfucker. How bad is it?" he screamed, trying to stop the blood with his hand.

"You're going to be okay, just relax." Fratelli took several deep breaths as she continued to sit atop the woman's back.

"That's fucking Bailey Buckholtz. What the hell?" he demanded. Blood ran down his arm and splattered onto Fratelli's jacket as he circled behind her. He raised his foot and drove his heel hard into Bailey's ass.

"Stop it," Fratelli screamed at him. "Get us some help."

McManus staggered over to the park's yellow Emergency Call Box located at the head of the steps and called.

EASTER SUNDAY
APRIL 4, 2010 · 1020 HRS.

Soon sirens were heard in the distance. Bailey was beginning to move, but Fratelli grabbed her neck and held it against the gravel trail. "What the fuck are you doing here?"

Bailey answered feebly, "Another pretty boy. Like all of them." She took a huge breath. "They just think with their dicks." She gulped "I don't know what you saw in that guy."

"What guy?" Fratelli asked, pushing Bailey's face harder into the gravel.

"I loved you, Trish," Bailey said. "Cassidy ruined the life we had together…I'm in love with you. Don't you understand?"

What the fuck. Something's not right here, Fratelli looks pale and lost. "What do you mean, 'Cassidy ruined your life?'"

Bailey tried to shift around to talk to him, but Fratelli wouldn't release her. "She's crazy, McManus."

The sound of a siren and car tires sliding on gravel drew closer.

"I told him that I loved you. I told him to leave you alone," Bailey said.

"Oh, my God," Fratelli gasped. She pulled her hand from off Bailey's neck to cover her own mouth.

McManus saw a cloud of dust and the flash of a black and white radio car.

Bailey spat and struggled to get free. "He started talking about you, Trish. He was so arrogant. Then he said it was gonna cost him too much money and you weren't worth it.'"

McManus felt his heart drop into his stomach. Then he saw Grogan running from his radio car down the trail toward them. *What the fuck is he doing here?*

"You meant nothing to Cassidy," Bailey taunted Fratelli. "I loved you. To him, you were nothing more than a little plaything…"

Stunned, McManus stood next to Grogan and listened to Bailey's story unfold.

29

The phone awoke McManus in his condo, and he opened his eyes. *This is another nightmare, isn't it? Oh yeah, the stitches are real, fourteen sewn across my shoulder and collar bone.* He lay in bed listening to the sound of the phone.

Bailey had been taken into custody and transported in Grogan's radio car to the Hall of Justice. Grogan had notified communications about an "X to the Hall" he was transferring. He also mentioned over the air this was a suspect in the Cassidy murder. *Dipshit got what he wanted: a battalion of photographers, and scores of TV lights greeted him in the basement of the Hall. He was in his glory while I was at the General getting treated.*

McManus rolled out of bed, answered the phone, and took it with him to the kitchen. It was Lahey.

"I'm looking for your girlfriend. She's not answering her phone. She with you?"

McManus sighed. "Last time I saw Fratelli, was when I was sitting in your office and you were hustling her into an interrogation room."

McManus put the phone on Speaker and squeezed a bottle of Blanton's between his knees. He worked the stopper free with his good arm and swigged an eye-opener straight from the bottle.

The shock and hurt I saw on her face was more than I could bear.

"Here's the deal," Lahey said. "Buckholtz copped to the whole thing. We even found her on the video from Cassidy's funeral at St Anne. Then she returns to the crime scene. It's classic. The guilty conscience needs to confess."

"Good work, guys," McManus said with a sarcastic tone in his voice.

Lahey hesitated and then continued. "She told us she'd been really pissed off at Cassidy. He'd mocked Fratelli at the sister's birthday party. And Bailey wasn't having anything of it."

That Bailey was one scary character. I'm sure throwing my flowers all over the firehouse was just the tip of the iceberg. "What'd Cassidy say?"

"We really don't know that. What we do know—at least what Bailey told us—was that she'd caught them together and thought her head was going to explode. Then she started stalking Cassidy, following him out to the golf course on Christmas Eve."

Lahey coughed on the phone and continued, "Cassidy was out there after closing, hitting tee shots on the fourth hole. His wife Gina had told us he used to go to the course often just to see if he could make an Eagle two on the par four. He was walking that cart trail searching for a lost ball when she got him in the neck—just like she tried to get you."

Holy Fuck! She thought we were just alike, that I wasn't any different, any better than Cassidy.

Silence.

"McManus, are you still there?" Lahey asked.

"Yeah," he said and took another swig of Blanton's. "How about the castration? She cop to that, too?"

"Yeah, said she wanted to hurt Cassidy as much as he had hurt her."

"That lady must have been in a lot of pain," McManus said coldly.

"Said she didn't finish the job because she heard somebody coming."

"The Russians?"

"Probably, but Buckholtz said she didn't see anyone. She did tell us some guys were speaking a foreign language." Lahey coughed again.

"She escaped by picking up Cassidy's golf bag and posing as a golfer. At some point, she said she threw the weapon into the bushes and made her way back to her car parked up on El Camino del Mar. We checked the vehicle, and, sure enough, Cassidy's clubs were in her trunk."

McManus exhaled, feeling the Blanton's boiling in his stomach. "Sounds like she has a decent insanity defense. Heat of passion, Involuntary Manslaughter, just like old Danny boy got."

Another long silence.

"There's another thing you should know if you haven't figured it out already." Lahey went on. "Though Fratelli's legally innocent of anything, in the court of public opinion and in the firehouses around town, your girlfriend is a dead woman walking when the full story gets out."

What can I say? Do I really want to hear all this? I love the woman and didn't want that spoiled.

"We've scheduled a press conference at four to announce the arrest," Lahey said.

McManus' spirits picked up. *Oh, great! At least, I'm going to get credit for the arrest.*

"But Deputy Chief Turner called to make sure you don't show up…It's his call, Phil."

"What the fuck," McManus screamed into the phone. "Do you *happen* to know why?"

"Sure do. You didn't win any friends down here on the fifth floor with your drinking. Turner doesn't think it's appropriate to honor a cop when he's just returned to work after a sixty-day suspension. You're no hero, Phil."

McManus felt bile rise up from in his stomach and burn into the back of his throat. He spit it onto the carpet.

"Oh…and there's another thing," Lahey said. "That little shit Grogan's been down here at the Hall trying to gain some yardage."

"Whoa. What the fuck, you gotta be shitting me," McManus said as he threw the bottle of Blanton's at the fireplace. He smiled when it shattered, but the explosion of glass made Carly bark and scamper under the bed.

McManus put the phone down, got on his knees, and gently pulled her out. He sat back down on the bed with Carly on his lap. He patted her head as he picked up the phone.

"You there, McManus?"

"I got to listen to more of this bullshit, Lahey?"

"You don't have to, but I'm sure you want to know Grogan's politicking to get credit for the arrest. He's claiming he was on-duty and heard the confession—but he's not getting any traction."

McManus felt a pounding in his head and his eyes water. *Could things get any worse?*

"People are indifferent to you, Phil, but they hate that asshole. He's got no friends, not a one. I'm writing a scratch to the Chief about his behavior. Maybe I can get him some days off."

"How was he there, anyway? He just works nights."

"He made a trade with Pimentel on the day watch, so he could have Easter dinner with his in-laws."

"Fuck me."

"Calm down," Lahey said.

"Why?"

"Because in our arrest report, you're getting a bone thrown your way."

"What do you mean?"

"I'm putting you in for a meritorious, Phil. The Gold Medal of Valor. Even with your injury—and the fact you almost bought the farm—you effected the arrest of a dangerous murder suspect. You're gonna get your day in the sun. You're going out on top, Phil. Then, you're gonna fuckin' retire."

MONDAY
APRIL 5, 2010 · 1430 HRS.

McManus parked department vehicle 024 next to the hydrant in front of Starbucks on California Street and went inside. Despite the pain in his shoulder, his pride motivated him to report for duty. *I just want to be in uniform and working while that bullshit press conference goes down at the Hall. It's the principle of the thing. Fuck 'em.*

He waited in line and felt his heart beat faster when he saw one cinnamon sticky bun left in the display case. But, with three people in front of him, he didn't dare get his hopes up.

"Excuse me, Officer," a woman's voice came from behind.

McManus turned and saw a woman in her 30s with a baby carrier and a diaper bag slung over her shoulder. At her side stood two children, a boy who looked to be about six and a girl a couple years younger. *Why's she pissed at me?*

"Is that your police car parked in front of the hydrant?"

"Yes, ma'am," he said trying to smile.

She continued to glare at him. "How come you get to park there?"

McManus shrugged. "For emergencies, ma'am. Someone's breaking into a house or nabbing a kid. You want me to run a block back to get my car?"

"Well...I had to walk a block with all this stuff and these guys."

McManus nodded. "Yes, ma'am, I understand your frustration," he said with a nervous tinge to his voice. He turned back to the counter and was now first in line. The sticky bun was still in the display case. McManus turned back to the woman.

"Would your kids like that last sticky bun as my treat?" he asked.

"No. Thank you."

McManus nodded and placed his order. Then he walked along the side wall and found the same table he and Fratelli had shared. No sooner did he sit down, than his phone rang.

I can't believe it. He smiled at her name on his phone screen.

"That your radio car in front of Starbucks?" Trish Fratelli asked.

What a relief to hear her voice. "Yeah, Trish. Where are you?"

"Wait there. I need to talk to you."

A moment later, Fratelli's rocket bike drowned out Paul Desmond playing "Take Ten" on the Starbucks speakers. McManus saw her park the bike on the sidewalk next to the hydrant in front of his radio car. He looked down and noticed the coffee swirling in the cup held by his jittery fingers.

Fratelli walked in looking around. When their eyes met, she pulled off her helmet.

Her eyes are so red and swollen. Shit, she looks like she hasn't slept at all. McManus stood up to greet her.

She walked forward and hugged him.

Oh, I really want this. But it feels like she's barely holding herself together. "Trish, you okay?"

She took a step backward and eyed him like a pit bull. Then she blew out her breath and set her crash helmet on an empty seat at the table. After taking the empty chair next to McManus, she ran her fingers through her hair. "I don't know how to answer that one, Phil."

McManus reached across the table and brushed her cheek with the back of his hand. She gave him a surprised look, and then reached for that hand and held it.

He said nothing, but gave her a look that asked, "Why?"

Fratelli read his expression. Her eyes widened, "Why?" she responded "If there's a 'why question,' it's why haven't I tried to kill myself, yet."

They stared at each other while they each pulled their hands back.

"You don't want to do that, Trish. Didn't work for me."

"I know," she said in a dismissive tone.

McManus folded his hands on the table and squeezed them together. "Where do we begin?" He raised an eyebrow as if to tell her that he had a lot to say. "I know about your plan to use Bailey and that gay persona to cover your affair with Cassidy." A wry smile crept across his lips. "Actually, that was quite clever. Like you said, 'Guys don't have a clue.'"

He braced for her rebuke. Fratelli's eyes darted away, and she said nothing. He waited.

When she finally looked at him again, he smiled at her reassuringly. "We're on an even playing field, here, Fratelli. Two people, both with dark secrets."

"Some darker than others," she said. "I got one person killed and someone else looking at the gas chamber. Ugh. Meanwhile, I've destroyed my family and any relationships I had with people at work."

"I don't care, Trish," McManus said quickly, his voice tinged with pain and fear. "You have me in your life. We're both hurting here."

Fratelli blinked back tears.

"We don't have a lot of wiggle room. But we do need to be honest with each other," McManus said.

She covered her mouth with her fingers and stared down at the table. "This sounds so stupid, but I did love him," she blurted out.

McManus' heart dropped like an anchor splashing into the sea.

"I fell in love with him in high school. He's all I ever wanted. It pissed me off when my sister got the man I wished was mine."

How could you love a fucking sociopathic asshole like him? McManus looked past her and out the window to avoid making eye contact.

"It's the truth," she said. "You know how he was."

Yeah, but do you *know how he was?* McManus continued to gaze out the window.

"Look at me, damn it." Her demanding voice caught the attention of people standing in line at the counter.

McManus snapped around and saw the tears on her cheeks. *I so much want that pleading look to be sincere. Or is she just trying to manipulate another guy?*

"I'm never going to be able to explain this. It was just crazy, stupid love, McManus. Aren't you capable of understanding that?"

He frowned. *I can't believe something so good could be so fucked up!*

Fratelli dropped her chin again. Neither spoke.

McManus brushed a tear from his own eye, and then reached out to her. She took his hand. He strained to hear her voice over the noise of the coffee shop.

"It's a complicated story, McManus. Bailey was the last in a string of 'beards' I used to cover up my affair with Pete," Fratelli's voice fell off.

"They didn't know anything initially, but eventually they'd figure it out and leave. Bailey was different. She fell in love…and she got jealous."

McManus blew his breath out.

After a moment's pause, Fratelli stood up. "Phil, I've gotta go. I'm working a trade with a guy from 6 tonight 'til 8 tomorrow morning. Should be a lot of fun."

McManus' jaw tightened and he stared into her expressionless eyes. "Okay, Trish, this time I want you to listen to me. This is as bad as it gets, but we're gonna get back up. We're gonna play through this pain. All I've ever heard in my life is, "Don't get your hopes up, just when things go good—they go bad.' But, there is something greater than pain, and that's love."

Fratelli shrugged and reached over to the empty seat to pick up her crash helmet. "Come on McManus…this is the real world, not Turkey Day."

McManus' heart pounded as he looked at her. "We're gonna get through this thing because I do love you, Trish. And I'm willing to make it work if you are." *I want to say more, but what else is there?*

Fratelli nodded. "I don't know, McManus, I used to think someday I'd find real love. I mean, like the almost perfect partner. Shit, that's a joke…Sorry, but I just need to focus on what to do next."

Fratelli pulled on her helmet and walked toward the door. *That's it, huh? No kiss, no hug. No nothing.* "Trish," he called to her, and she turned around. He pulled out a business cards from his uniform pocket and quickly scribbled "Call Me!" on the back.

Fratelli took the card and glanced at it. She put it in her pocket and then waved him away as she walked outside to the rocket bike.

McManus slumped back into the seat and watched through the window as she switched on the rocket bike's ignition. An instant later, the orange motorcycle thundered to life. The sound reverberated inside his head.

Fratelli pushed the bike off its stand, jerked the throttle once, then held on tight as she rocketed off the curb and out onto California Street like a fighter jet catapulted from a carrier deck.

McManus sat at the table and closed his eyes. *Shit. Just like a star blazing across the sky for a few intense seconds, and then it's gone... What the fuck!*

He strained to hear the rocket bike for as long as he could until there was no sound. *Why's it always come down to the same old crap? Turn the fuckin' page and move on, you stupid shit...*

"I've decided to file a complaint against you, Officer."

McManus looked up just in time to see the woman with the baby carrier and two kids take his picture with her cell phone.

"The contempt you have for the law and your job is disgusting," the woman said. "It was bad enough to watch you flaunt your authority and park in front of a fire hydrant. But I'm sorry. To allow your woman friend to recklessly ride out of here like that—that needs to be reported to your superiors. This city pays you good money, to say nothing of those obscene pensions you get. I don't know how you can sit there drinking your coffee like nothing happened."

Before McManus could reply, the woman's young son, with his two front teeth missing, interrupted. "Mom, can we go now?"

The mother glared down at him, then looked back at McManus as the roar of fire engines on California Street wailed past the Starbucks.

"You haven't heard the last of this," she said shifting the weight of the baby carrier.

"I'm sure I haven't." He watched the woman take her son's hand and lead her children out the door.

Fuck me. What else can go wrong today? That damn press conference is probably over by now... Wonder what the fallout will be?

"Richmond Six, Headquarters calling Richmond Six."

Speak of the Devil...here it comes... His attention shifted to the staticky voice calling from the radio speaker dangling from his shoulder. "Richmond Six," McManus answered.

"Richmond Six. Respond to the intersection of California and Arguello...California and Arguello... Report of a 519... Motorcycle versus a Muni bus. Fire department and ambulance are en route. Do you copy?"

THE END

ACKNOWLEDGMENTS

This book was written using the amazing power of the Three S's: sensitivity, synchronicity and serendipity. The people I needed help from to write this story all miraculously appeared in my life at exactly the moment I most needed them. The story was written when I was going through The Dark Night of the Soul, transitioning from a 23-year career working as the team photographer for the San Francisco 49ers back to the "real world."

I want to thank the people who unselfishly and without hesitation contributed their insights and made this story a reality.

Dr. Carol Adrienne, noted life coach and the acclaimed author of the book, *The Purpose of Your Life and The Celestine Prophecy: An Experiential Guide,* worked with me and urged me to pursue writing. Three amazing editors: Holly Payne, Caroline Paul and Linda Jay; my outstanding book midwife and publishing consultant, Ruth Schwartz, aka The Wonderlady; cover and book designer extraordinaire Tom Joyce; social media maven and general manager, Shari Weiss; and the Bay Area's best web designer and artist Abigail Gorton.

Lt. Arthur Gerrans, SFPD retired, Sgt. Maureen Barron, SFPD, Inspector Ron Morehen, SFPD and SFFD retired, Sgt. Bob Del Torre, SFPD retired, Jerrod Marshall, Rohnert Park Public Safety Department, Battalion Chief "Big Mike" Cunnie, SFFD retired; San Francisco's best tour guide Mark Kasulen; Dr. Larry Dietz and Dr. Barbara

Murphy. Social profiler, Steven Raymond Salisbury, Lincoln (SF) #43—DB. And to Jeff Paquette, Lincoln (SF) #82—End, who had four interceptions and caught the winning TD pass to beat Bal, 27-26, in the last nine seconds at Kezar Stadium, Friday, October 27, 1967—after further review, the cosmos picked up the flag and awarded us the win.

Beth Huizenga and Janna Barkin, yoga teachers and renowned spiritualists; superb videographer and editor Robert McIntosh; miracle working portrait photographer Danielle Buoncristiani, whose father Capt. Al Benner, the "Cop Doc," founded the SFPD Officer Stress Unit. Jill Shay and my FIT and yoga sisters at Rolling Hills Club; Randy Gibson, my physical therapist who helped pull me through some very dark days. Terrell Lloyd, San Francisco 49ers team photographer, who continued to reach out. My barrista friends at the San Marin Starbucks, who make my Grande Americanos and are great company. And artist Eduardo Aguilera, who built and unfortunately has had to rebuild McManus' spiritual touchstone, the magnificent Lands End Labyrinth. Thank you Eduardo for your gift to San Francisco and to Colleen Yerge, now the keeper of the Lands End Labyrinth.

And finally my wife, Rosemary, and my children Rocky and Niki, who had the patience and love to deal with a sports photographer for 35 years—only to then deal with a writer.

Again, thank you and *namaste* to all.

Bill Fox
Novato, California, 2015

ABOUT THE AUTHOR

Bill Fox was a San Francisco Police officer in the 1970s. He is the former team photographer for the San Francisco 49ers and is the author of *Field Photo: 25 Years on the San Francisco 49ers Sideline.* He lives in Novato, California.

Photo by: Danielle Buoncristiani

Bill@Kezarbooks.com
Facebook: Bill Fox
Twitter: @BillFoxwriter
Instagram: PhilMcManus74
Websites: Billfoxwrites.com
Landsendthebook.com